Dedalus European Classics
General Editor: Mike Mitchell

Stranded
(En Rade)

Stranded
(En Rade)

by J.-K. Huysmans

Translated and with an introduction and notes by
Brendan King

DEDALUS

Published in the UK by Dedalus Limited,
24-26, St Judith's Lane, Sawtry, Cambs, PE28 5XE
email: info@ dedalusbooks.com
www.dedalusbooks.com

ISBN 978 1 903517 84 0

Dedalus is distributed in the USA by SCB Distributors,
15608 South New Century Drive, Gardena, CA 90248
email: info@scbdistributors.com   web: www.scbdistributors.com

Dedalus is distributed in Australia by Peribo Pty Ltd.
58, Beaumont Road, Mount Kuring-gai, N.S.W. 2080
email: info@peribo.com.au

Dedalus is distributed in Canada by Disticor Direct-Book Division
695, Westney Road South,Suite 14, Ajax, Ontario, LI6 6M9
email: ndalton@disticor.com web, www.disticordirect.com

Publishing History:
First published in France in 1887
First published by Dedalus in 2010

Translation copyright © Brendan King 2010

Printed in Finland by WS Bookwell
Typeset by Dedalus Limited

A C.I.P. listing for this book is available on request.

The Translator

Brendan King is a freelance writer, reviewer and translator with a special interest in late nineteenth-century French fiction. He recently completed his Ph.D. on the life and work of J.- K. Huysmans.

His other translations for Dedalus include *Là-Bas, Parisian Sketches*, *Marthe* and *Against Nature*. He also edited the Dedalus edition of *The Life of J.- K. Huysmans* by Robert Baldick.

Contents

Introduction

En Rade (*Stranded*) is J.-K. Huysmans' most underrated and most misunderstood novel. Written when he was at the height of his creative powers, it was published in 1887, mid-way between the two seminal works for which he is now best known, *A Rebours* (*Against Nature*) of 1884 and *Là-bas* of 1891. But the novel's radical approach to its depiction of the world, its hallucinatory blurring of the lines between reality and illusion, between the waking state and the dream state, confused contemporary critics and the reading public alike. Its bizarre dream sequences seemed too florid, too other-worldly to sit comfortably within the mundane bounds of Naturalism, while the sometimes brutal scenes of country life seemed too closely tied to the world of material reality to belong to the metaphoric landscapes of Decadence and Symbolism.

Sustained by this fundamental confusion about which literary genre the book belonged to, *En Rade* has never been satisfactorily integrated into the general schema of Huysmans' work. While some critics, such as Ernest Seillière, Léon Daudet and Pierre Cogny, felt the book marked a return to Naturalism, a regressive step back from *A Rebours*, others, unable to classify it as either Naturalist or Decadent, have simply "tended to see the novel as a confused juxtaposition of the two modes," as Charles Bernheimer puts it in *Decadent Subjects* (2002).

But it is a mistake to think of *En Rade* as existing in a kind of literary no-man's land, falling between the Naturalist mode of the early novels and the Decadent mode of *A Rebours* – still less is it a step back into Naturalism. Such misreadings ignore the subversive way in which Huysmans uses the conventions of Naturalism, both in his descriptions of the real world – as in his depiction of the crumbling château where the fabric of reality itself seems to be dissolving even as it is being described – and in his evocations of the dream world, where Naturalistic details are used to reify the purely imaginary and give it concrete substance. As J. H. Matthews argues in '*En Rade* and Huysmans' departure from Naturalism' (1964):

> In *En Rade*, naturalistic techniques are frequently turned back upon themselves. They function *à rebours*. Their purpose, consequently, is not to clash with the fantastic descriptions of the dream universe into which Jacques's exhausted mind retires, but to account for them… Just as Huysmans uses Naturalism to discredit reality, so, in this novel, he uses it to lend credence to the unreal.

From this perspective we can see that *En Rade* represents the next phase in Huysmans' search to find a literary form that could encompass both the subjective world of psychological reality and the objective world of material reality. It looks forward to, and in many ways is a precursor of, *Là-bas*, the novel in which Huysmans defined his theory of "spiritual naturalism", which was a formal attempt to synthesise the mundane and the transcendent by tracing parallel routes, one "in the air", the other "down below", and applying the processes and methods of Naturalism equally to the world of psychological and spiritual experience as to everyday reality.

Dreams – and their antitheses, nightmares – were a major impetus in this formal development, performing an analogous liberating function for Huysmans' imagination as drug experiences have done for certain other writers and artists. During the 1880s Huysmans read a wide range of books on the subject and was familiar not only with the psychological studies of Radestock and Wundt, which contained substantial sections on the physiology of dreams, but also works such as P. Max Simon's *Le Monde des rêves* (*The World of Dreams*) and X. B. Saintine's imaginative *La Seconde Vie: rêves et rêveries, visions et cauchemars* (*The Second Life: dreams, daydreams, visions and nightmares*), a book of stories and prose sketches inspired by dream events. Indeed, a number of French critics have drawn parallels between the historical overview of dreams given in Chapter III of *En Rade* and Sigmund Freud's introductory chapter to *The Interpretation of Dreams*, published over a decade later in 1900.

Huysmans was also fascinated by dreams as a subject for his writing. In his reply to Zola's criticisms of *A Rebours* in May 1884, for example, he said that he regretted not having "set the entire book in a dream," and over the next few years the visionary aspect of dreams and the dream-state became a kind of critical yardstick by which he measured the quality of his aesthetic experiences. Writing to the symbolist poet Jules Laforgue in September 1885 to thank him for sending a copy of his book *Les Complaintes*, Huysmans praised the evocative phrases in the poems that "opened up dream-provoking vistas". And when Jules Destrée sent him some pages of Lautréamont, Huysmans wrote back to say that he was captivated by Ducasse's "nightmares *à la* Redon", and mused about "what a man who wrote such fearful dreams" could possibly do for a living. Perhaps the clearest indicator of how significant dreams were to his ideas at this time can be seen in the way he used them to define the distinction between his own aesthetic approach and that of Zola's. In a letter to the Dutch writer Arij Prins in March 1886, a few months before he started work in earnest on *En Rade,* Huysmans explained that there was an "immense difference between Zola's ideas and mine...he is, in short, a materialist. I am not; basically I am for the art of dreams as much as the art of reality."

It was during this period, too, that Huysmans began writing down his dreams in a notebook, his *carnet vert*, for later analysis and use in his work. In effect, *En Rade* became the vehicle by which aspects of this new material, liberated from his unconscious, found expression in literary form.

Acting as both a complement to and a catalyst for these new ideas was Huysmans' continuing fascination with art, and in Odilon Redon, the "prince of mysterious dreams", he believed he had found an artist whose work embodied dream-like visions in their most powerful form. As he enthusiastically remarked to Destrée in a letter of December 1885, after having seen some of Redon's unpublished work in the artist's studio:

> You really have to have seen them to understand
> just how far this art of dreams can go...

Huysmans used what he saw as Redon's hallucinatory "art of dreams" as a springboard for his own literary experiments. For example, a piece he wrote in 1885 – nominally a review of an album of work by Redon – took the form of a daydream or reverie, in which the narrator is transported by a series of Redon's images spread out before him. The resulting text is a stunning evocation of the dream-state, with its strange associations and juxtapositions of ideas and images. Huysmans included it in the second edition of *Croquis parisiens* (*Parisian Sketches*), under the title 'Cauchemar' ('Nightmare'), and significantly the piece also contains elements that would reappear in two of the dream sequences in *En Rade*. The reference to a Redon landscape looking like a Beer and Mädler map of the moon, for example, was expanded into the dream where Jacques and Louise find themselves walking on the surface of the moon; while a reference to the print, 'The Juggler', in which "imperceptibly squinting pupils bounced around like billiard-balls", became an image that Huysmans reworked to disturbing effect in Jacques's final dream of a beautiful woman whose eyeballs repeatedly fall out of, and then bounce back into, their sockets.

Ironically, the very reason *En Rade* seemed so incomprehensible when it was first published – its dream-like blend of subjective and objective reality – is one of the reasons it is now generating a resurgence of critical interest. Huysmans' attempt to represent the complex relationship between reality and the perception of reality, between conscious thoughts and unconscious dreams, resonates much more with modern sensibilities than it did with those of its original readers. With its proto-Freudian viewpoint in which reality is subjective, problematic and contingent, in which neurosis and anxiety shape perceptions of the world and find their expression in dreams and in the symptoms of disease, *En Rade* is now seen as a text that goes far beyond the narrow genre divisions of Naturalism and Decadence, and as a consequence it is finally getting the critical attention it deserves.

The Writing of En Rade

Huysmans made his first visit to the small village of Jutigny, in the department of Seine-et-Marne, 60km south-east of Paris, in 1882. Here, he discovered the imposing ruin of the Château de Lourps, which stands on a hillside overlooking the valley of the River Voulzie, midway between the village and the railway station at Longueville. Attracted to the château as much by its symbolic as its picturesque qualities, he used it first as the birthplace and ancestral home of Jean Floressas des Esseintes in *A Rebours*, then as the suitably ruinous backdrop to Jacques

Marles' existential crisis in *En Rade*.

Huysmans didn't get a chance to explore the château more closely, however, until two years later, in July 1884, when he decided to spend some of his annual summer holiday in a nearby house, belonging to the château's owner. Initially he hadn't been very optimistic about his forthcoming visit, and in a letter written just before his departure on 11 July he told Stéphane Mallarmé:

> I leave tomorrow for an authentic village and I shall probably stay there for three weeks, unless I find it just too boring. This I may well do, as I'm not much of a countryman and have always preferred art and artifice to wide open spaces...

As it turned out, he discovered that life in the country had its compensations and a week or so after his arrival he wrote to Zola in almost enthusiastic terms:

> I'm writing to you from the depths of the country-side, where I'm living amid the peasants...I landed here on the 12th at Jutigny, a canton of Donnemarie, where I found a country cottage prepared for me that looks like the stage set of *L'Auberge des Adrets*, with its great fireplace, wood-beamed ceiling, and tall iron-hinged dressers. I'm now settled in and am savouring the pleasure of doing absolutely nothing, apart from chatting to the local rustics who are really interesting...I miss Paris a bit because I don't really have a feeling for the countryside, but it's doing me good here and I'm poulticing my tortured nerves before my return...For my part, I'm not writing

anything, but I'm taking notes on all the fascinating people around me, and it's worth the effort – I went with one of them to buy a calf at the market at Bray-sur-Seine, an extraordinary operation that lasts an hour and is accompanied with potations of white wine. Insults are exchanged all the time, and finally they decide on the calf that was picked out right at the beginning! What a crafty and stupid lot they are!

Among these notes were descriptions of Jules and Honorine Legueux, an aging peasant couple who leased a farm on the Lourps estate and who he would later portray in *En Rade* as Antoine and Norine. In between times, Huysmans also began to explore the deserted château and despite its parlous state, or perhaps because of it, he "thought it had possibilities as a rural Thebaid", as Robert Baldick puts it, and accordingly arranged to rent some rooms in it the following year.

This time, Huysmans was joined by his mistress, Anna Meunier, the younger of her two daughters (not by Huysmans), Antonine, and Anna's sister Joséphine. He even invited his new friend Léon Bloy to stay for a few days. Bloy duly arrived at the beginning of September, complete with his own pillow and blankets, and in the course of the four days he spent there the two men talked animatedly on the lawn while Antonine played ball and the two women rested indoors. This tranquil, almost homely, image is very different from the picture of life at the Château de Lourps given in *En Rade,* and it serves as a reminder to those who see Huysmans' novels simply as an autobiography in fictional form that the connection between the life and the work is not always a straightforward one. Nevertheless, as can be seen from a long letter Huysmans wrote to Alexis Orsat in

August 1885, this holiday did provide much of the incidental detail that would find its way into *En Rade*, and which would give it its air of verisimilitude:

> My dear Orsat,
> I am holed-up in the moribund Château de Lourps, an aristocratic château with ancient moats, towers and grounds, all of which are in a very sad state. Of the 200 or so rooms that comprise this ruin, there are about 5 or 6 that are habitable. The grand rooms of the lower floor are falling to pieces and the rooms in the garret, with their broken windows through which the wind blows like a gale, are inhabited by birds that make a huge racket. As for the grounds, they've returned to a state of nature. In short, it's a romantic ruin, absolutely silent and solitary, eaten away by moss and ivy, an immense building with cellars and dovecotes cooing with pigeons and swallows, battered by the winds, but with an air of nobility in its distress. I'm more or less camped in two Louis XIV-style rooms, two of the newer rooms in this barracks, north-facing and looking out onto the woods that are part of the château's grounds.
>
> That's the dream aspect – now the other side of the coin: Naturalism in the run-down realm of the old Marquis de Saint-Phale! It's like the raft of the Medusa! Just imagine, the butcher from Savin refuses to climb up the hill to us, even for money, and we have to put a basket at the end of the avenue (a fifteen minute walk) so that the baker can leave us a loaf as he passes – and to cap it all, you have to

struggle with a formidable well, use every ounce of strength in your arms in order to get water, because we're so high up.

In spite of everything we're beginning to get organised, getting provisions as if for a sea voyage, stacking the hams in the cellars in case of rain. That would mean starvation. I'm waiting for some wine. In 7 or 8 days this struggle for life will come to a close.

I can see you shiver, my dear friend, at this not very Gargantuan resumé, but all in all we eat meat and eggs every day and are doing pretty well.

Against that, *la bourgeoise* [Anna] is feeling dead-tired at the moment. She isn't sleeping well – and is gripped by terror at night in this abandoned ruin with no locks on the doors. The gigantic dark corridors, the echo of footsteps, and the noises made by birds all terrify her as soon as night falls. I only hope she'll get over it and doesn't listen to the gossip of the locals, who think the château has been haunted ever since the last of the Saint-Phales died.

At the moment, Joséphine is having a nap, I'm nodding off, and Tonine, worn out by her little games, is snoozing with her fists tightly clenched.

Well, that's our news. Recently we've taken to dining in Jutigny and drinking a bit more than usual. During the day, I explore the delightful woodland paths, I sit reading on the lawn, I live in perfect peace. In the evening, when we're by ourselves, bezique helps to pass the time, and of course there's always the bed...

> I'm still on my honeymoon with solitude. I hope it'll last…
>
> But the postman has arrived, and since it's a mile to the post office at Jutigny I'll finish this off in a hurry…Fortunately the old postman is a drunkard and Anna is plying him with wine while I write this.

Appropriately enough, the first reference to "a novella" that would eventually turn into *En Rade* also appears in a letter written from the château during this visit. In response to a query from Arij Prins, Huysmans admitted that his novel about the Siege of Paris was "still a long way off" and that he'd had to "delay its completion until some indeterminate time in the future," as he had so little time to work on it:

> The truth is that at the moment I'm preparing a new edition of *Croquis parisiens*, which is out of print – an expanded edition with 9 or 10 new pieces I've finished. Then I've still got a novella to write, to complete a book of three stories that I'd like to get done by January next.

The harassed tone in his voice was partly the result of anxieties about money, something that would be reflected in *En Rade* in Jacques's constant worry over the state of his finances. The bookbindery Huysmans had inherited after the death of his mother in 1876 was not doing well, and he was worried that if it went into bankruptcy he would not only lose his job at the ministry but his pension as well. As a consequence, he spent much of 1885 and 1886 writing journalism to make money, convinced as he was that it was "impossible to have a financial success with an artistic novel in this era of cheap Americanised literature", as he put it in a letter to Destrée.

Despite Robert Baldick's claim that Huysmans visited Lourps again in the summer of 1886 the evidence suggests otherwise. Suffering from neuralgia and rheumatism, Huysmans seems to have remained in Paris, working on his novella based on his experiences at Lourps with Anna the previous year, and the stream of letters he wrote to Prins during the summer and autumn, all postmarked from Paris, bears this out.

It is difficult to know how much of the overall structure of *En Rade* Huysmans had already planned before he made the decision, in October 1886, to start publishing it in serial form. Nevertheless, there are elements of the novel that can be dated and which reveal a glimpse of the chronology of the writing process. For example, in June 1886, Huysmans published 'Esther, a fragment' in *La Vogue*, a new literary periodical which, despite only surviving for a couple of years, was at the vanguard of the Symbolist movement, publishing contributions from Stéphane Mallarmé, Villiers de l'Isle Adam and Arthur Rimbaud. It is unlikely that the piece, which he incorporated wholesale into *En Rade* as the dream sequence in Chapter II, had been originally conceived as part of the novel, as he later made some changes to it in order to make it conform to other references in the text.

Although in early July Huysmans had complained to Prins that the novella "was going very slowly" and that it was "so difficult to get it up and running", by mid-August 1886 he seems to have got as far as Chapter V, Jacques's dream voyage across the surface of the moon. Huysmans himself seemed very pleased with it as a piece of writing, and in a letter to Prins he describes being "…worn out from working on the moon – you know that there are some dreams in my new book and among them there's a trip to the moon. I think I'm doing something a bit special,

because I'm getting carried away by my subject – fuck Verne!"
By the end of the month he'd finished the chapter and, as he put
it in another letter to Prins, had "fallen back into the down-to-
earth filth of my peasants."

Progress slowed a little in September, due partly to a
"prodigious cold in the head" and partly to "a couple of
administrative affairs" at the ministry, whose "pointless stupidity
is annoying me", as he complained to Prins. When it was all over
he decided to take some leave, and he informed Destrée on the
17th of October that:

> I'm on leave from work until the end of the month
> and I'm writing, shut up at home. Just imagine, my
> novella – half-dream, half-reality – is turning into
> a novel, and the first chapters are to appear next
> month in the *Revue indépendante*…

Huysmans didn't tell Destrée the reason for his sudden
decision to publish in serial form a book he hadn't even finished,
but in a letter to Prins written at the same time he was a little
more forthcoming:

> Having had need of money, I made a deal with the
> *Revue indépendante* to serialise my wild novella,
> *En Rade,* which has become a novel. However, the
> first two chapters are due to appear in November
> and I've only got five chapters finished – in other
> words, I've got three months head start, but I've got
> to get a move on, as I've also got various articles to
> write in order to earn some money.

Huysmans' admission that he'd only got five chapters

completed, two weeks before the first chapters started appearing in print, means we can be fairly certain that he didn't know exactly how the novel would end until fairly late in its composition. One of the novel's key symbolic events is the sickness and lingering death of the cat that Jacques and Louise had rescued from Norine, as it serves as a grim parallel to Louise's illness and Jacques's anxieties about it. Huysmans based the incident on the death of his own cat, *Barre de rouille*, which occurred at the end of November 1886, and which he described in a letter to Destrée:

> Nothing new here apart from the death of *Barre de rouille*, my cat, which you saw, and which I had to put out of his misery yesterday with strychnine – the unfortunate animal had paralysis and suffered like a martyr. It's very annoying – I'd got so used to living with this silent, toilet-trained being that my apartment now seems empty. Now I'll have to go and find and train another one.

The first reference to the cat in the novel is in Chapter IX, published in the March 1887 issue, so we can assume that the idea of using the cat's death as a device must have come to him relatively late in the book's development, otherwise he would have introduced the animal into the novel earlier.

Another significant late change was that of the main character's name. In the manuscript used to typeset the serial version of the novel, the name 'Gastin de Quélaine' has been crossed out and 'Jacques Marles' inserted. Huysmans may have simply decided to change to a less aristocratic-sounding name in order to avoid drawing parallels with *A Rebours*. But the change also signifies a considerable shift of sociological and political perspective in a book simmering with conflicts between middle-class and working-class codes of behaviour, and between urban and rural values.

En Rade was the first of Huysmans' novels to be serialised before publication in book form, and he didn't find the experience a happy one. Not only was he increasingly under pressure to meet the *Revue*'s deadlines as the book progressed towards its end, he also had to put up with interference from the editor, who censored certain scenes by cutting out words he thought readers would find objectionable. Writing to Prins at the end of March 1887, Huysmans warned him:

> Don't read the last two chapters in the *Revue*. They've been neutered...I'm definitely not going to publish my novels in serial form again. It's too annoying. Pieces chopped about for modesty's sake don't work. They just seem idiotic.

As the final deadline approached, Huysmans grew increasingly frantic about finishing the book, as can be seen from a series of hurried letters:

> Sorry for not having acknowledged sooner the arrival of your letter and the cigars, but I've been in a terrible flurry of work, trapped by the *Revue* as the last two chapters of *En Rade* have to be delivered by the 25th. And I'm doing them now! By the devil, never again will I give a novel to a paper before having finished it!
>
> (Huysmans to Arij Prins, c. 10 March 1887)

> I'm overwhelmed with work. I've put in a terrible effort to get *En Rade* finished, as it has to be

completed by the 1st of April for the next issue of the *Revue*.

But I am shattered…

I will finish now as I have to dive back into the last chapter. I hope it turns out OK.

(Huysmans to Arij Prins c. 20 March 1887)

I didn't write to you earlier, my dear Lemonnier, because I've been in a terrible flurry of work – in an urgent haste to finish my novel *En Rade*, driven into a corner by the *Revue indépendante* which I couldn't keep waiting.

Now I've just written those felicitous words: the end!

You know what that means!

It is the only really good literary moment in one's life…

(Huysmans to Camille Lemonnier, March 1887)

At the end of 1885 Huysmans had somewhat rashly signed a deal for all his future books with a young publisher, Victor Stock, a highly symbolic move given that his previous publisher, Charpentier, was also Zola's and closely linked with the Naturalist movement. Stock wasted no time in getting the novel out in book form and a week after telling Prins he was just finishing the last chapter, Huysmans informed him the book was already at the printers. It was published on the 26th of April: the same month as the final two chapters appeared in serial form.

Contemporary Critical Responses to En Rade

In November 1886, after the first two chapters of *En Rade*

appeared in the *Revue indépendante*, Huysmans got a foretaste of the critical reaction his novel would provoke when it was published in book form six months later. As he explained in a letter to Arij Prins:

> It's funny, everyone here is exasperated by this book which basically seeks to play a double role – a portion of real life on one hand, and a portion of dream on the other. So the Naturalists are exasperated by the dream aspect, and the idealists by the Naturalism of my peasants.
>
> It's worse than with *A Rebours*, I have everyone against me, the novelty of it frightens them…Even Goncourt is surprised by it. As for Zola he finds my peasants very good, but the apparition of Esther, the naked woman you'll see in the second chapter, monstrous. On the other hand, Villiers is delighted and is learning the apparition of Esther by heart, so are Mallarmé and Bloy. As for d'Aurevilly, he understands nothing of it, neither the peasants nor the dreams.
>
> Damn it all, what a hotchpotch of opinions!

Given that Huysmans already had a dubious reputation as one of the most extreme of Zola's Naturalist disciples, and that the book contained some scenes of an obviously controversial nature, it is not surprising that *En Rade* attracted its fair share of negative criticism. Much of this criticism tended to be divided between those who found the formal construction of the novel incomprehensible, and those who were outraged by its 'obscene' subject matter. Those in the first camp included Téodor de

Wyzewa,[1] who, in his review in the *Revue indépendante* of June 1887, expressed admiration for the 'Naturalist' parts of the book, but admitted he was unable to see how the dreams fitted into its overall schema:

> Why did Huysmans add to this marvellous book three or four poems in prose, one of which – the biblical dream of Esther – is written in a very rich style, but which has no actual connection either with the subject of *En Rade*, or with the state of mind of Jacques Marles? I think the author started the project of a quasi-symbolic novel offering a continual juxtaposition between lofty visions and base reality, but during the course of writing he got carried away by the artistic desire to construct a work of homogenous realism, which is what – aside from certain exceptions – *En Rade* is. And I think that these exceptions – Esther, the voyage to the moon, the dream in Chapter X and the fantasy about ptomaines – are just the remains of this original plan, preserved in that of the new...

By contrast, *La Revue Bleue*, a literary and political periodical with a liberal, democratic agenda, criticised the book from a moral perspective, attacking Huysmans' aesthetics for undermining decent values in a progressive society:

> M. Huysmans is of that school which disdains all

---

1 By coincidence, Huysmans had discussed Wyzewa's critical capacity in a letter to Prins five months before this review was published: "He [Wyzewa] is a strange character, the son of a Pole and a Russian woman – what his ideas are I don't know – his attacks on Dostoievski seem to me to be as stupid as they seem to you, and his criticisms peevish and pretentious."

the arts of composition and which rebels against the ancient precept that all works of literature should have a beginning, a middle and an end. This same school also proclaims that there is neither beauty nor ugliness, and that everything, even if it is awful, disgusting and – what is worse still – insignificant and stupid, deserves to be described... By heaven! women, avert your eyes! Grown men, don't look! I will quickly draw a veil over two – all too Naturalistic – scenes. First scene: "Meeting between a cow and a bull", or "Nothing is hidden". Second scene: "Eleven months later", or "The difficult birth of a calf". But let us stop there; how thankful I am to have drawn the curtain, let me assure you, because it's as frightful as anatomical nakedness and obstetrical truth. The bovine race clearly holds no mysteries for M. Huysmans, and he reveals those mysteries with glee...Are these subjects which should tempt an artist? Come on, raise your eyes, Monsieur Writer, a little less preoccupation with the body and a little more preoccupation with the soul...

(*La Revue Bleue*, 17, September 1887)

In a similar fashion, *La Liberté*, another paper hostile to what it saw as the deleterious moral effects of Naturalism, used its review to mount an extended attack on the movement in general and Huysmans' style in particular:

Amid the deluge of novels which has rained down, and which continues to rain down so as to threaten to submerge bookshops for the next 20 years, one is often obliged to make a difficult choice. I received, a few weeks ago, a volume which I had the idea of presenting to my male readers – I am excluding my female readers – though obstacles got in the way of the promise I made to myself. If I say I'm excluding my female readers it is because the work is not precisely a box of chocolates. I will dredge up a description of some ruins so you can judge for yourselves straight away.

"In short, the infirmities of a hideous old age – a mucilaginous discharge of rainwater, blotchy plasterwork, rheumy windowpanes, fistulous stonework, leprous brickwork, the hemorrhaging of all kinds of filthy detritus – had hurled itself at this wreck, which was dying alone and abandoned in the hidden solitude of the woods."

Now tell me: Is this the kind of book that's been written for a lady?

...Théophile Gautier was a great artist who did not understand the word malice; he wrote for the pleasure of art, following the great aesthetic rules that he himself invented, and always in the realm of the marvellous or of pure beauty. The Naturalists resemble him more closely than they think, because they too like to artistically fashion their sentences, only they do it with filth. I might be mistaken, but it seems to me that the generations to come will be astounded at the pains they have taken to sculpt their trifles out of such disgusting material. The Naturalist's study is comparable only to a torture chamber...

(*La Liberté*, 19 August 1887)

Despite such outpourings of abuse, *En Rade* nevertheless attracted some of the most positive and laudatory reviews Huysmans had yet received. One of the most insightful of these was written by the Symbolist poet Henri de Régnier, who perceived that Huysmans was trying to capture both the physical and the spiritual aspects of existence, and he even anticipates the "parallel paths" concept of spritual naturalism that Huysmans would formulate in *Là-bas*:

> Three extraordinary dreams dominate the book, opening a window onto unknown perspectives, parallel to normal existence and establishing another, mysterious and inexplicable, a sudden blooming of obscure seeds in the soul, of forgotten events that divide and then join together, that metamorphose or combine at random.
>
> (*Écrits pour l'art*, 7 June 1887)

As a poet, de Régnier was also captivated by Huysmans' rich literary style:

> In these strange dream pages, as in the rest of the novel, M. Huysmans is the master of an extreme, personal style, where words, in sentences whose harmoniousness and straight-forwardness is deliberately slightly slipshod, take on extraordinary meanings and an unexpected precision, reinforced by incisive and penetrating epithets.

The review concluded on an effusive note that would probably have pleased Huysmans more if he'd had more respect for de

Régnier's talent as a poet:

> Such is *En Rade*. I will add that nowhere has the author better demonstrated his qualities of style, precision and irony, and, among the books this year which have imposed their attention on, and dominated, the ephemeral tide of print, *En Rade* is showing itself to be one of the best, the most precious and worthy of the writer, lifted up above everything else by the scrupulous self-consciousness and the complex and captivating talent that is J.-K. Huysmans.

Another positive review came from the pen of a young writer associated with the Naturalist movement, Lucien Descaves, who would later become Huysmans' literary executor. As a Naturalist, Descaves's approach is almost the opposite of that of de Regnier's, concentrating on the novel's literary realism, both in terms of physical description and psychological accuracy:

> Huysmans excels in these excavations [of the human mind] and I do not know any pages, among the works of older writers, in which a more troubling lucidity is revealed than in his implacable exposure of those "mysterious impulses that circumscribe the outer limits of desire, that are nurtured, cultivated and sheltered in the most secret sewers of the soul." (*Revue Rose*, July 1887)

For Descaves, the book's excursions into the phantasmic and the realm of dreams were psychologically realistic descriptions of neurotic states, rather than signs of a decadent imagination.

If, for de Régnier, the dream sequences opened "a window onto unknown perspectives, parallel to normal existence", illuminating a world that was "mysterious and inexplicable", for Descaves, by contrast, they represented simply the symptoms of some psychological or neurotic disorder:

> These three morsels of literature are not as far-fetched as some people think, if you take into account the heady influence of the immense abandoned château on someone like Jacques, who is the victim of an over-sensitive nervous system.

Descaves also spent a considerable amount of time trying to defend Huysmans against the charge of decadence:

> What ignoramuses they are who see an analogy between Huysmans' style and the poetic effusions of the Decadents...I'm staggered to think that anyone could compare his nervy, agile language, which throbs with colour, which unites fancy with self-control...to the pitiful clowning of those jokers of the literary circus-ring.
>
> ...Huysmans is now in full command of a literary form that since *Les Soeurs Vatard* has undergone a bracing therapy of cold-showers and massages, a cure I'd recommend to the young misses of the Decadence.

Despite some reserves about the novel's title, which he thought too condensed and slightly misleading, Descaves finished on a positive note:

> No matter, all in all, this is a fine, consoling novel,
> assured of the longevity reserved for works of this
> scale. *En Rade* has its designated place in the great
> wine cellar of literature, next to the *grand crus*
> of Château Flaubert 1869 and Château Goncourt
> 1881.

There were other positive reviews, most notably Gustave
Geffroy's long and considered assessment in *La Justice*, and
Louis Montchal's take on the philosophical character of the book
in the *Génevois*, but perhaps the most strikingly idiosyncratic
review of *En Rade* was that by Léon Bloy which appeared in two
issues of *L'Art moderne,* on the 8th and 15th May 1887. Written
in Bloy's typically overblown, apocalyptic style, the review
itself became the subject of comments in the press. Along with
Bloy's articles on *A Rebours* and *Là-bas*, it was republished
in *Sur la tombe de Huysmans* (1913), a book which perfectly
embodies Bloy's extreme, contradictory personality: while the
first two articles are lavish in their praise, the last two bristle
with contempt: Bloy fell out with Huysmans shortly after *En
Rade* was published and he nurtured his grudge until his own
death in 1917.

At the time of writing the review, however, Bloy was still
captivated by what he called this "extraordinary book". Bloy
tended to judge Huysmans' novels according to how closely
they approximated to his own views, and in *En Rade* Bloy saw
his own loathing for the common run of humanity reflected back
at him:

> Never has anyone gone so far in his disgust for
> life, in his desire to hurl abuse at his fellow man,
> and, at the same time, never has such a complete

surfeit of the human farce been expressed with such a glacial irony. *A Rebours* has certainly been surpassed. The new novel is not only even more bitter, more desolately negative about every earthly joy, but its very style has been super-refined and sublimated...

If Descaves had made a point of trying to put some distance between Huysmans and the Decadents in his review, Bloy was equally keen to separate Huysmans from any connection with Zola and the Naturalist camp:

What significance does the lazy qualifier 'Naturalism' have when we're dealing with a novelist carried away by his vocation, whose sole ideal is to embrace sensible reality as it has never been embraced, to reflect, to transmit, to transcribe in high relief the normal sensations or the symbolic images of life, and who really has no need of the trappings of any literary school to be persuaded that every colour in the box is necessary to the artist who wishes to paint everything?

Huysmans' intellectual genesis was like that of most of the writers of his generation; if one absolutely must attribute a master to him, it's Flaubert one must name, and what's more, the hermetic Flaubert of *L'Education sentimentale*, the one nobody reads anymore. Flaubert and Goncourt for the language, Baudelaire for the spiritual decadence, and Schopenhauer for the black pessimism, such are the incontestable influences that, at the beginning, shaped this champion of contempt.

As for Zola, his contribution is imaginary and counts for nothing in the vocation of this artist who differs so profoundly from him, in spite of their illusory confraternity. One would need the intellectual poverty of a newspaper critic to imagine that an inspirational connection exists between that burly lout and this delicate inventor, this distiller of ideas and sensations, this aristocrat of analysis, who ornaments his style with a tortured psychology that would demoralise even a king's executioner!

Like Descaves, Bloy also fastened on Huysmans' psychological acuity. But while Descaves saw what the author was doing in prosaic terms – Huysmans was simply the "official receiver in the bankruptcies of life" – to Bloy, Huysmans was a "moralist who wasn't afraid to uncover souls and to examine hearts with the speculum of his imperturbable analysis":

The purely psychological sections of *En Rade* are such that one really has to direct the reader straight to the sensations he'll experience there, without lessening their impact by giving even the shortest extract here. Certain of these explorations into the dark night of the soul – in the seething abysses of which reside what Huysmans calls "the unconscious ignominy of refined souls" – will make your hair stand on end and give you a shudder of agony as if you'd fallen into a crater. His wholly justified detestation of affected familiarity could not have been denounced in a more exquisitely atrocious fashion, nor sarcastically administered by a more diabolical pen. As I said at the beginning, this book will give you the shudders.

Bloy's enthusiastic response was in sharp contrast to that of Zola, who was astute enough to see that *En Rade,* following in the wake of the radical departure of *A Rebours,* represented a further shift away from the fundamental values and aesthetics of Naturalism. Zola never publicly published his opinion of *En Rade*, but in a letter to Huysmans of June 1887 he formally outlined his criticism, which, like his response to *A Rebours*, was a mix of positive and negative points that left Huysmans in no doubt as to what he really felt:

> At last, I've managed to re-read *En Rade* in book form, and how much it gains from not being fragmented, even though those fragments were quite long! In its complete form it seems if not simple, at least neater. You have some superb things in it, the most intense perhaps that you've ever written. The whole peasant section stands out in extraordinary relief. It's not at all that I don't like dreams[2] – that of Esther is assuredly an exquisite thing and complete in itself – but to be honest, I should have preferred the peasants on one side and the dreams on another. That, no doubt, was too banal, yet what an astonishing novella, what a masterpiece worthy of *A Vau-l'eau,* you have with your peasants just by themselves! It seems to me that the contrast you wanted hasn't come about, or at least that it has

2 Interestingly, Zola would write his own dream novel, *Le Rêve*, a year or so later in 1888. This anomalous book, which Huysmans lambasted in a letter to Prins as "imbecilic" and "ridiculous", had a seemingly conventional moral and an even more conventional plot, which Huysmans mockingly summarised as "a young girl, pure, heavenly, dreaming of her prince charming, but who lacks money!!!"

come about with a confusion that isn't art. Perhaps
it's me that's mistaken, but I'm just giving you my
honest impression as a friend. No matter, you are
a proud artist, and there aren't many novels which
have as powerful an aroma as yours.

Once again, it is interesting to see how Zola tries to accentuate
the aspects of the novel that accord with his own aesthetic ideas
and downplay those to which he feels antithetical. It is curious,
too, that while Huysmans had told Prins in November 1886
that Zola found the Esther dream "monstrous", Zola himself
specifically singles out the Esther dream for praise. Whether
Zola is being disingenuous in his letter, or Huysmans was
exaggerating to Prins for effect in his, is difficult to determine.

Unfortunately, Huysmans was not always the best advocate
of his own novels. This was especially true with *En Rade*
and his reply to Zola's criticism is frequently cited as proof
of the book's artistic failure. However, Huysmans' negative
assessment of his work often had less to do with his sense of its
critical success or failure as with the aesthetic sensibilities of his
correspondent, and his views tended to change according to the
prejudices of the person he was writing to, be it Zola, Goncourt
or Mallarmé. With *En Rade*, Huysmans was in the difficult
position of wanting to put some distance between himself and
the Naturalist movement, but to do so without breaking publicly
and acrimoniously with Zola. As a result, he replied to Zola in
conciliatory fashion, much as he had done after the publication
of *A Rebours* and the older writer's criticism of that novel as a
literary dead-end:

Thanks for your kind letter about *En Rade*. I'm
very glad to see that the book didn't displease

> you. As to your opinion on the unequal legs of this
> pair of trousers, one down-to-earth, the other up-
> in-the-air, it is, alas, mine too. Your comments are
> absolutely right. My method was a preconceived
> idea, a division fixed in advance; the day, reality; the
> night, dreams. And it should be noted that given this
> idea, I'd have done infinitely better to have applied
> it in all its rigour, to write alternately a chapter of
> reality, then one of dreams. It wouldn't have been
> much better and wouldn't have prevented the jolts
> between the two, but it would still have been better
> than strewing those three long, devilish chapters
> that have an air as if they've happened by chance
> onto the fork.

This attempt to downplay the novel's formal innovation, as if trying to paper over the aesthetic differences he had with Zola, is in stark contrast to his comments written a few months earlier to Prins, who he felt was more on his artistic wavelength:

> What a laugh. I hear people saying: "But one bit
> doesn't follow on from the other!" or "It's a very
> bumpy ride!" Damn it, I know it's a rough ride
> because that's how I wanted it…

A sign of Huysmans' growing influence on the literary scene in England during this period is the increasing number of reviews he received in English papers. Although there was obviously nothing that could match the virulence and enthusiasm of Bloy's review, surprisingly, given the often prudish reaction of the English press to the liberties French novelists took with moral proprieties, *En Rade* received some generally favourable, if slightly misguided, notices:

> Among the other Christmas books issued is one
> by Messrs. Tresse and Stock, called *En Rade*, by
> M. J. K. Huysmans. The work is not only well
> written, but is neatly printed, and the text almost
> invites one to read. It is a study of the "ups and
> downs" of a Parisian household in the country, and
> the author shows his knowledge of peasant life
> to be as accurate as his Balzac-like acquaintance
> with metropolitan manners and customs. Here
> and there in the volume there are a few Zolaesque
> sentences which might have been expurgated, but
> M. Huysmans has not allowed himself to follow
> the author of *La Terre* too closely in his modes of
> expression, and he very prudently stops short where
> M. Zola would be tempted to go on. *En Rade* is, on
> the whole, a healthy study of peasant life.
>
> (Daily Telegraph, 30 October 1887)

The unnamed reviewer of the *Saturday Review* (the paper for
which Arthur Symons, one of the great promoters of Huysmans
in England, would later write), even revealed a hint of insider
knowledge about the uneasy relationship between Zola and
Huysmans, noting that:

> As for M. Huysmans, we have always suspected
> that he is a young man of an exquisite but carefully
> concealed humour. We are sure of it since, following
> his revered master, M. Zola, with humble steps, he
> has in *En Rade* described at great length the coming
> into the world of – a calf. The parody on *Pot-bouille*

37

could not be better.

(*Saturday Review*, 6 August 1887)

Despite this wide range of opinion, *En Rade* didn't have as much of a critical impact on Huysmans' peers as *A Rebours* had, nor did it produce the shockwave of public outrage and notoriety – and hence larger sales – that *Là-bas* would a few years later. Huysmans' own perception was that his book was being ignored, and he put the unfavourable response down to the fact that *A Rebours* had stirred up a whole section of the press against him and that it was taking its revenge by trying to "bury him", as he put it in a letter to Prins. Huysmans always tended to think that the press was against him, but this time it seems that there was at least some justification for his sense of paranoia. In July 1888, *Le Parisien* noted, not without a hint of gloating, that:

> Last year, M. Huysmans gave us *En Rade*, a book of a very distinct and personal colour: subtle and strange states of mind in stagnation, illuminated by a miraculous verbal suggestivity and a surprisingly acrobatic style, an irritating breath of nervous intensity. A silence as of death fell on this book...

Note on the Translation

As is nearly always the case with Huysmans' novels, the book's title presents as many difficulties as the text itself. In French, *rade* can literally mean a harbour, and in the novel Huysmans uses the word three times, in each instance referring to the idea of finding a metaphorical harbour or shelter from the rough seas of life. The phrase *en rade*, which doesn't actually appear in the novel, has two contrasting meanings: on the one hand it is used to describe a ship that is laid up for repairs or anchored in the 'roadsteads', the calm waters outside a harbour, while on the other it is also applied to boats in a harbour that have been abandoned or that are no longer seaworthy. For Jacques Marles the Château de Lourps embodies both these meanings of *en rade*: it is not only the place where he hopes to find shelter from the financial storms of his life in Paris, it is also the place where what he refers to in the novel as the ship of his marriage gets stranded and runs aground. As Charles Bernheimer puts it in *Decadent Subjects* (2002): "the *rade* can be thought of as a temporary home, a refuge, a protected haven, but it is also the opposite, a place where one is abandoned, left behind, left homeless and exposed."

This translation is based on the French edition contained in Volume IX of Huysmans' *Oeuvres complètes* (Paris: Crès 1928-34). I have also consulted the critical edition produced by Jole Morgante (Istituto Universitario di Bergamo, 1987), which compares the published text with the manuscript of the serialised version that appeared in the *Revue indépendante*, as well as the edition of *En Rade* in *Romans* (Vol. I, Robert Laffont, 2005) which contains useful notes and an introduction by Dominique Millet-Gérard. Although there are two extant manuscripts of

Introduction

En Rade, both in private hands, only one, that used by Jole Morgante, has been examined, the other, having been temporarily "misplaced" by its owner, has never been studied critically. To avoid cluttering the text with footnotes, extensive notes and references are provided at the back of the book for those who wish to consult them.

Selected Bibliography in English

Antosh, Ruth. *Reality and Illusion in the Novels of J.-K. Huysmans.* Amsterdam: Rodopi, 1986.

Baldick, Robert. *The Life of J.-K. Huysmans.* Oxford: Clarendon Press, 1955. Revised ed. Dedalus Books 2006.

Banks, Brian. *The Image of Huysmans.* New York: AMS Press, 1990.

Bernheimer, Charles. 'Huysmans: Writing against (Female) Nature.' *Poetics Today,* 6 (1-2), 1985: 311-324.

Bernheimer, Charles, 'Huysmans: syphilis, hysteria and sublimation.' In *Figures of Ill Repute: representing prostitution in nineteenth-century France*, Duke University Press, 1997.

Bernheimer, Charles. *Decadent Subjects: The Idea of Decadence in Art, Literature, Philosophy, and Culture of the Fin de Siècle in Europe.* Baltimore: Johns Hopkins University Press, 2002.

Gordon, Rae Beth. 'The Function of the *métaphore filée* in *En Rade.*' *Nineteenth-Century French Studies*, 21(3-4) 1993.

Grigorian, Natasha. 'Dreams, Nightmares, and Lunacy in *En Rade*: Odilon Redon's Pictorial Inspiration in the Writings of J.-K. Huysmans.' *Comparative Critical Studies,* 2008 (5): 221-233.

Laver, James. *The First Decadent, Being the Strange Life of J.-K. Huysmans.* Faber & Faber, 1954.

Lloyd, Christopher. *J.-K. Huysmans and the fin-de-siècle Novel,* Edinburgh University Press, 1990.

Matthews, J. H. '*En Rade* and Huysmans' Departure from

Naturalism.' *Esprit Créateur*. 4 (1964).

Mayer-Robin, Carmen. 'Carcass or Currency? Marketing Ptomaines in Huysmans' *En Rade*.' *Currencies: Fiscal Fortunes and Cultural Capital in the French Nineteenth Century*, Eds. S. Capitiano, L. Downing, P. Rowe, N. White, Peter Lang, 2005.

Ziegler, Robert. 'Subterranean Skies: the Vertical Axis of Huysmans' *En Rade*.' *Stanford French Review*, Vol IX, 2, 1985.

Stranded
(En Rade)

I

Night was falling; Jacques Marles quickened his pace; he'd left the hamlet of Jutigny behind him and, following the interminable road that led from Bray-sur-Seine to Longueville, he looked to his left for the footpath a peasant had pointed out to him as a shortcut up to the Château de Lourps.

'Life's a bitch,' he murmured, hanging his head, and despairingly he thought about the deplorable state of his affairs. In Paris, his savings lost due to the unpardonable bankruptcy of a too ingenious banker; on the horizon, a menacing succession of bleak tomorrows; at home, a pack of creditors, scenting disaster, baying at his door with such fury that he'd had to flee; at Lourps, his wife Louise, sick, taking refuge with her uncle, the caretaker of a château owned by a wealthy high-street tailor who, while waiting to sell it, was leaving it untenanted, unrepaired and unfurnished.

It was the sole refuge on which he and his wife could now count; abandoned by everyone they knew, ever since the whole debacle began they'd thought about finding a shelter, a harbour, somewhere they could drop anchor and take counsel during a momentary truce, before returning to Paris and renewing the struggle. Jacques had often been invited by old Antoine, his wife's uncle, to come and spend the summer at the empty château. This time he'd accepted. His wife had got out at the town of Longueville, on the borders of which stands the Château de Lourps; as for him, he'd stayed on the train as far as the station at Ormes, where he'd alighted in the hope of recovering some debts.

He'd called in on a friend there, insolvent, or so he'd said; had endured heated protestations and vague promises, but in the end met with a straight refusal; so without further delay he was retreating to the château, where Louise, who'd arrived in the morning, should be waiting for him.

He was tortured with anxieties; his wife's ill-health had bewildered doctors for years; it was a sickness whose incomprehensible phases baffled the specialists, a perpetual jumping between periods of wasting and periods of obesity, emaciation giving way in less than a fortnight to a plumpness that would disappear just as quickly; then there were the strange pains, surging up like electric sparks in her legs, twitching her heels, piercing her knees, wrenching a spasm and cries of pain, a whole panoply of symptoms ending in hallucinations, in fainting fits, in such bouts of debility that she seemed to be on her last gasp when, by some inexplicable volte-face, the patient regained consciousness and felt herself alive again. Ever since that bankruptcy, which had thrown her and her husband on the scrapheap, out on the street without a sou, the sickness had intensified and spread; and the sole observation that they could make was this: that her physical weakness seemed to abate – her colour returning and her flesh becoming firmer – whenever a troublesome or alarming issue ceased; the sickness seemed above all mental, events aggravating it or keeping it in check depending on whether they were ominous or auspicious.

The journey had been singularly distressing, interspersed with fainting fits, shooting pains, and a terrible mental confusion. Time and again Jacques had been on the point of abandoning the trip, of getting out at the next station to stay at some inn, reproaching himself for having dragged Louise off without waiting a bit longer; but she was determined to remain on the train, so he tried to reassure himself, telling himself that she would have died in Paris if he hadn't taken her away from the horrors brought on by lack of money, from the shame of insulting demands and threatening summonses.

The sight, at the station, of old Antoine waiting for his niece with a cart to pick her up and carry their cases had been a relief to him, but now, harassed by the monotony of the flat road, he let himself go, obsessed by an anguish which he could see was exaggerated but which oppressed him and imposed itself on him all the same; he almost dreaded arriving at the château from fear of finding his wife suffering still more or even dead. He debated with himself, had an urge to run in order to dispel his fears all the quicker, but he remained, trembling on the road, his legs sprightly and sluggish by turn.

Then the external spectacle of the landscape stemmed the flow of these internal visions for a few minutes. His eyes fastened on the road, sought to see ahead, and this concentration distracted his heartfelt anxieties and stilled them.

On his left, he finally made out the path that had been pointed out to him, a path rising and snaking up as far as the horizon. He skirted a small cemetery with walls topped by pink tiles, and started down a track furrowed by two frozen cartwheel ruts. Around him stretched rows of fields, the borders of which blurred and merged in the twilight. On the hillside, in the distance, a huge building filled the sky, like an enormous barn with its hard, black outline, above which silent streams of red cloud were flowing.

'Almost there,' he said to himself, because he knew that behind this barn, which was in fact an old church, lay the Château de Lourps hidden by woods.

He took heart again, watching the advance towards him of this building pierced by windows which, facing each other across the nave, were ablaze with the clouds' trails of fire.

This black church, pierced by the red of those windows whose circular, star-shaped traceries of lead were like gigantic spiders' webs hanging above an inferno, appeared sinister to him. He looked higher up; the scarlet waves continued to unfurl in the heavens; lower down, the landscape was completely deserted, peasants snug, animals stabled; in the whole expanse of the plain, if one listened, one could hear nothing but the faint barking of a dog far off on the hillside.

A languid sadness overwhelmed him, a sadness different from that which had gripped him during the journey. The personal character of his anxieties had disappeared; they had spread, diffused, lost their particular essence, had in some way passed out of him and combined with that inexpressible melancholy exhaled by sleepy landscapes in the drowsy peace of evening; this vague and indistinct feeling of anguish, precluding thought, cleansing the soul of precise fears, numbing its tender spots, assuaging by its mystery the certitude of specific pains, comforted him.

Having arrived at the top of the hill, he turned round. Night was still falling. The immense landscape, without depth during the day, was hollowed out now like an abyss; the bottom of the valley vanished in the blackness, seemed to go down forever, while its edges, brought closer by the gloom, appeared less broad; a funnel of darkness began to take shape where, that afternoon, the slopes of a corrie had descended in a gentle incline.

He lingered in the mist; then his thoughts, which had been diluted by the mass of melancholy that surrounded him, caught up with him and, becoming active again through cohesion, struck him to the heart with a sudden blow. He thought of his wife, shivered, and began walking again. He was approaching the church; by the main gate, at a bend in the road, he made out the Château de Lourps a short distance in front of him.

This sight dispelled his anxieties. A sudden curiosity about the château – which he'd heard spoken of for so long without ever having seen it – gripped him for a second; he stared. The war-like clouds in the sky had fled; the imposing *fortissimo* of the sunset had given way to the mournful silence of an ashen sky; here and there, however, the odd unconsumed ember glowed red among the smoke of the clouds and lit the château from behind, striking the haughty ridge of the roof, the lofty form of the chimney and the two towers topped with candlesnuffer bonnets, one square, the other round. Illuminated like this, the château seemed like a burnt-out ruin in which a badly extinguished fire was still smouldering. Inevitably, Jacques was reminded of the old yarn spun by the peasant who had shown him the way. The winding path he'd followed was called the Path of Fire because it had been marked out long ago by the whole village of Jutigny trampling across the fields at night, running to the rescue of the blazing château.

The sight of this château that still seemed to be burning dully exacerbated his state of nervous agitation, which had been steadily growing since the morning. His shudders of apprehension – momentarily interrupted but now resumed – and his twitches of anxiety increased tenfold. He feverishly rang at a little door pierced into the wall; the noise of the yanked bell soothed him. He listened, his ear flat against the wood of the door; not a sound of life came from behind the wall. Immediately his fears ran riot; he hung onto the bell-pull, feeling faint. At last, over a crunch of gravel, clogs clattered; there was a screeching of old iron turning in the lock; someone was pulling vigorously on the door which was juddering but didn't budge an inch.

'Well push then!' said a voice.

He struck it a hard blow with his shoulder and leaned on the door as it gave way into darkness.

'It's you, nephew,' said the shadow of a peasant who held him in his arms and scraped his unshaven cheeks against

Jacques's.

'Yes, uncle, where's Louise?'

'She's out back, gettin' things prepared; aye, young man, out here in the country it's not like it is in the city; we don't have no pile of gadgets to make things easy like you do.'

'Yes, I know; so how is she?'

'Louise? Well, she's with Norine, they're scrubbing, they're sweeping, they're knocking everything about…unfortunately. Still, it keeps 'em amused; they're 'aving a grand time, sometimes they laugh so 'ard I don't know what's goin' on!'

Jacques breathed a sigh of relief.

'We'll go and find her, my boy,' continued the old man. 'We'll give 'em a hand, 'cause Norine has to go and look after the cattle; we'd better get a move on or we'll get soaked. You got here just in time – look at the sky, it's going to pour down!'

Jacques followed Uncle Antoine. On the way, he looked around him. They were walking down invisible paths lined with trees, betrayed by the brushing of bent branches; in the lighter part of the sky, threaded by ragged clouds of tulle, needle-shaped foliage like that of pine trees rose up to formidable heights, bristling treetops whose trunks, buried in shadows, could no longer be discerned. Jacques couldn't figure out the shape of the garden he was crossing. Suddenly, there was an opening, the trees gave way and the night became a void, and, at the edge of the clearing, loomed the pale mass of the château, from the doorway of which two women were advancing.

'Eh now then, how goes it with you?' cried Aunt Norine, who, with a mechanical gesture like a wooden doll, threw her stiff arms around his neck.

Jacques and Louise understood one another without exchanging a word.

She was getting better; he was returning without money,

empty-handed.

'Norine, did you put the wine to cool?' said old Antoine.

'Aye, and thinkin' you wouldn't be late, I was just about to serve the soup.'

'So, it's all ready up there?' added the old man, turning to Louise.

'Yes, uncle, but there's no water.'

'Water? No lack of that round 'ere! I'll go and fetch you a bucket.'

With a couple of strides, Aunt Norine vanished into the darkness; old Antoine plunged into the trees in the opposite direction; Jacques and his wife were left alone.

'Yes, I'm feeling better,' she said, kissing him; 'all this exertion has bucked me up; but let's go upstairs, I've managed to find the one room in the whole château that's just about habitable.'

They entered a prison-like corridor. By the glimmer of a match he'd struck, Jacques could make out enormous hewn walls, covered in soot and pierced by cell doors, overarched by a sheer, ribbed vault, as if carved out of rock. A dank odour like that of a cistern filled the corridor, the flagstones of which wobbled at every step.

The passage made a sharp turn and he found himself in a gigantic hall whose painted faux marble panels were peeling, in front of a staircase with a banister of wrought iron; he went up, looking at the square stone stairwell pierced by very small, six-paned windows.

Through the broken glass the wind rushed in, stirring the shadows gathered beneath the vault, rattling the doors on the upper floors, their hinges groaning in the breeze.

They stopped at the first floor. 'It's here,' said Louise.

There were three doors: one opposite them, one in a recess

to the right, and one in a recess to the left.

A ray of light was filtering under the first. He went in and immediately an inexpressible feeling of unease gripped him; the room into which he'd entered was very large, the walls and ceiling covered by a wallpaper simulating a vine trellis, harsh green diamonds against a brackish background. Panels of grey wood surmounted the doors, and above the Griotte marble fireplace, framed in the same grey wood, was a small greenish mirror whose silvering had sagged, pitting its quicksilver surface with commas.

By way of flooring, tiles that had once been painted orange, and along the partition walls, cupboards whose paper-covered doorframes were riddled with scratches and gashes.

Even though someone had swept the room and opened the window, a smell of old wood and crumbling plaster, of wet flax and the cellar was exuding from this dead room.

It's sinister here, thought Jacques. He looked at Louise; she didn't seem dismayed by the room's icy solitude. On the contrary, she was examining it with complaisance and smiling in the mirror, which reflected her face back at her, discoloured by its green tinge and pockmarked by the holes in its silvering.

And in fact, like most women, she was feeling excited by the spontaneity of this haphazard encampment, this gypsy-like set up, pitching her tent no matter where. That childish happiness a woman has in breaking a habit, in seeing something new, in contriving some clever scheme to secure a bed for the night, that need to think on her feet, that compulsion to mimic the nomadic life of a touring actress – which every middle-classs woman secretly envies so long as it's watered down, with no real danger and doesn't last very long – that self-importance of the dependable quartermaster entrusted with finding food and lodging, that maternal instinct for sorting out sleeping arrangements for her man, who has only to stretch himself out when all is ready, had acted powerfully on her and braced her nerves.

'The furniture isn't up to much,' she said, pointing to an antique wooden bed in the alcove, on which a bolster and a straw mattress lay, and then to the middle of the room to two straw-bottomed chairs and a round table, obviously rescued from the garden because the legs had swollen and the table-top had started to peel under the effects of sun and rain; 'but still, we'll see tomorrow about getting anything we're missing.'

Jacques assented with a nod of the head; with a glance he took in the room, most of which was taken up with his open trunks all along the wall; decidedly, a shower of gloom was falling from this too-high ceiling over the cold tiled floor.

Louise thought her husband was brooding over his money problems; she kissed him. 'Come on, we'll pull through despite it all,' she said. And seeing he was still worried: 'You must be hungry, let's go and find my uncle, we'll talk later.'

Back on the landing, Jacques half-opened the doors to the left and right; he could make out huge, endless corridors from which rooms emanated; everything was in a state of complete neglect, as cold as the grave, walls crumbling, battered by wind and rain.

He went downstairs but then suddenly stopped: a cacophony of rusted chains, of screeching, ungreased wheels, a grating of complaining pullies shattered the silence of the night.

'What's *that*?'

'It's uncle drawing the water,' she said laughing, and then explained that water was scarce at this height and that a single gigantic well, sunk in the courtyard, supplied the château; 'it takes five minutes by the clock to bring the bucket back up; what you're hearing is the sound of the rope straining against the winch.'

'Hey, there!' shouted old Antoine, as soon as they reached the courtyard, 'here's the water and it's cold 'cause it's come straight out the chalk,' and he grabbed the enormous, sploshing wooden bucket, and carried it at arm's length as if it were a feather; then, rejoining them, he added: 'Let's go and see Norine because I've an idea she's getting impatient and she'll give us a right telling off if we keep her waiting much longer.'

The night was dark and damp from the rain. They walked in single file along a path, hands raised to fend off the swishing blows of branches in the blackness, following in the footsteps of the old man who made his way as calmly and surely as if it were broad daylight.

Eventually a star-shaped light, very faint, twinkled, gradually got bigger, then spread out and became more diffuse the closer they got; before long, it resolved itself into the dull, flat square frame of a window. They had reached a one-story cottage, comprised of a single room. In the large fireplace, beneath a cowl whose shelves were weighed down with painted crockery, a fire of vine branches crackled loudly under a simmering cast-iron cauldron, a fierce smell of cooked cabbage permeating from beneath its dancing lid.

'Sit yourselves down there,' said Aunt Norine, 'are you hungry?'

'Certainly are, auntie.'

'Ah well, that's that then!' she said, employing the practically meaningless expression the peasants from this part of Brie used all the time.

'Taste that for me, nephew,' said old Antoine, 'and tell me what you think; it's wine from my Graffignes grape harvest.'

They clinked glasses and drank an acidic rosé wine, spoiled by an irritating dusty taste wines often have when they're fermented in vats once used to store oats.

'Yes, it tastes a bit of oats, that vat played a trick on me,' sighed the old man, smacking his lips; 'here in the country it's not like the city, we ain't got no wine from far off places in our silos; but even so, it's as good a drop of wine as you'll taste, you know.'

'Oh, we're in no position to be fussy; in Paris, uncle, we drink only mediocre wines in which few fresh grapes ever find their way.'

'Is that so, is that so?' Then, after a pause, he added: 'You could be right all the same, young man.'

'Ah well, that's that then!' sighed Aunt Norine, clasping her hands together.

Old Antoine pulled his penknife from his pocket, opened it and cut up some bread.

He was a small old man, thin as a beanpole, gnarled as a vine and swarthy as old boxwood. His wizened face, cheekbones streaked with red veins, was pierced by two glaucus eyes flanking a bony nose, short, pinched and twisted to the left, beneath which opened a large mouth harrowed with very clean sharp teeth. Two bushy sideburns descended on either side next to ears that stuck out from his skull; all over his face, above his lips, in the hollows of his cheeks, in his nostrils, on the nape of his neck, sprouted thick hairs stiff as the bristles of a brush, greying like the dense hair he would sweep under his cap with his fingers. Standing up, he was a little stooped, and, like most of the peasants in Jutigny who have worked in the peat bogs, he had the legs of a horseman, bowed in an arc. At first glance, he seemed stunted, undersized, but looking at the taut arch of his chest, his muscular arms, the tanned pincers that were his fingers, one could imagine the strength of this grasshopper who wouldn't buckle even under the heaviest of burdens.

And Norine, his wife, was even more robust; she, too, was over sixty; taller than her husband, she was even thinner: no belly, no bust, no backside, and hips like pick-axe blades, there was nothing of the woman about her. Her yellow face, criss-crossed with wrinkles, furrowed with lines like a road map, crinkled like a piece of material around her neck, was lit by two eyes of an unusually light blue, piercing eyes, youthful, almost obscene in that face over which furroughs and grooves marched at the slightest movement of her eyelids or mouth. Added to which, her straight nose was pointed like a blade, and its tip followed the direction of her gaze. She was at once disturbing and ridiculous, her bizarre gestures adding to the unease of her too-bright eyes and her receding, toothless mouth. She seemed to be worked by a mechanism that lacked joints, she stood up in a single movement, marched like a corporal, offered her hand like one of those clockwork automatons; and, when seated, without being aware of it she would affect poses so comical it got on your nerves, adopting the dreamy attitude of ladies represented in paintings from the First Empire, eyes raised to the heavens, left hand touching her mouth, elbow cradled by the palm of her right hand.

Jacques examined this couple whose rugged, swarthy features were even more clearly accentuated by the feeble light of a rustic candle, tall as a church taper, than by broad daylight.

At that moment both of them had their noses in their soup and were licking the last drops straight from the bowl. They wiped their lips with the backs of their sleeves and the old man refilled the glasses; then, picking his teeth with his penknife, he started to complain:

'It'll maybe 'appen tonight.'

'Maybe it will,' replied Norine.

'I reckon on sleeping in the cowshed, what do you think?'

'Well if she calves, she'll calve, but you can't rightly know when she'll calve; oh, no one would believe how much she's sufferin', my poor Lizarde …there, listen!'

And indeed they heard a muffled lowing that cut through the silence of the room.

'It's the same as with people, they get contractions,' Aunt Norine added, and she explained wearily that Lizarde, her best cow, was about to drop a calf.

'Really?' said Jacques, 'but a calf should fetch a nice price; for you it's a bit of a godsend.'

'Well, yes…of course…but it's just that she has a hard time calving; it might come on her during the night and not be done till tomorrow evening; and what's more she's got a nasty inflammation, if the calf dies and anything bad happens to Lizarde that'll be nearly five hundred francs lost. So, we've a right to be worried, believe me.'

And they started on the habitual grievances of peasants: 'It's hard to make a living here, you break your back and what does the land give you in return? Barely two-and-a-half percent. If we weren't raising cattle, what would've become of us? Nowadays you can buy wheat for next to nothing, thanks to foreigners. We'll end up having to plant poplars,' continued the old man, 'that brings in a franc a foot every year on its own. By God, it's not like you lot in Paris, no disrespect to you mind, where you can make a pile of money for doing next to nothing!'

He broke off and reached over to the candle, the wick of which was sputtering. 'Now why's it cracklin' like that?' he said, and he closed his knife over the wick, cutting the charred end between the blade and the groove in the handle.

'Come now,' he added, 'aren't you eating?'

'Yes…yes, I am…No, aunt, really, I've had enough,' and he tried to fend off the old woman, who wanted to put another haunch of rabbit on his plate.

But she let it slide off the spoon all the same.

'Sure you'll eat it, just you see; you haven't come here to fast, I reckon,' and after a moment's silence she sighed: 'Ah well, that's that then!' and suddenly got up and went out.

'She's going to see Lizarde,' said the old man, in response to the astonished looks of Jacques and Louise. 'If it comes tonight, well I don't know what can be done; the herdsman'll be too far away at that hour, the poor beast'll be half dead before he even sets off; ah, God damn it!' and he shook his head, striking the table with the handle of his knife.

'And what about you, young man, you're not drinking at all. Is my wine offending you?'

Jacques could feel his head starting to spin in this little room, which was filling with scorching fumes from the vine branches burning in the fireplace.

'I'm suffocating,' he said. He got up, half opened the door, and inhaled a gust of fresh air, a gust perfumed with the sharp odour of damp wood to which was mixed the warm, ambergris-like fragrance of cow dung. 'That's good,' he said, and he lingered on the threshold of this country night where you could barely see two steps in front of you; vermiculated threads of rain were falling in front of his pupils, dilated in the blackness, but this murky vision lasted only for a moment because the night lit up in the distance; a flash of fire drilled through the gloom, stretched out into a blade, and a large gash of light cut across Aunt Norine, who became immense, her body bent in two as if it were hinged, her legs lying flat on the grass, her torso and head straight up in the treetops.

She was coming towards him, preceded, in fact, by her shadow, which was being animated by the lantern.

'Well, auntie, how is Lizarde?'

'I certainly don't reckon it'll be tonight; she'll calve shortly around midday tomorrow.'

They went back in and sat at the table again.

'Here, see what you think of that,' said the old man, offering some of the terrible local cheese, a 'dry cheese' as they called it, a kind of hard Brie the colour of an old molar, giving off a smell of decay like an outside privy.

Jacques refused. 'Louise is asleep on her feet,' he said, 'we'll go to bed.'

'Well we haven't heard much out of you tonight, my girl, and that's a fact; but sleep ain't so pressing that we can't all have a cup of mint tea,' and Aunt Norine poked the fire, muttering: 'It's got a frozen arse, this kettle…' while the old man took out a sachet of herbs from the cupboard.

'There's nothing better for the stomach,' he affirmed as he selected the leaves; but the Parisians grimaced when they tasted his infusion, which was like rinsing with mouthwash.

They preferred the cognac Aunt Norine brought out in a medicine bottle; then, at their insistence, old Antoine pulled his clogs back on, lit a lantern, and led them back to the château.

II

On entering the bedroom Louise collapsed into an armchair; the overexcitement of the day was at an end: she felt exhausted, mind empty, bone-tired.

Jacques pulled back the covers so she could get into bed, then put his suitcase on the table, and, sitting opposite her, sorted his papers, leaving the task of tying them up and and putting them in the cupboard till the next day.

Despite his long journey he experienced none of that exhaustion that warms the limbs, instead he felt weak, overcome by an infinite mental lassitude, by a boundless despondency.

With his elbows on the table, he stared at the candle whose tiny flame failed to pierce the darkness of the room, and an indefinable sense of unease began to haunt him; it seemed to him that, behind him in the blackness, there was an expanse of water and the breeze from its lapping waves was freezing him.

He stood up and shuddered, explaining away this shivering by the perennial damp, the impermeable chill of this room.

He contemplated his wife; she was stretched out, pallid, on the mattress, eyes half-closed, the sudden relaxation of her nerves making her look ten years older.

He went to check the doors; the bolts didn't work, and, in spite of his efforts, the keys stubbornly refused to turn; he ended up pushing a chair against the door to prevent it opening, then he returned to the window, scanned the darkness through the glass and, worn out with worry, went to bed.

The bed was lumpy and the bolster pricked him with its spiky barbs of straw; he squeezed into the space by the wall so as not to wake his sleeping wife, and, lying flat on his back, before extinguishing the candle, he examined the wall of the alcove, papered like the rest of the room in trellis wallpaper.

He applied himself to trying to numb his anxieties through some pointless and mechanical activity; he counted the diamond-shapes on the partition, carefully noted the added bits of wallpaper where the pattern didn't match; suddenly, a bizarre phenomenon occurred: the green lines of the trellis-work began to undulate, and the brackish background of the panelling started to ripple like flowing water.

And this lapping motion of the previously immobile partition became more pronounced: the wall, now liquid, oscillated, though without spreading; presently, it expanded upwards, burst through the ceiling and became colossal, then its flowing stonework parted and an enormous breach opened up, a tremendous arch through which plunged a road.

Little by little, at the end of this road, a palace rose up which drew nearer, then reached the panelling, pushing it aside, reducing this liquid portico to the status of a frame, rounded at the top like a niche, and straight lower down.

And this palace, with its layers of terraces rising into the clouds, its esplanades, its lakes bounded by banks of bronze, its towers ringed with battlements of iron, its domes lamellated with scales, its sheafs of obelisks with their tips permanently capped by snow like mountain peaks, silently split open and evaporated, and a gigantic hall appeared, paved in porphyry and supported by vast pillars with capitals finialled with bronze colocynths and golden lilies.

Behind these pillars stretched side galleries with floor tiles of blue basalt and marble, corbels of hawthorn and cedarwood, and panelled ceilings, gilded like reliquaries; then, in the nave itself at the end of the palace, rounded like the stained-glass apse of a basilica, other columns sprang up, spiralling into the invisible architraves of a dome and disappeared, as if exhaled into the immeasurable bounds of space.

Around these columns, linked by copper-red espaliers, a vineyard of precious stones rose up in a confusion of entangling steel tendrils and twisting branches whose bronze bark oozed a translucent sap of topazes and an iridescent resin of opals.

Everywhere was climbing with vine leaves cut from individual gems; everywhere was a flaming inferno of incombustible vines, an inferno fed by the mineral embers of leaves carved out of different glimmers of green: the light green glimmer of emerald, the grassy green of peridot, the sea-green of aquamarine, the yellowy-green of zircon and the greeny-blue of beryl; everywhere, high and low, from the tips of the vinepoles to the base of the stalks, there were vines sprouting grapes of rubies and amethysts, bunches of garnets and almandines, chasselas-like clusters of chrysoprases, muscat sprigs of olivines and quartz; they irradiated fabulous bursts of red lightning, violet lightning, yellow lightning that rose up in a tower of fiery fruit, the very sight of which suggested the realistic illusion of a grape harvest ready to spit out from under the screw of the winepress a must of dazzling fire!

Here and there, amid a chaos of foliage and creepers, these vines were spreading in every direction, grabbing onto branches with their tendrils to form cradles, at the ends of which dangled symbolic pomegranates, their bronze-red calyxes caressing the tips of phallic flowerbuds springing up from the ground.

This inconceivable vegetation was illuminating itself from within; on every side obsidian and prismatic stones inlaid into the pilasters were refracting and dispersing the glimmer of precious stones which, simultaneously reflected by the porphyry flagstones, seemed to strew the paving with a shower of stars.

Suddenly, as if it had been furiously stoked, the inferno of this vineyard roared; the palace was illuminated from base to summit, and, borne aloft on a kind of bed, the king appeared, motionless in his purple robe, standing erect beneath his hammered gold breastplate, spangled with emeralds and studded with gems, his head covered by a turriculated mitre, his beard forked and twisted into braids, his face the reddish grey of lava, his boney cheeks protruding beneath hollow eyes.

He was looking down at his feet, lost in a dream, absorbed by some inner dispute of the soul, weary perhaps of the futility of omnipotence and the unattainable aspirations to which it gives rise; in his moist eyes, clouded over like a lowering sky, you could sense the dearth of all joy, the obliteration of all sorrow, the extinction even of that hatred that sustains, and of that cruelty whose pleasures are blunted by prolonged indulgence.

Finally, he slowly raised his eyes and saw, standing in front of an old man with a bald cranium, beady eyes deep-set over a bulbous nose and flabby, hairless cheeks stippled like chicken skin, a young girl, head bowed, breathless, silent.

Her head was uncovered and her exceptionally blonde hair, bleached by salts and tinted by the play of mauve reflections, encased her face like a tight helmet, covering the tips of her ears and coming down over her broad forehead like a short visor.

Her exposed neck was bare, without a single jewel or gemstone, but from her shoulders to her heels a tight dress accentuated her figure, clinging to the shy swellings of her breasts, emphasising her small nipples, lineating the undulating circumlocutions of her body, lingering at her hips, creeping over the light curve of her belly, flowing the length of her legs which, placed together, were outlined by this sheath, a hyacinth-coloured dress of violet-blue, ocellated like a peacock's tail and dotted with eyes in which sapphire pupils were mounted in irises of silver satin.

She was small, scarcely mature, almost boyish with a hint of puppy fat, very delicate and very frail; lines of lilac make-up, smudged underneath to soften them, tapered back from her flower-blue eyes towards her temples; her painted lips sparkled against her supernatural pallor, a pallor acquired through the deliberate bleaching of her complexion; and the mysterious odour that was emanating from her, an odour comprised of complementary but distinguishable essences, was evidence of this artificial whiteness in that certain perfumes break down the pigments of the skin and permanently alter the tissue of the epidermis.

This odour floated around her, surrounded her as it were with a halo of aromas, evaporating from her flesh in wafts, now light, now heavy.

Over a primary layer of myrrh, a dark odour with its resinous, musty smell, its bitter, almost surly effluvia, was superimposed an essential oil of citron, impatient and fresh, a green perfume that held in check the solemn essence of Judea balsam whose musky tint dominated, but was in turn constrained, as if enslaved, by the red emanations of olibanum.

Standing thus in her dress strewn with blue flames, steeped in fragrances, her arms behind her back, her head slightly tilted, her neck taut, she remained motionless, but from time to time a shudder ran through her and as the material moved with her heaving breasts the sapphire eyes of her dress trembled, their pupils sparkling.

Then the man with the bald, egg-shaped head went up to her and with both hands seized her dress, which slid down and the woman sprang forth, completely naked, white and lustreless, her breasts barely formed, her nipples circled with a ring of gold, her slender legs seductive, her belly embossed at the navel with a golden stud and, further down, mauve reflections shimmered as on the hair of her head.

In the silence of the vaults, she took a few steps, then knelt, and the deathly pallor of her face intensified still more.

Reflected in the porphyry tiles, she could see her naked body; she saw herself as she was, without muslin or veil, under the relentless gaze of a man; the fearful deference that a short while ago had made her tremble before the silent scrutiny of a king, analysing her, examining her with deliberate relish, able, if he chose to dismiss her with a gesture, to insult that beauty which her feminine pride considered indestructible, consummate, almost divine, was now transformed into the desperate modesty, the shocked anguish of a virgin delivered up to the mutilating caresses of a master she didn't know.

A fear of this irreparable embrace, bruising the skin she'd ennobled with balm, crushing her inviolate flesh, deflowering and violating the secret chalice of her womb, and – surpassing any vain feeling of conquest – a sense of disgust at this ignoble sacrifice made with no surety of the future, with none of those hesitations of the personal love-affair, those passionate affectations of the soul that beguile the physical pain of such a wound, overwhelmed her; and as she held her stance, arms and legs apart, she glimpsed beneath her, mirrored in the dark paving-stones, the golden crowns of her breasts, the golden star at her belly, and, between her parted thighs, one more point of gold.

The king's gaze bored through this childlike nudity, and slowly he extended towards her the tulip-shaped diamond of his sceptre, the tip of which she, almost fainting, kissed.

The enormous room began to sway; billows of fog began to unfurl, like those smoke rings that, at the end of a firework show, cloud the trajectories of flares and conceal the flaming parabolas of rockets; and, as if borne aloft by this mist, the palace rose up, becoming larger still, took flight, disappearing into the night-sky, scattering pell-mell its seed of precious stones into the furrows of blackness, where, far above, glimmered an incredible harvest of stars.

Then, little by little, the mist dissipated; the woman reappeared, head thrown backward, completely white against the king's purple robe, her bust arched under the red arm that, like a poker, thrust into her.

***

A loud scream broke the silence, echoing under the vaults.

'Uhh…what is it?'

The room was black as pitch. Jacques lay stupefied, his heart beating, his arm gripped by clutching hands.

He stared into the darkness: the palace, the naked woman, the king, all had disappeared.

He came to his senses, stretched out his hands and felt his wife beside him, trembling.

'But what's the matter?'

'There's someone on the stairs.'

Immediately, he was back in the world of reality; it was all too true, he was in the Château de Lourps.

'Listen!'

Through the ill-fitting door he heard the sound of footsteps on the stairs, first brushing lightly on the steps, then almost tripping and finally banging heavily against the rails of the banister.

He jumped out of bed and seized a box of matches. He must have been asleep for a long time because the candle that had lit the room was now used up; the wick was lying flat, drowned in its own wax which had wept green stalactites down the brass candlestick; he took another candle from a packet which fortunately he'd brought in his luggage, stuck it in the holder and grabbed his cane.

His wife had also risen and put on her petticoat and slippers.

'I'm going with you,' she said.

'No, stay here,' and moving the chair, he opened the door.

Now let's see, he said to himself, scrutinizing the floor above, it would probably be better not to cut off my line of retreat. He hesitated; a slight noise below in the hallway made up his mind; he went forward, gripping his cane, and at the turn of the stairs, plunged down.

Nothing. In the flickering gleams of the candle, only his shadow was moving, winking up at the vaulted ceiling, stretching out head first down the stairs.

He reached the final steps, skirted the entrance hall, pushed sharply on the huge double doors, the noise of which rumbled like a peal of thunder throughout the empty house, and entered a long room.

He was in the ruins of the dining room; the stove had been ripped out of its recess, the plasterwork of which, felted with dust, was crumbling amid enormous spiderwebs, hanging down like little bags in all the corners: florets of mould mottled the partition walls covered with a lacework of cracks, and the alternating black and white flagstones on the floor were disintegrating, some chipped, others split.

He opened yet another door and went into an immense drawing room, devoid of furniture, its six windows barricaded by shutters that had once been painted; damp had absolutely wrecked the room's wainscotting; whole sections of woodwork were crumbling into dust; the splintered remains of the parquet floor lay on the ground amid a sawdust of old wood the colour of muscovado sugar; pieces of the partition walls were reduced to powder, which fell like fine sand if one so much as stamped the floor with one's foot; fissures snaked down the panels, cracked the friezes, zigzagged the doors from top to bottom and criss-crossed the fireplace, where a lifeless mirror had slipped from its tarnished frame now turned red and almost powdery.

In places, the ceiling was split, revealing rotten shingles and laths; in others, it had retained its stucco but leaks had sketched, as if with streams of urine, improbable landscapes on it in which, like a relief map, cracks simulated canyons and rivers, and the bulging, flaking plaster the peaks of Cordilleras and Alpine ranges.

Every now and again, something would creak. Jacques would turn around abruptly, shining his candle in the area the noise had come from, but the dark corners of the room he explored hid no one, and, on all sides, whichever door he opened revealed only a succession of silent, mildewed rooms, smelling of mausoleums, airless and slowly turning to dust.

He retraced his steps, postponing until daylight an examination of each of these rooms in detail, telling himself he'd board them up if it were possible. He crossed the rooms he'd already been through, turning around at every step, because the walls were settling and making new cracking noises.

The tension induced by this fruitless search put his nerves on edge; the mournful solitude of these rooms gripped him and, along with it, an unexpected, dreadful sense of fear, a fear not of known, certain dangers, for he felt his panic would have evaporated if he'd found a man crouching in a corner, but a fear of the unknown, a nervous terror provoked by the disturbing noises in this desert of blackness.

He tried, without success, to be reasonable, to make light

of this weakness in imagining that the château was haunted, his mind deliberately seizing on the most preposterous, the most fantastic, the most insane ideas in order to reassure himself, in order to demonstrate in this peremptory way how inane such fears were. But whatever he tried, his sense of unease increased. Even so, he managed to repress it for an instant by conjuring up the vision of an immediate threat, of a sudden hand-to-hand struggle; he entered the corridor, searched it feverishly, swearing angrily, wanting at all costs to discover a real danger to save himself from his fear.

Despondent, he'd just decided to go back upstairs when a thunderous noise suddenly resounded on the stairs above his head; he moved towards it. Something huge was filling the stairwell, agitating the air within it.

The candle flame, as if jerked by a gust of wind, guttered, darting acrid jets of smoke, shedding hardly any light; Jacques barely had time to step backwards, brace his legs and lash out hard with his hawthorn cane at the whirling mass that plummeted down on him with a shriek.

This was answered by another shriek, that of Louise who had come out and was leaning over the banisters, terror-stricken.

'Watch out! Watch out!'

Like the roaring blast of a forge, two circles of flaming phosphorus plunged towards him.

Again, he stepped back and struck, stabbing as if with a sword at the two holes of fire, slashing as if with a sabre, striking with all his force the howling mass which was thrashing about, butting against the walls, rattling the banisters.

Finally he stopped, exhausted, and stared in a daze at the corpse of an enormous screech owl whose clenched talons had streaked the panelling with drops of blood.

'Phew,' he said, wiping away the spots of red that speckled

his hands, 'lucky I had my cane,' and he went upstairs to his wife who, whiter than a sheet, had collapsed into a chair. He sprinkled her face with water, helped her back into bed, explaining awkwardly to her in a panting voice that the château was deserted, that the sound of steps in the distance had been the sound of wings brushing the walls of the stairwell, knocking against the balustrade, and scratching against the vault. She smiled softly and stretched out, shattered, on the straw mattress.

He himself felt no need of sleep. Although his legs were trembling and his fingers were so limp and numb he was incapable of clenching his fist, he preferred to remain dressed and wait for the dawn in a chair.

And then he experienced an inexplicable confusion of thoughts, like a rosary of ideas comprised of diverse and ingenious beads that had unravelled and was now rattling around in his brain with no thread linking them, no coherence.

His first thought was how lucky he'd been in piercing the bird's skull and in not having his eyes pecked out. And what about that naked woman glazed with gold, blotted from his memory on awaking, like a drawing rubbed out with an eraser? How could he have produced such a dream? – Ah, the dawn was taking so long to break. – His arrival in the countryside had begun so badly. Certainly, he was going to find it difficult to settle in here, because judging from first appearances this isolated château, far from any village, had little to offer. What an appalling situation he was in, all the same, and what, once he'd returned to Paris, could he do to earn a living? Nonetheless, Aunt Norine had extraordinary eyes! But still, how could he explain that strange dream? If only that friend he'd helped out in the past had paid him back a little of the money, but no, nothing! – Poor woman, he said to himself, looking at Louise, lying pallid in bed, eyes shut, lips gaunt.

Then, standing up, he stared out of the window; the day was finally dawning, but so crepuscular and so pale. To circumvent the incoherence of these melancholy ideas, he forced himself to sort out his papers and tie them into bundles; he ended up dozing off, his head on the table, and then woke up with a start.

The sun was now up; his watch said five o'clock. He sighed with relief, took his hat, and went downstairs on tiptoe, so as not to wake his wife.

III

He stood for a moment, dazzled, on the doorstep. Before him stretched a vast courtyard seething with dandelion heads, their bristling dried cilia moulting onto the green leaves that crawled over the gravel. To his right was a well, surmounted by a kind of tin pagoda that tapered up to an iron crescent resting on a sphere; further off, rows of peach trees were set along a wall and, above them, was the church, whose mild grey outline was in places obscured beneath a shiny lattice of ivy, and in others by the marigold-yellow velvet of accumulations of moss.

To his left and behind him was the château, immense, with a two-storey wing pierced by eight windows, a square tower enclosing the staircase and, at right angles, another wing, its lower casement windows shaped like Gothic arches.

Debilitated by age, crackelured by rain and blasted by the north wind, this building thrust up its facade, illuminated by warped triple-barred casements with glass the colour of water and topped by a roof of brown tiles marbled white with bird droppings, in a pale wash of daylight that was bleaching its weather-beaten stone skin.

Jacques forgot the funereal impression he'd felt the night before; the sun's rays applied a coat of make-up to the old château, the imposing wrinkles of which now grinned with gold-fillings of sunlight from walls smudged with the rouge of rusty Y-shaped iron ties spaced equally along the rugged epidermis of its stucco.

That deathly silence, that sense of resignation that had gripped his heart during the night was gone; the long extinguished life of this place, betrayed by the uncurtained windows opening onto bare corridors and empty rooms, seemed ready to be reborn; it would be enough simply to air the rooms, to awaken with the sound of human voices the dormant sonorities of those bedrooms, for the château to relive an existence that had ceased years ago.

Then, as the young man was examining it, inspecting the façade, discovering that the upper floor and the roof dated from the eighteenth century while the foundations went back to the Middle Ages, a great commotion made him turn, and, raising his head, he noticed that the round tower, glimpsed the night before, wasn't joined to the château at all as he had thought. It was separated off in the poulty yard and was serving as a pigeon loft. He approached, clambered up a dilapidated staircase, drew the bolt on the door at the top and looked inside.

The sudden panic of frantically beating wings above him in the tower startled him, and at the same time a prodigious whiff of ammonia stung the mucous membrane of his nose and his eyelids. He recoiled, barely able to make out through his tears the interior of the pigeon loft, honeycombed like the inside of a beehive and furnished in the middle with a ladder mounted on a swivel; as he retreated he glimpsed a snow of white feathers whirling in a shaft of light falling from an open skylight at the top of the tower all the way to the ground.

The birds that had fled the dovecote had taken refuge on the roof of the château; they were all flapping and stretching their wings, strutting about and preening themselves, and as they moved in the sun their backs glinted metallically, their quicksilver breasts shone pale green and pink, their satin throats quivering *flamme de punch* and cream, saffron yellow and cinder grey.

Some of the pigeons took flight, circling round the tall chimneys on the uppermost part of the château, and then all of a sudden this garland of birds broke up and settled again onto the tower, covering its roof with a cooing feather headdress.

Jacques turned his back to the château and, in front of him, at the far end of the courtyard, he saw an insanely overgrown garden, a riot of trees, rising madly into the sky.

As he got closer, he could make out ancient flowerbeds cut into almond-shapes, though their outlines had barely survived. Of the box shrubs that once bordered them, some were dead while others had shot up like trees and seemed, as if in a cemetery, to be giving shade to graves lost amid the grass. Here and there, in these ancient ovals overrun by nettles and brambles, old rosebushes could be made out, now reverted to their wild state, strewing this tangle of green with the reddish olives of budding rosehips; further off, potato plants, arrived from who knew where, were running to seed, as were poppies and clover that had doubtless blown in from the fields; lastly, in another bed, clumps of wormwood were lashing tufts of wild grass with an aromatic hail of golden seeds.

Jacques walked towards a patch of lawn, but the grass was dead, suffocated by moss; his feet sank into it, snagging against hidden roots and stumps that had been buried for years; he tried to follow a path the line of which was still visible, but the trees, left unpruned, were barricading it with their branches.

This garden must once have been planted with fruit trees and blossom trees; hazels as big as oaks and sumacs with small dark-purple berries, sticky as blackcurrants, entwined their branches around the paralysed tops of old apple trees, their trunks split, the wounds poulticed with lichen; bladdernut bushes waved their gauze-bandage seedpods beneath bizarre trees that Jacques knew neither the name nor the origin of, trees stippled with grey balls like soft nutmegs from which protruded little clawed fingers, clammy and pink.

Amid this tumult of vegetation, amid these rockets of greenery exploding at will in every direction, conifers were sticking out: pines, firs, spruces and cypresses; some were gigantic, shaped like the serried roofs of pagodas, balancing the brown bells of their cones; others were pearled with little red berries, while others still were pebbled with bluish ribbed buds; and all were holding up masts bristling with needles, flaring out enormous trunks scored with gashes from which oozed, like globs of melted sugar, tears of white resin.

Jacques advanced slowly, pushing aside the shrubs, stepping over the tufts; soon the way became impassable: the lower branches of the pine trees blocked the path, spreading out and curling over the ground, killing all the vegetation beneath them, strewing the earth with thousands of brown needles, while shoots from old vines had leapt the gap from one side of the path to the other and, clinging onto the trunks of the pines, were creeping around them, snaking their way up to the treetops and brandishing, high above in the sky, triumphant bunches of green grapes.

He stared, amazed, at this chaos of plants and trees. How long had this garden been left abandoned? Here and there, great oaks, pushed askew, criss-crossed each other and, dead from old age, served as supports for parasitical plants that coiled between them, connecting up into delicate webs held together by loops, hanging like nets of green meshing filled with a rustic haul of foliage; further on, wild quinces and pear trees were in leaf, though their enfeebled sap was too sluggish to produce fruit. All the cultivated flowers in the beds were dead; it was an inextricable skein of roots and creepers, an invasion of couch-grass, an onslaught of wild vegetables from seeds carried on the wind, inedible legumes with stringy marrow, with flesh deformed and soured by their seclusion in fallow soil.

And a silence, occasionally interrupted by the cries of startled birds and the leaps of disturbed rabbits fleeing, hung over this uprising of wild plants and weeds, this riot of nature, now mistress at last of a patch of ground manured by the massacre of cultivated species and aristocratic flowers.

He thought gloomily about this cynical thuggery of nature, so slavishly copied by mankind.

It's not a pretty sight, whether it's a mob of plants or of people, he said to himself; he shook his head, then jumped over the low branches and pulled aside a fan of greenery, which sprang back behind him, blocking the route again; he came up against an iron gate. It turned out the garden wasn't, as it had seemed, very big at all, the main grounds began beyond the gate; a stately avenue of trees, disfigured by felling, ran down through the woods to a simple oak door with an iron grill, giving access to the road to Longueville.

He pushed against the gate; it shuddered but didn't give way; a tangle of crackling moss stalks obstructed it at the bottom while climbing plants entwined round the iron bars, the bell-flowers of bindweed perfuming the air with a scent of almonds; he turned round again and beat his way back through the thickets of an old bower, the dead branches of which snapped and flew up like shards of glass; finally he reached a breach in the wall, went through, and found himself on the other side of the gate.

There, he noticed the traces of ancient moats, some of which still preserved the remains of gargoyles, their spouts stuffed with yarrow, their necks throttled by strands of morning glory and the spiralling tendrils of wild vine, and then he came across the edge of a copse of chestnuts and oaks. He plunged down a path, but soon the route became impenetrable; ivy was devouring the wood, covering the ground, filling up hollows, flattening out tussocks, suffocating trees; it spread overhead like a large-meshed sieve and beneath his feet like a ploughed field of dark green, mottled here and there by bright vermillion plumes of euphorbia.

A sensation of dusk and cold descended from this dense vault of trees which sifted out the golden light of day, allowing only a violet glow to filter through to the gloomy expanse of ground; a pungent, acrid smell, something like the scent of boar's urine, rose from earth that was rotten with leaves, churned up by moles, undermined by roots and sodden with water.

That sensation of damp that had chilled him the night before when he first set foot in the château gripped him again. He had to stop because his feet were stumbling into holes, getting entangled in ivy snares.

He retraced his steps, followed the edge of the copse and skirted the back of the château, which he hadn't seen before. This side, deprived of sunlight, was dismal. Seen from the front, the château was still imposing, despite its shabby appearance and its dilapidated façade; in broad daylight its old age even came to life, becoming gentler and more welcoming so to speak; seen from the back, it appeared dreary and frail, dark and squalid.

The roofs that were so bright in the sunlight, with their swarthy complexions speckled by white fly guano, became as unspeakably dirty in the shade as the bottom of a neglected birdcage; and beneath them everything was rickety; the gutters, full of leaves, crammed with tiles, had split, inundating a stucco flayed by the north wind with chewing-tobacco spit; the brackets of the downpipes were broken and some hung askew, waving their empty sleeves in the air; the windows had been broken, the staved-in shutters hastily nailed back together, braced with planks of wood, and the *persiennes* were teetering, stripped of slats, lopsided from the loss of hinges.

At the bottom, a shattered flight of six steps, with a hollow gap underneath full of tangled weeds, led to a broken door, its splintered boards rejoined and patched, as it were, by the blackness of the sealed vestibule behind it.

In short, the infirmities of a hideous old age – a mucilaginous discharge of rainwater, blotchy plasterwork, rheumy windowpanes, fistulous stonework, leprous brickwork, the hemorrhaging of all kinds of filthy detritus – had hurled itself at this wreck, which was dying alone and abandoned in the hidden solitude of the woods.

That dazzle of gleaming daylight, that shower of sunshine that had stilled the high wind of anguish which had buffeted him the day before, was over. An indescribable sadness gripped his heart again. The memory of that terrible night he'd spent in this ruin revived, coupled with a sense of shame, now that it was brighter and the clarity of day was reflecting through his mind, from having been so profoundly unnerved by that interlude in the shadows.

And, in spite of it all, he again felt overcome by a peculiar uneasiness. This isolation, this dank wood, this cloudy, purple light decanting through the treetops affected him in the same way that the gloomy chilliness of the château had, recalling its morbid, latent sense of melancholy.

At the memory of his absurd fight on the stairs with the screech owl he shuddered, and at the same moment felt annoyed with himself for doing so. He tried to justify himself, conceded that he'd been in an unusual state of mind, that he'd given in to external impressions against his better judgement, tormented by flayed nerves in revolt against his reason whose wretched failings had, nevertheless, dissipated with the break of dawn.

This inner struggle overwhelmed him. He quickened his pace to try and escape it, hoping that his unease would disappear if he was somewhere less sombre.

He strode towards a lane, mottled by rays of sunlight, which he could make out at the far end of the château and the copse, and his theory seemed to be proved right as soon as he reached this path, which separated the grounds of the château from the common land belonging to the parish. He felt a sense of relief; the grassy embankment being dry, he sat down and with a quick glance took in the towers, the orchards and the woods, and he forgot his troubles, suffused as he was by the sudden numbing warmth of this countryside whose subterranean exhalations were thawing his soul.

This respite was of short duration. The march of his thoughts, retracing the terrifying paths they'd been down the night before, began again, only more coherent and more precise. Now that he was out of this wood – the atmosphere of which, by returning him to an imaginatively analogous milieu, had aroused sensations similar to those he'd endured in the château the night before – he blushed at his apprehensions, angry with himself at his anxieties and his fears.

That vague feeling of shame he'd just experienced when he was in the copse thinking about the events of last night decided him: now that he was breathing calmly, in the sunlight, he would no longer allow himself to feel, as he had under the icy arches of ivy, those involuntary shudders that had run down his spine in the château. He tried to divert his thoughts from this track, to hurl them down some byway far from the countryside, far from the Château de Lourps; but still they returned to his present life, leaping over the childhood years he was evoking, over the image of Paris he was trying so hard to conjure up, even over his money problems, which he summoned to assist the illusion.

He shrugged his shoulders, realising that his mind wasn't going to be led astray, that it wouldn't, in spite of all his efforts, distance itself from that imperious night; so he forced himself at least to try and deflect his fears, to steer his thoughts and fix them on the only event of that night whose recollection he didn't find unbearable. He closed his eyes to better isolate himself and thought again about that astonishing dream he'd seen unfold in front of him while he was dozing.

He sought to explain it to himself. Where, in what period, in what hemisphere, in what country could that immense palace have been constructed, with its domes shooting up into the clouds, its phallic columns, its pillars emerging from a paving of hard, shimmering water?

He wandered among age-old fables, among ancient legends, stumbled through the mists of history, picturing vague Bactrias, hypothetical Cappadocias, speculative Susas, imagining inconceivable peoples over whom this monarch in red, gold-turbaned and covered in gems, could have reigned.

Little by little a glimmer of light sprang up in his mind; recollections from holy books adrift in his memory joined together, one to another, and converged on that book in which Ahasuerus, at the promptings of a declining virility, stood before the niece of Mordechai, that venerable procurer, that blessed intermediary of the God of the Jews.

The characters illuminated by this glimmer of light, sketched in by his memories of the Bible, became recognisable; the silent king searching to slake his carnal thirst, and Esther, steeped in spices, bathed in oils and dusted with powders during the previous twelve months, led naked by the eunuch Hegai towards the redemptive bed of a nation.

And the symbolism was also revealed by the huge Vine, sister to carnal Nudity by way of Noah, and sister to Esther: the fruit of the Vine combining with the allure of woman to save Israel, by extracting an all-important promise from the lustful drunkenness of a king.

This explanation seemed reasonable, he thought, but how had Esther's image come to assail him when there were no circumstances that could have revived such memories, so long extinct?

Not as extinct as all that, he added, since, if not the text, at least the subject of the Book of Esther is coming back to me now so clearly.

In spite of everything, he persisted in searching for the sources of this dream in the more or less logical connection of ideas; but he hadn't read any books with passages that might stimulate a possible reminder of Esther; he hadn't seen any engravings or paintings whose subject matter might induce him to think about her; he was therefore forced to accept that his reading of the Bible had been incubating for years in one of the corners of his memory so that, once the period of gestation was over, Esther burst forth like a mysterious flower in the land of dreams.

All this is very strange, he concluded. And he remained pensive, because the unfathomable enigma of the dream haunted him. Were these visions, as man had long believed, a voyage of the soul outside the body, a flight beyond the world, the wanderings of a spirit escaped from its carnal lodging and roaming at will in an occult region, in a past or future limbo?

Within their self-contained madness, did dreams have a meaning? Was Artemidorus right when he maintained that the dream is a fiction of the soul, signifying some good or evil, and did old Porphyry understand rightly when he attributed the elements of a dream to a daemon warning us, while we sleep, of the traps that waking life has in store?

Do they predict the future and summon up events to come? Was the time-honoured mumbo-jumbo of oneiromancers and necromancers not so completely mad after all?

Or was it, as modern theories of science hold, a simple metamorphosis of real-life impressions, a simple distortion of previously acquired perceptions?

But then how can one explain through memory alone those flights into regions unsuspected in the waking state?

Was there, on the other hand, a fundamental association of ideas so tenuous that its connecting wire escaped analysis, a subterranean wire operating in the darkness of the soul, transmitting the spark, illuminating its neglected cellars in a sudden flash, linking chambers uninhabited since childhood? Did the phenomena of dreams have a closer relationship to the phenomena of real life than it was possible for man to conceive? Or was it simply just a sudden, unconscious vibration of encephalic tissues, a residue of mental activity, the hangover of processes in the brain creating embryonic thoughts and spectral images, passing through the murky sieve of a partially arrested mechanism ticking over as one slept?

Ultimately did one have to acknowledge supernatural causes, to believe that the designs of Providence were inciting these incomprehensible vortices of dreams, and in the same breath accept the inevitable visitations of incubi and succubi, all those far-fetched hypotheses of the demonists, or was it better to stop at material causes, to ascribe exclusively to external triggers, to disorders of the stomach or involuntary movements of the body, these wild ramblings of the soul?

In the latter case, it was essential to have no doubts as to science's pretension to explain everything, to convince oneself, for example, that nightmares are engendered by bouts of indigestion, dreams of Siberia by the chilling of the body when the covers slide off and leave it bare, and dreams of suffocation by the weight of one's blankets, to acknowledge too that the common illusion a sleeper has when he starts in his bed, imagining himself tumbling downstairs or falling into a void from the top of a tower, is solely due, as Wundt affirms, to an unconscious stretching of the foot.

But even assuming the influence of external stimuli, of a faint noise, a light touch, or a smell lingering in the bedroom, even admitting considerations of hyperemia or the speeding up and slowing down of the heart, even if one acquiesces in Radestock's belief that it is light from the moon that determines whether the sleeper experiences mystical visions or not, none of this would explain the mystery of how the psyche liberates itself and swiftly flies off to magical landscapes under new skies, to resurrected cities, to palaces of the future and regions yet to be, above all none of this would explain the fantastic appearance of Esther at the Château de Lourps.

It's enough to unsettle anyone, he said to himself, nonetheless it's clear that whatever opinion they profess, the experts are floundering.

These fruitless considerations had at least diverted the stream of his thought, which was straying away from its original source; the sun began to warm his back and, without his realising it, a joyous fluid began to circulate through his veins. He got up and looked behind him at the landscape stretching out at his feet as far as the eye could see, completely flat for miles, a landscape quartered by two wide roads into a long white cross, between the arms of which, rippling in the wind, was a multi-coloured haze of green rye, violet alfalfa and pink sainfoin and clover.

He felt the need to walk, but he didn't want to return by the same route; he followed the line of the walls zigzagging up an incline, advancing slowly, hunching over, listening to the lazy buzzing of the air, inhaling the earthy odour of the wind that was sweeping across the path. He was walking now among apple trees and vines. Suddenly, he noticed a half-open gate and found himself in an orchard, at the end of which loomed the candle-snuffer tower of the pigeon loft.

'Hey there!' said a voice to his left, as the rumble of a wheelbarrow bore down on him.

It was Aunt Norine.

'Now then! How's it going with you this morning, nephew?' And she rested the handles of the wheelbarrow on the ground.

'All right…so where's Uncle Antoine?'

'He'll be workin' in the yard at this hour, doin' the coppa.'

'Doing what?'

'The coppa.'

Aunt Norine burst out laughing at the confused look on Jacques's face: 'Why, he's cleaning the dirty cauldron with sandstone.'

Jacques finally understood: 'Oh, the copper…'

'Aye coppa, that's what the cauldron's made of.'

'And your pregnant cow…?'

'Don't talk to me about that, my boy; poor beast, when I think what a torment it is for her, what a strain…but it still ain't budging. I'm just off now to see the herdsman on account of her.'

And she continued on her way, bolt upright beneath her straw hat, chest flat beneath her smock, her haunches jerking with a martial air in time with her military step, elbows trembling from the effort of pushing the wheelbarrow in front of her.

'See you later…hey, over there!' and with a movement of her head she indicated a little path to follow, at the end of which he indeed glimpsed Uncle Antoine, in a pool of sunlight, scouring a copper cauldron.

His fingers scraped against Jacques's when they shook hands.

'I've just left Louise,' said old Antoine, placing his cauldron on the ground.

'So she's up, then?'

'Aye, seems she didn't have a good night,' and he added that the evening before last, he and his wife had to slaughter two screech owls in order to prepare the bedroom.

'Oh, it ain't dangerous here…there ain't no thieves,' he added after a moment's silence as if talking to himself or repeating the reply to one of the questions Louise had no doubt asked him; 'all the same, you shouldn't be taking your constitutionals near the woods at night, you know.'

'Really, why's that?'

'Well, because there are poachers who don't like it when you disturb them.'

'But, in your capacity as steward I'd have thought you should be chasing them off.'

'No doubt, no doubt, but in this 'ere game, my boy, I'd just be wasting my time; isn't it better that they eat the rabbit…or sell it to me for a good price?' And the old man winked. 'Now let's see, sit yourself down, you've got time because your wife will be miles away by now; she's gone to Savin with my sister…you know, Armandine, my blood sister…she's taken her in the cart to buy some provisions; she won't be back before one o'clock.'

Jacques sat down next to old Antoine on the trunk of a tree.

He recognised now the little house in which he'd dined the night before. By the light of day it seemed to him shabbier and even more contemptible, with its threadbare thatch, its stable door and rickety sheds propped up against it, full of bales of fodder, wine barrels and spades.

The smell of the cowshed reached him, warmed by a sheet-metal sky that had dried up during the night and was now flat and cloudless, of an almost harsh blue. Jacques ended up not listening anymore to the old man, who was lapsing into patois, his face gilded by the reflections from his cauldron.

Absent-mindedly, he rolled the hollow stem of a dandelion between his fingers, flicking away the seeds that blew onto his trousers; then he watched the hens, speckled black hens that would peck the earth with the tip of their beaks, scratch furiously with their star-shaped claws and then start pecking again with sharp stabs; here and there, chicks darted past like little rats whenever the cock came near, suddenly sticking out his neck and ruffling his feathers as if about to fly off.

He ended up falling asleep, intoxicated by the smell of manure and cow-pats; the crowing of the cock dragged him out of his torpor; he opened one eye: old Antoine was now rummaging about in the shed. Jacques yawned, then was distracted by a flock of ducks walking towards him, waddling from side to side. A few feet away they stopped, turned sharply and started thrusting the lemon-yellow pincers of their beaks into a piece of old wood, chipping off the bark and swallowing wood lice, which, now exposed, were hastily scurrying away.

'Now then, no sleeping,' said Uncle Antoine, 'come with me as far as Graffignes, that'll wake you up.'

But the young man refused; he preferred to go and look round the rooms in the château.

He was, in fact, curious to examine the interior of the building and to try and ascertain before nightfall if it was possible to set up in a room that was more secure and less depressing.

He was feeling exhausted from his railway journey, from his long walk, from his sleepless night. It seemed to him as if there were a fire in the palms of his hands and hot flushes coursed over his temples. As he made his way back, he reasoned with himself: if he'd been agitated by this vague and overpowering sense of fear, infatuated by this preoccupation with security and this need for vigilance, haunted by that inexplicable dream which still obsessed him even now, it was all simply due to his state of mental enervation and fatigue, to a sense of disequilibrium that had been primed by worries and cares, and triggered by the sudden change in his surroundings.

'A good night's sleep will rid me of this malaise but in the meantime,' he said to himself as he went into the entrance hall of the château, 'let's have a look at the downstairs rooms.'

He entered the gloomy kitchen, lit only by those tiny windows one sees in theatre-sets of dungeons, with its arched vault, its low doors rounded at the top, its cowled fireplace, its quarry-tiles; then he came across a series of sinister-looking cellars, compacted earth floors pitted by erosion, the marly soil pierced by eyes of black water; he turned back, returning by way of the rooms he'd passed through the night before; they seemed to him even more dilapidated, even more cankered by saltpetre, even more of a demolition site in the sunlight which was bathing the mouldy shreds of paper hanging off the walls; then he started on the other wing and wandered through its deserted rooms. They were all the same, immense, topped by high ceilings, with ruined parquet floors revealing rotten joists, stinking of fungus and smelling of rats. 'They're uninhabitable,' he said to himself; finally, he ended up in a very large bedroom, adorned with two fireplaces, one in each corner.

This room was superb, with its grey wood pannelling set off with fine filletwork, its doors surmounted by decorative lintels, and its two large windows with closed shutters.

'Now this is more like it! Let's have a closer look.'

He loosened the window latches, breaking his nails against the shutters which gave way with a groan. But he was left disappointed: the room had preserved an appearance of health in the shadows, but in the daylight it was incredibly run-down and shabby; the domed ceiling was sagging; raised blocks of parquet flooring were standing on end; the paper-covered doors of the cupboards were torn, exposing mildewed linen that looked like laudanum poultices; a coffee-coloured sweat ran continuously along the rotting strips of skirting board, and enormous rosaries were strung out along the friezes – the rosary threads being mimicked by a network of cracks and the beads represented by pale blisters of mould.

He went over to the alcove, noticed that it was furrowed by woodworm and plagued by termites. One punch and the whole thing would crumble. What a ruin! – this room was perhaps the most neglected of them all. A small door situated near the alcove attracted his attention; it opened onto a dressing room lined with shelves; a strange smell emanated from this room, the smell of warm face-powder beneath which filtered a very faint scent of ether.

This musty odour almost moved him, for it stirred in him pampered visions of a vanquished past; it seemed to be the last emanation of those forgotten perfumes of the eighteenth century, those scents founded on bergamot and citron which, when they evaporate, leave a whiff of ether. The spirit of perfume bottles unstoppered in the past returned and bid a plaintive welcome to the visitor of these dead rooms.

This was probably the dressing room of that Marquise de Saint-Phal which old Antoine, in the course of his visits to Paris, had often mentioned.

And this bedroom was no doubt also hers. Peasant tradition portrayed the marquise as slender, delicate, languid, almost pitiful. All these details sprang into his mind, one after another, uniting to form the powdered image of a young woman daydreaming in a Bergère armchair, warming her feet and her back, between the glowing hearths of the two fireplaces.

How long ago all that was! The frigid charms of the woman were now sleeping in the graveyard close by, behind the church;

the bedroom, too, had passed away and stank of the grave. It seemed to him that he was violating a sepulchre, the sepulchre of a defunct past, a way of life that was dead; he closed the shutters and the doors again, made his way to the stairs and went up to the first floor as far as his bedroom, then turned right and began to explore the other wing.

His astonishment grew; it was a veritable maze of doors; five or six opened onto a long corridor; he would push one door open and, in a darkened room, three more, all closed, would immediately appear; and all led onto storage areas, dark recesses that were connected together by yet more doors and which generally ended up in a large, well-lit room overlooking the grounds, a room in tatters, full of debris and refuse.

What neglect! he thought. He came out again and inspected the other wing; albeit without much hope, he went through new doors into other rooms, getting lost in this labyrinth, coming back to his starting point, going round in circles, bewildering himself in this tangled mess of closets and rooms.

He was making a considerable racket just by himself; his steps resounded in the emptiness like the boots of a battalion on the march; rusty door hinges squealed at every push and the shaken windows rattled.

He was starting to get exasperated by all this noise when, at the far end of the château, he came across an immense room furnished with shelves and cabinets. He pushed back the shutters of one of the casement windows, and in a stream of light, the character of the place became apparent.

It was the château's former library; the bookcases had lost their panes of glass, shards of which crunched under his shoes whenever he moved; the ceiling was bulging in places, flaking, raining down a scurf of plaster over the powdered glass sanding the floor in tiny gleams; behind him the young man noticed an elder tree growing into the room through a broken window, its branches dusting the growths and swellings caused by the dampness of the walls. From top to bottom, everything was decomposing, crumbling, peeling, rotting, while in the air enormous garden spiders, their backs branded with a white cross, were hanging, dancing silent chaconnes one opposite the other, at the end of their threads.

As in the bedroom of the marquise he fell into a reverie; this library, now so dilapidated, must have once been alive. What had become of all the marbled calfskin, all the coarse-grained morocco, cavalry blue or burgundy, edam red or myrtle green, the goatskin bindings adorned with heraldic bearings on the top boards and gilded along the edges? What had become of the indispensable map of the ancient world, with its four angel heads blowing swollen-cheeked at each of the cardinal points? What had become of the tables made of rosewood and kingwood, furniture ornamented with spiral legs and ormulu casters?

Like the meadows, like the woods now carved up by the peasants, they had no doubt disappeared in a deluge of looting and auction sales!

'Well, I've had enough,' he sighed, closing the door; 'my wife's right; in this immense château, there's only one room that's fit to live in.'

He found his way back to the main corridor and, once back on the stairs, went up to the attic. He no longer had the heart to walk through the garrets. He merely half-opened a door, saw the sky emerging through the unplugged gaps between the tiles, and came back down, thinking to himself that, in comparison, the room Louise had chosen was quite pleasant.

But this impression didn't last long; it evaporated as soon as he went to their window. This casement looked out on the back of the château, next to the dark woods devoured by ivy. He felt a shiver run down his spine, and made his way over to the courtyard.

He prowled round the château, looking to see if, with more secure fastenings, he could find a proper refuge, from the night, from marauders and from wild animals; although the doors refused to open properly without a kick or a shove, most had lost their keys or had to be shut with latches that no longer had catches or were deprived of bolts. He inspected the surroundings; the grounds weren't even separated off from the woods; no walls, not even a hedge; anyone at all could get in.

It's really too primitive, he thought; then, overcome with tiredness, he went into the garden, stretched out on the lawn, and, once again, under the vibrant brightness of the sky, his spirits returned, because the direction of his thoughts, like those of everyone who is physically tired, changed according to purely external sensations. He breathed a sigh of contentment and dozed off, his back snugly set against a cushion of moss, his face gently cooled by the resin-scented fanning of the pines.

IV

The next day at dawn, around four in the morning, the bedroom door burst open with a fist blow. Waking with a start, the terrified Jacques and Louise saw Uncle Antoine standing before them, exuding the cloacal odour of warm manure.

'Nephew,' he said, 'the waters 'ave broken!'

'What waters?'

'Why the calf's, of course! What'd I tell you? Norine's run to the village to get the herdsman; I can't be everywhere at once and I'm afeared Lizarde'll calve before they get up the hill.'

'But,' said Jacques as he slipped on his trousers, 'I'm no midwife and I don't know what to do with a cow in labour, so I don't really see that I can be much help to you.'

'Oh yes you can; your wife can light the fire and warm some wine for Lizarde, and you can give me a hand while we wait for Norine and François to arrive.'

Louise made a sign to her husband; then she said: 'I'll follow you, go on ahead while I get dressed.'

On the way, Jacques couldn't help laughing as he looked at his uncle's face, pockmarked with black spots.

'What's that on your face?'

The old man spat into his hand, rubbed it on his cheeks and examined it.

'Oh…it's fly-shit. I slept the night in the cowshed, and believe it or not nephew where there's cows, there's flies.'

And, bending his short legs, he quicked his pace, muttering to himself, rubbing his fingers in the bristles on his chin, then scratching his head beneath a cap greasy with cow-muck.

When he opened the door of the cowshed, Jacques reeled. A caustic fug of ammonia streaming with thousands of flies pierced his eyes like needles and bored into his ears with its continuous buzzing. The cowshed, dimly lit by a skylight, was too small to hold its four cows, which were squeezed in, one against the other, on a litter of straw smeared with pats of excrement.

'My poor Lizarde, my poor creature!' moaned old Antoine, going up to the one that was lowing feebly and looking at him, head twisted round, with her huge, vacant eyes. And, shoving aside the others with his boot, he stroked Lizarde and spoke to her softly as if to a child, bestowed tender names on her, called her 'my baba, my girly,' and entreated her to bear up to the 'sweet pangs' of birth, swearing to her that if she pushed hard it would only last a moment, after which she'd be back to her normal size.

Scratching his head again, he said to Jacques: 'It's just that she's getting closer and closer to droppin' the calf! God in heaven, what the bloody hell's Norine up to? I suppose while we're waiting I could always prepare the cord for pulling the calf out with;' and, as Lizarde continued to low, while twisting his skeins of hemp he went on about how fond he was of her and what fine udders she had, no doubt in order to comfort her.

'If you tried to milk 'er, nephew, well, she'd barely give you a drop. She only lets herself go with Norine; she'll give it all to her; aye, they don't love you unless you loves them! Lizarde's like everyone else, she loves those who take care of 'er.

'And the others are just the same,' – and he pointed at the three cows who he called out to by name. 'Beauty', 'Patch,' and 'Blackie' stared with indifference at their companion, who was now lowing, her head raised toward the skylight.

'I could always grease her passage, that'll give her some relief,' said old Antoine as if to himself; he poured some oil into a bowl, then lifting up the tail with one hand, smeared the creature's inflamed genitals with the other.

'Ah, there you are!' he said, twisting round towards Louise, who had just come in. 'Be quick and warm up some wine, and prepare some bran mash in the bucket. What's the matter with you?' – and seeing his niece blanch, he grumbled between his teeth: 'Damn females, they're certainly not much help to a man!' Louise was turning white, for the terrible smell of the cowshed made her feel ill. Jacques was helping her to the door when the sound of voices announced the arrival of Aunt Norine.

'Well, well,' cried Antoine, ignoring his niece's indisposition, 'not a moment too soon! If you've been gone an hour, you've been gone two; so what the hell kept you?'

'I came as sharp as I could,' said the herdsman, who raised his cap when he saw Jacques.

And he entered the cowshed, deafened by Norine's squeals as she kissed her cow on the chops and the animal's lowing, which had become more frequent and more prolonged.

'I reckon this'll be it,' said the herdsman, who took off his long-sleeved waistcoat and pushed his cap back on his head.

The pointed outline of hooves could be made out against the diaphanous balloon emerging from the cow. The herdsman split the membrane and the hooves appeared, not totally raw, but a bit bloody, like those badly-cooked sheep's trotters that are served in cheap restaurants; and Jacques, standing in the doorway, watched as the two men each inserted a bare arm, cord wrapped around their hands, into the cow's hindquarters, and began to pull, cursing and swearing, while the animal shook the cowshed with her bellowing.

'Goddamn it, pull harder man! No, no, to the right! By God, the bugger weighs a ton!' And suddenly an enormous, sticky mass tumbled out, amid the splatter of placental discharge and mucus-membrane, onto a prepared pile of straw, while the gaping red gash beneath the cow's rump closed up again, as if worked by a spring.

'In God's name hold the damn brute!' growled Uncle Antoine as he rubbed down the calf, which was trying to get up on its front legs and butting its head in every direction.

Norine came in with a steaming bucket of wine.

'You haven't put any oats in it have you?' asked the herdsman.

'No, François.'

'That's good, because otherwise it ferments you see; some hempseed if you've got it, but no oats.' And they put the bucket near the animal, who was back on her feet, her vulva bleeding stalactites of pink mucus.

Lizarde lapped up the wine in one go. Then Norine knelt down and started to milk her; she looked like she was ringing bells, and beneath her fingers, wet with drops of milk, the teats squirted out a yellow slush, bubbling with froth.

'There, drink that,' she said to the cow, which swallowed the juice from its own udders in a couple of licks.

'For a calf, it's a good-looking calf,' said the herdsman, drying his fingers on a handful of straw; Aunt Norine was still ecstatic, her hands clasped over her belly.

The cow began to low again.

'Oh come on, you can stop moaning like that now, you brute,' complained Norine.

'Give the ol' bitch a belt on the snout!' replied Uncle Antoine, wiping his forehead with the back of his sleeve.

There was no more 'baba' or 'girlie' now, no more affectionate nicknames, no more inducements to calve well; the delivery had been an easy one and the calf had been born healthy: as their pecuniary anxieties subsided, so too did their kindness.

There was nothing to do now but sit back and have a

drink.

They returned to the cottage, and Norine took a medicine bottle full of brandy from the cupboard and filled their glasses; everybody clinked glasses and emptied them in one go.

Then Antoine seized on the moment to talk with the herdsman about some of the region's celebrated cow deliveries.

'Now then, François, tell my nephew how many men were needed to deliver Constant's cow.'

'Well, sir,' said the herdsman turning to Jacques, 'it needed eight all told, and strong men at that! Oh, I worked up a sweat that day, I can tell you! Yes, I 'ad to…begging your pardon, sir… stick my arm up the beast's arsehole in order to turn the calf round and make it come down the right passage, and no word of a lie there's only a fiddly bit of skin that separates 'em.'

'That's why,' said old Antoine, 'you're spoken of round here as a herdsman who knows what's what…'

'Aye, and the times I've said: "There's nowt more to be done, you can fetch the vet from Provins but it won't be worth his while coming…"; and he knows it all the same, that man, because once he gets there he barely has time to spit before he's back in his cart on his way home.'

'Ah well, that's that then!' cried Norine, with an approving nod.

Jacques was staring at the herdsman while he was talking. He was a small crooked man, scrawny and bandy-legged, with a stern profile like Bonaparte's and bright eyes that, along with the wry smile on his clean-shaven mouth, betrayed an incorrigible cunning whenever he laughed. On his feet he wore slippers – which they called 'bamboches' in this part of Brie – made from plaited strips of black and white material, a stripey blue shirt, a waistcoat with black lustrine sleeves, a pair of corduroy breeches held up by a leather army belt, a tin horn slung bandolier fashion, and a whip dangling from one shoulder.

'Another drink,' suggested Norine, and again they clinked glasses. François wiped his lips with the back of his hand and, after a few more bits of advice, he hobbled off down the hill.

Then, pressed by questions from his nephew, old Antoine talked about the herdsman; he explained that he was now rich. 'Oh, that's a cushy job, that is! See, he buys a two-year-old bull for four hundred francs, and sells it again for six when it's four years old: and during all that time, his stud being the only one in the village, he makes a packet!'

And he listed all his profits: two francs per cow per year, plus a bushel of wheat and rye, eggs at Easter, a soft cheese when the cow calves, as well as wine at harvest time. 'And what does he have to do for all that, I ask you? Keep his bull so it's always keen, lead the beast from the village to the meadow, and look after its bumps and bruises if it gets any. Oh, yes,' continued the old man, deep in thought, 'it's a cushy job. François is doing all right for himself…'

'But how many cows are there in Jutigny?'

'Well, I reckon at the moment there's two hundred and twenty-five.'

'And inhabitants?'

'That'd be around four hundred, my boy.'

There was a short period of silence. Louise and Norine returned from the cowshed where the young woman had finally ventured to look at the calf.

'If you could see how sweet it is,' she said to her husband, 'would you believe it, it drinks from a glass!'

'Yes, if you force it into its mouth and wiggle it!' replied Aunt Norine who didn't seem very enthusiastic about this civilised method of drinking.

'We don't do things here like everywhere else,' continued

the old man in a school-masterly tone. 'We don't let them suckle; they get lost a bit more often, but this way they don't keep following their mothers around and they don't graze.'

He started laughing. 'Do you remember, Norine, old Martin the greengrocer? – he's up in Jutigny,' he added, turning to Jacques, 'throwing his money away. He thought he was right clever just because he'd been to Paris; he didn't realise that you only fatten a veal calf with milk. He says to me: "Hey, old man, why are you putting a wicker muzzle over your calf's snout?" And when I says to him, "So it don't eat the grass," he just laughed in my face.

'Well, when he took his calf off to market in Bray, Achille says to him, after inspecting his calf's pink eyelids, "You've got yourself a red-blooded republican there, but it's no use to me," and all the other butchers told him the same thing…and he still has his grass-eating calf to this day!'

'So, a veal calf needs to be anaemic, completely undernourished,' Jacques asked, 'for it to sell?'

'Of course, my boy, if it wasn't, its meat wouldn't be edible!'

'It's got to turn to fat or else it'll be too bloody,' said his wife, backing him up. 'Listen, there's someone ringing at the gate beyond; oh, don't bother getting up…it's open; he only needs to give it a shove.'

And, indeed, after a bang, footsteps could be heard. Jacques stuck his head outside and made out a fat, short-legged figure with a limp.

'It's the postman!' said old Antoine.

'Ah well, that's that then!'

The man was wearing a huge straw hat encircled by a black ribbon on which the word 'Post' was painted in red letters, and over his blue canvas smock with cuffs dyed madder-red, he carried a satchel. He returned their greetings, wiped his feet, put down his walking stick, and said:

'You are Monsieur Jacques Marles?'

'Yes.'

He held out a letter and then rebuckled his sack.

'I've a notion you wouldn't say no to a drink,' said Norine.

'Certainly,' he said.

'And how many glasses have you drunk since you started your rounds?' asked old Antoine with a laugh.

'Oh, I've definitely not drunk more than seven.'

'Seven!' cried Louise.

'Him? My girl, he could down ten more without being any drunker than he is now!'

The postman's expression was both humble and proud at the same time. 'Yes, but it's only 'cause I eat,' he said modestly.

'You hear that, Louise? if you had any leftovers he'd polish 'em off in the time it takes to serve 'em; I don't know where you put it all.'

The man shrugged, and, as they were bringing him some bread and cheese, he pulled out his penknife; he carved himself a chunk of bread big enough to feed a regiment, put a bit of the piss-smelling mould they called blue Brie on it, and devoured the lot in enormous mouthfuls.

Between times, his jaws full, cheeks swelling in a constant ebb and flow beneath each temple, he complained about the length of his rounds, although his route was pretty good all the same; all the proprietors were down at the moment staying in their châteaux and that meant he often had further to walk, like coming out as far as this one, for example, but he was dealing with good honest people who never forgot their postman...

Jacques, immersed in the reading of his letter, looked up at this attempt to angle for a tip, but the postman, whose eyes were shining and dancing, so to speak, beneath a brow furrowed with wrinkles, was sycophantically going on about the largesse of the rich. Over at the miller's place in Tachy, they always gave him a bit of pie and a bottle of wine, and sometimes they kept him some of the stew from the day before; at the château up in Sigy, it was even better; the gardener treated him to fruit and salad, and the lady of the house saw to it herself that he always had a bite to eat and never left with a thirst on him; everyone liked him, moreover, because they knew who they were dealing with; then, when they returned to Paris again, they always remembered his little family, for he had two children, and it's all you can do as a postman to make ends meet...

Wearied by this verbiage, Jacques folded his letter and thought about his growing troubles. A friend who had undertaken to watch over his business affairs in the capital had written him an unsettling letter.

It was certain now that he wasn't going to get his money back; his creditors had united and taken steps in order to seize his possessions; and what's more Credit Lyonnais refused to honour some promissory notes he was hoping to convert into cash. Things aren't going well, he thought.

'Let's go and have some lunch,' said Louise, who was watching him.

'Well,' she resumed when they were alone, 'what does Moran say?'

He passed her the letter and she shook her head.

'How much money have we got left?' he asked.

'Not much, eight hundred francs at most, because there's already been some expenses,' and she added with a sigh, 'and that's not the end of it either!'

'Why's that?'

She went into some explanations. First, it had been necessary to spend about fifty francs on kitchen utensils and crockery. Next, they had to buy supplies of coffee, brandy, sugar, pepper, salt, candles and coal, a whole range of purchases that would have been otherwise difficult to get in this isolated château.

Besides, the question of food was becoming unnecessarily complicated. The butcher at Savin, the only butcher for miles around, was absolutely refusing, as were all the other shopkeepers for that matter, to come as far as the château because it wasn't on their route; as for the woman who comes on Saturdays from Provins with supplies of vegetables, chickens and eggs, the egg-woman as they call her, she declared she didn't want to knacker her horse climbing up the hill.

It was only the baker who consented to supply bread, and even then it was on the understanding that he'd leave it down below by the gate of the château, at the end of the avenue on the road to Longueville, at five o'clock in the evening.

'That'll be very convenient,' observed the young man. 'Whenever it rains we'll be eating soggy bread, nothing but sops.'

'We'll buy a basket with a cover and put stones on it.'

'But look, Uncle Antoine eats bread too. Why the devil can't he buy ours when he gets his?'

'You wouldn't like that. Norine brings back several loaves at a time, so after five or six days, it's as hard as rock. You know it as well as I do.'

Jacques made a despairing gesture.

'As for the wine,' she continued, 'we're having to have a barrel sent from Bray-sur-Seine; anyway, uncle's harvest was poor last year so if there's too much for us he's offered to pay us back for half the barrel.'

'And how much will it cost, this barrel?'

'About sixty francs.'

Jacques sighed.

'I don't know…what was your uncle going on about when he told us we'd find plenty of everything here?'

'He doesn't know us. He probably thought we'd live off a few potatoes and some fruit, like he does.'

'The only clear thing in all this is that every day, whatever the weather's like, we're going to have to run around the countryside for miles just to find a lamb chop and some cheese. But what about Jutigny or Longueville, aren't there any shops in those dumps?'

'No, they get their supplies from Savin. Nevertheless,' she continued, 'I'm hoping we'll get things organised in the end because aunt Armandine, Antoine's sister, knows a poor family in Savin whose little girl isn't going to school at the moment; for a price which still has to be agreed they'll send the child here each morning, we'll give her a shopping list and she'll bring things back after her lunch, in the afternoon.'

Jacques was beginning to think that the vaunted economies of life in the country were a delusion, and that solitude, so seductive to evoke when you live in the middle of Paris, becomes unbearable when you experience it, far from anywhere, with neither domestics nor a carriage.

And in his mind he went through all the disadvantages of the château: the threatening aspect of its surroundings, whether from people or animals; its icy dampness; its lack of comfort and the dearth of drinking water; then there were the other privations that annoyed him. He'd searched the labyrinth of its rooms in vain for one of those confessionals of the body, those rooms designed to carry away its secret evacuations. He had finally discovered, downstairs near the marquise's bedroom, a small water-closet, but it was in such a state of dilapidation that it wasn't safe to enter.

And that was the only one.

He had expressed his astonishment to Uncle Antoine, who had at first been taken aback, then looked at Norine.

She'd stamped her feet in delight and slapped her thighs.

'If you want to take a shit, nephew,' she said between gulps of laughter, 'just find a spot outside wherever you want, like we do!'

This simplistic way of resolving an embarrassing problem just exasperated the young man even more.

And he fumed about it for the rest of the day, which slipped by, moreover, without him noticing the hours draining away.

He was still being cushioned by the sedative effect of the countryside; he didn't feel that boredom of inactivity that hangs over too-familiar rooms or in front of already seen landscapes; he was still in that period of sluggishness, that blissful weariness induced by fresh air, which blunts sharp stabs of anxiety and bathes the soul in a drowsy, fainting sensation, in a dull feeling of vagueness; but if the warmth of the mornings acted on him like a dose of opium, like a sedative, the chill gloom of twilight dispersed that tranquillity which gave way, as it had on the first day, to an unsettling malaise, to a disturbing, unshakeable dread.

That evening, after dinner, he had gone down with his wife into the château's courtyard, and, sitting on folding chairs, they had watched in silence as the tired garden retreated back into itself and went to sleep; and even though he still experienced that sense of distraction which detached his mind from any idea he wanted to fix on, he felt the mysterious humiliations of fear welling up in this spiritual twilight. He looked at Louise. My God, how pale she was! He shivered, because her drawn features betrayed the continuing progress of her neurosis, and he dreaded the next attack of this indomitable sickness amid the isolation of these ruins.

And so this almost cosy uneasiness, caused by his inability to govern himself, transformed itself in Jacques into a clearly-defined anxiety; his scattered thoughts regrouped around his situation and that of Louise. He withdrew into his memories, looked back over his life, recalled the good years they had spent together. In order to marry her he'd had to quarrel with his family, composed of wealthy businessmen indignant at the lower-class origins of this woman, her peasant ancestry squaring badly with the middle-class values of his father. He'd overcome these prejudices, had accepted without regret a complete break with parents whose tastes and ideas he despised and whom he previously only visited at rare intervals anyway.

For their part, they considered him mad; 'A good-for-nothing, yes, but not yet mad,' thought Jacques, who was aware of his family's opinion. Yes, it was true, he was a good-for-nothing, incapable of interesting himself in the kind of jobs other men coveted, unfit to earn money, or even to hold onto it, indifferent to the lure of public honours and the attainment of high office. It wasn't, however, that he was lazy, because he'd done an immense amount of reading, his scholarship was wide-ranging but too sporadic, ingested without any precise aim, and consequently held in contempt by utilitarians and the idle rich alike.

The question he was striving to excise from his preoccupations, the question of knowing by what stratagem he could earn his daily bread in the future, assailed him more sharply and more doggedly now that his eyes fell on his wife, slumped in her chair and no doubt tortured by similar fears herself.

He rose and took a few steps in the courtyard.

The night, now closing in, was distorting the nave of the church opposite, which passed through all the shades of black:

from the darkest, made darker still by overcast shadows from areas overrun with ivy; to a less profound, more washed out black in places where the walls were bare; and then paler still within the window frames, whose opposing glass panes seemed to contain a sombre, cloudy water.

Jacques was contemplating this slow melting of stonework into the darkness when, from the top of the church a bird rose up like an eagle, described an amazing parabola with wings outspread, and then fell from the sky into the woods with a dull sound as the ruffled branches cracked.

'What's that?' asked Louise, who came and pressed herself against her husband.

'Just a screech owl, no doubt. They breed in the bell-tower of the church.'

He took his wife's arm and they walked around the courtyard, gripped by the vast silence of the countryside, that silence composed of the imperceptible noises of animals and plants that you can only hear if you concentrate.

The night, now more opaque, seemed to be rising up from the earth, drowning paths and undergrowth, condensing on scattered bushes, coiling around the disappearing trunks of trees, coagulating in their twigs and branches, filling in the holes between leaves, fusing them into a single clump of shadow; thick and dense lower down, the night gradually evaporated in proportion as it reached the sparse tops of the pine trees.

Finally, above the church, the garden and the woods, high up in the harsh sky, welled the cold water of the stars. Most seemed like frozen springs of light, and those that burned most fiercely were like inverted geysers or hot springs of glimmering water in reverse. There was not a shimmer, not a cloud, not a wrinkle in this firmament, which suggested the image of a solidified sea sprinkled with liquid islets.

Jacques suddenly felt faint in his whole body, a dizziness induced by staring into the vastness of space.

The immensity of this silent ocean, with its archipelagoes illuminated by feverish fires, almost left him trembling, overwhelmed by a sensation of the unknown, of the void, faced with which his stifled soul took fright.

Louise had also let her eyes wander among those distant abysses, following her husband, whose eyes, adulterated by the mirage of his own fixed vision, deceived him, perceiving brightly coloured constellations, at random and at will, even when they weren't there: the lilac and yellow stars in Cassiopeia, Venus as a green planet, the red terrain of Mars, the blue and white suns of Orion.

Guided by her husband, she fancied that she too saw them; and she was left breathless from the effort, dazed when she thought of what was before her eyes, feeling in her stomach a kind of anguish that was flowing into her legs, now unsteady and limp, feeling exactly as if a hand was pulling her slowly inside-out, from top to bottom.

'I don't feel well,' she said, 'let's go back.'

And from behind the château the moon rose up in its turn, full and round like a gaping well descending into the depths of an abyss, and bringing up to its silver surface buckets of pale fire.

V

It transcended all boundaries, receding endlessly as far as the eye could see, an immense desert of dried plaster, a Sahara of congealed whitewash, in the centre of which a circular mountain was rising, gigantic, from its rugged slopes, riddled with holes like a sponge, glistening with lumps of mica like sugar grains, up to its ridged crest of hard snow, scooped out in the form of a bowl.

Separated from this peak by a valley whose smooth floor seemed to have been moulded from a clay of white lead and chalk, another mountain thrust its pewter-coloured, funnel-shaped summit up to prodigious heights; you might have said of this mountain, dented like repoussé-work, swollen with enormous bumps, that it was a colossal wave, just breaking at the top, boiled in the fires of innumerable furnaces, whose bubbling turmoil, suddenly held in check and solidifying instantly, had been preserved intact.

It's obvious, thought Jacques, that we're in the middle of the Ocean of Storms, and these two monstrous chalices straining up to the heavens must be the crater-shaped summits of Copernicus and Kepler.

No, I haven't lost my way, he thought, contemplating the frozen milk of this almost flat surface, which became swollen and torulous only when you approached the foot of one of its peaks.

With a serene sense of assurance, he got his bearings: over there, what vaguely appears to be an enormous bay is the Sea of Humours, and those two horrible chancres guarding its entrance are unmistakeably the craters Gassendi and Agatharchides. And with a smile he thought that the Moon was a very strange country all the same, given that there was neither vapour, nor vegetation, nor soil, nor water, nothing but rocks and streams of lava, nothing but stratified craters and extinct volcanoes; so why then had the science of astronomy conserved those inaccurate names, those outdated and bizarre terms with which ancient astrologers had christened a succession of plains and mountains?

He turned to his wife, who sat hypnotised by this whiteness, and he explained to her in a few words that it would be imprudent to venture further south on this planet, because that's where the volcanic zone was, an agglomeration of extinct craters, sierras piling up one on top of the other, almost merging cordilleras that left barely enough room between their foothills for rugged paths that seemed to be hewn through slabs of limestone or bored through loaves of white lead.

He finally helped her to get up; she was listening to him, reading his lips, understanding his words but not hearing them at all, since there was no atmospheric medium on this planet devoid of air that could propagate sound; then, turning their backs on the landscape they'd just been contemplating, they climbed northwards again, following the chain of the Carpathians, crossing the Aristarchus crater, its ridges standing out against the horizon, barbed like a crayfish tail, serrated like a comb; they progressed easily, sliding rather than walking on a sort of frosted ice, beneath which seemed to be faint crystallised ferns whose veins and ribs gleamed like trails of quicksilver. They fancied they were walking over flattened undergrowth, over compressed brushwood, spread out under water that was diaphanous but solid.

They stepped out onto a new plain, the Sea of Rains, and here again, stationing themselves on a ridge, they overlooked a landscape, receding as far as the eye could see, that bristled with plaster Alps, swelled with salt Etnas and bulged with tubercles, that was blistered with cysts and scoriated like slag.

And just as on a relief map, immense peaks, countless Chimborazoes, swept across the plain: Euler and Pytheas, Timocharis and Archimedes, Autolycus and Aristillus, and, to the north, almost at the edge of the Sea of Cold, next to the Bay of Rainbows, whose rocky ridge curved round a smooth floor, burst the formidable Plato crater, the surface broken up for miles around by lava rising up in stucco rods and marble masts, descending in giant rolls of alabaster, tumbling down in a mass of white rocks, riddled with holes like coral and gleaming like sediment in a sieve.

You would have sworn that all this was self-illuminating; the light seemed to radiate from it, rising up from the ground, because high above the firmament was black, absolutely, intensely black, sprinkled with stars that burned solely for themselves, in one spot, without shedding a glimmer of light.

In essence, Aristillus resembled a Gothic city, its jagged peaks cutting like a saw, teeth upwards, into the starry basalt of the sky; and in front of and behind this city, two other cities were superimposed, blending the Moorish architecture of Granada with that of Heidelberg in the Middle Ages, intermingling one with another in a confusion of countries and epochs, minarets and belfries, obelisks and steeples, loopholes and crenellations, domes and machicolations, a monstrous trinity forming this dead metropolis, sculpted eons ago in a crater of silver by molten torrents of lava.

And on the ground, each of these cities projected harsh black shadows, shadows several miles long and resembling a mass of enormous surgical instruments, colossal saws, huge lancets, exaggerated probes, monumental ·needles, titanic trepanning tools, gigantic cupping glasses, an entire surgical kit for an

Atlas or an Enceladus, tipped out pell-mell onto a white cloth.

Jacques and his wife were dumbfounded, doubting the clarity of their eyesight. They rubbed their eyes, but as soon as they reopened them they were confounded by the same vision of a city painted in silver gouache against a background of night, and casting a spiky pattern of shadows shaped exactly like sinister instruments scattered on a white sheet, as if before an operation.

Louise took her husband's arm, and they went down onto the plain; turning to their right, they plunged into a small valley enclosed on one side by Timocharis and Archimedes, and on the other by the Apennines, the peaks of Eratosthenes and Huygens pushing out their demijohn bellies that gradually tapered upwards like winebottles, the uncorked necks of which were ringed with white wax.

'All the same it's strange,' said Jacques, 'here we are in the Marsh of Decay, and it isn't a marsh and it doesn't smell of anything! Though it's also true that the Ocean of Storms is perfectly dry, and the Sea of Humours, which you'd imagine would be as greasy as a lake of pus, is just an oversized faience plate with streams of grey lava for a crackle glaze.'

Louise flared her nostrils and inhaled the lack of air. No, there was no smell from this Marsh of Decay. None of those exhalations of calcium sulfide that indicate the putrefaction of a cadaver, none of that aroma of corpses deliquescing or of blood decomposing, no charnel house smell; just a vacuum, nothingness, a void of aroma and a void of sound, a negation of the senses of smell and hearing. And to prove it, with the heel of his shoe Jacques loosened some lumps of stone, which tumbled down, rolling just like balls of paper, without making a sound.

They advanced with difficulty; this undulating marsh, crystallised like a lake of salt, was pockmarked as if by giant smallpox, riddled with circular blemishes as large as those fountains built at Versailles during the reign of Louis XIV; in places, imaginary streams, rippled by the refraction of some unknown mineral, zigzagged with purple-grey streaks of iodine; in others, fake ponds, tinged an unhealthy bromine red, were linked by artificial canals; in other places still, pink cysts swelled like incurable wounds on this pallid flesh of ore.

Jacques consulted a map he kept folded up in the pocket of an English-made jacket which he didn't remember having put on until this moment. The map, published in Gotha under the auspices of Justus Perthes, seemed to him to be of indisputable clarity, with its shaded areas, its details in relief, and its Latin names: 'Lacus Mortis', 'Palus Putredinis', 'Oceanus Procel-larum,' borrowed from Beer and Mädler's old *Mappa Selenographica*, of which this was just a smaller scale copy.

Let's see, he said to himself, we've got a choice of two paths. Either we go down the channel formed by the edge of the Sea of Serenity and the gorge of Mount Haemus, or we go up via a pass through the Caucasus mountains as far as the borders of the Lake of Dreams, and then down again following the Taurus mountains until we get to the Jansen crater.

The latter route appeared to be easier and wider, but it lengthened the journey he had planned by thousands of miles. He decided they should thread their way through the path around Haemus, but what with its narrow walls of petrified sponge and white coke, and its ground swollen by hardened bubbles of chlorine like warts, he bumped into Louise at every step. Then they found themselves in front of a sort of tunnel and they had to let go of each other's arms and walk, one after the other, into this shaft like a crystal tube, the bright facets of which, like the points of a diamond, lit up the route. Suddenly, the vault rose higher, disappearing into the chimney of a blast furnace, stoppered at its summit an incalculable distance above them by a circle of black sky.

'We're almost there,' murmured Jacques, 'because this opening is the hollow peak of the Menelaus crater.' And, indeed, the tunnel came to an end and they emerged near the Acherusia promontory, not far from the Plinius crater in the Sea of Serenity, the contour of which resembled the belly of a pale figure, her navel represented by the Jansen crater, her girl's sex by the great V of a gulf, and the fork of her two spread legs, one clubfooted, by the Sea of Fecundity and the Sea of Nectar.

They advanced rapidly towards the Jansen crater, leaving on their left the Marsh of Sleep, tinged with yellow like a pool of coagulated bile, and the Sea of Crises, a plateau of sintered clay, the milky green colour of jade.

They scaled its steep slopes and sat down.

Then an extraordinary spectacle unfolded in front of them.

As far as the eye could see a silent, raging sea was rolling with breakers as high as cathedrals. On all sides were cataracts of congealed spume, avalanches of petrified waves, torrents of mute howling, a whole seething tempest compressed and anaesthetised in a single stroke.

It extended so far that the eye, confused, lost all sense of proportion, amassing mile upon mile, regardless of the possibilities of distance and time.

Here, sedentary whirlpools eddied in immobile spirals, descending into insatiable chasms in states of suspended animation; there, indeterminate sheets of foam, convulsive Niagaras, deadly columns of water were towering over abysses, their roars dormant, their surges paralysed, their vortices impotent and mute.

He began thinking, asking himself what kind of cataclysm could have frozen these hurricanes and extinguished these craters; what fantastical ovary compressor could have arrested the *petit mal*, the epilepsy of this planet, the hysteria of this moon, spitting fire, panting whirlwinds, rearing and convulsing on her bed of lava; in the wake of what unanswerable exorcism had cold Selene fallen cataleptic into this indissoluble silence, hanging for eternity under the immutable darkness of an incomprehensible firmament?

From what fearful seeds were these desolate mountains thus born, these calcinated, hollowed-out Himalayas? What cyclones had dried-up these Pacifics and scalped the unknown vegetation on their shores? What supposed deluges of fire, what vanished bolts of lightning had scarified the planet's crust, traced furrows deeper than riverbeds, and dug ditches into which ten Brahmaputras could easily have flowed?

And more distant, more distant still, other chains of mountains were emerging from the circle of imagined horizons, their interminable peaks brushing against the sky's cover of blackness, a cover resting solely on the nail-points of these summits, waiting for a supernatural hammer to drive them in with a blow and hermetically seal this indestructible box!

The plaything of some immense Titaness, of some enormous girl giant, an extravagant box containing icing-sugar replicas of storm-tossed plains, cardboard rocks and hollow volcanoes into the hole of which one of these children of Polyphemus could stick its little finger and thus lift into space the colossal framework of this incredible toy, the Moon was frightening to human reason, terrifying to human frailty.

And now Jacques began to feel that heaviness in the bowels, that contraction of the bladder induced by a prolonged fear of the void.

He looked at his wife; she was calm, and, with pince-nez held steady, was consulting, like an Englishwoman studying her tourist guide, the map that was unfolded on her knees.

This tranquillity, and this proof of having an actual living being near him, that he could touch if he wanted, allayed his fears. The vertigo that seemed to drag his eyes from their sockets, drawing them slowly towards the bottom of the abyss, faded now that his eyes rested on someone familiar, just two paces away, whose existence was tangible and certain.

Then he started to feel as hollow beneath his clothes as those tubulous mountains with no entrails of mineral, no heart of rock, no veins of granite, no lungs of metal. He felt light, almost fluid, ready to be blown away if the uncertain winds of this planet started up. All around him the aggravating cold of the poles and the appalling heat of the equators succeeded each other with no transition, without him even noticing it, because he had the sensation that he was at last rid of the temporary shell of his body; but a horror of this mournful desert, this tomb-like silence, this mute death knell, suddenly burst in on him. The tormented death throes of the Moon lying under the gravestone of the heavens unnerved him. He raised his eyes as if about to flee.

'Look over there,' said his wife innocently, 'it's all lighting up!'

Indeed, at that very moment the sun skimmed the mountaintops, their cracked ridges radiating white flame like molten metal. Glimmers of light were creeping all along the peaks, in the centre of which the cone of Tycho gleamed, awesome, opening its fiery pink mouth, grinding its glowing teeth, baying noiselessly into the imperturbable silence of an unhearing firmament.

'It's a more beautiful view than the one from the terrace at Saint-Germain-en-Laye,' continued Louise in an earnest tone.

'No doubt,' he said, surprised at his wife's stupidity,

which until then hadn't seemed to him to be so profuse or so emphatic.

VI

A few days passed. One morning, on going back up to his room after a walk across the fields, Jacques found his wife collapsed in a chair, face pale, arms hanging by her side.

'I'm all right, but I can't comb my hair. As soon as I lift my arm, I feel as if I'm going to faint; I'm not in any pain, on the contrary, it makes me very calm inside, very calm; but I feel so sad it's suffocating me.'

'I'm sure it's nothing,' she continued with a sigh, and with an effort of will, she stood up and took a step. 'That's strange, it feels to me like it's the floor of the room that's moving, that it's doing the walking.'

Suddenly, she let out a short scream and her right foot flung forward, with the quick, easy action of a French kickboxer.

Jacques carried her to the bed, where these kicks continued in succession, minute after minute, preceded by a scream; pains like electric shocks ran down her legs, fading away as if after the crackling jolt of a spark, only to return, running along her thighs and bursting out again in a sudden discharge.

Jacques sat down, knowing he was helpless against this sickness that had exhausted every conjecture, every prescription. He recalled the consultations with doctors who spoke of an incurable infection, of uterine metritis, who acknowledged its continuing progression in the wake of a spell of adynamia aggravated by rest and by sedatives, and that all the cauterisations, all the bloodletting, all the probing, all the distressing examinations, all the humiliating manipulations the unfortunate woman had had to undergo had been in vain.

After having descended into the body's crypt searching for traces of this numb sensation that habitually weighed on their patient, the doctors, anxious at not finding anything, changed their tactics, one after another attributing the malaise of the entire organism to an illness whose roots extended everywhere but were to be found nowhere. They prescribed stimulants and tonics, tried large doses of bromide, and resorted to morphine to deaden the pain, waiting for some symptom that would guide them, so they'd no longer have to grope around like this in a fog of vague, unknown illnesses.

The quacks, to whom one always turns when the irrefutable impotence of orthodox medicine reveals itself, didn't see things any clearer; at best, one of them had come across a remedy that seemed to regulate it, but what a remedy! Pressing a metal plate on the precise point of pain caused it to move, and one then had to follow it, give it chase, track it down, only for it to wind up eventually in some irreducible dead end from which it bounced back again, as if launched by a pliant springboard, into the tangled undergrowth of nerves.

On the other hand, a magisterium concocted by a Bolognese count, Cesare Mattei, and known within the schismatic circles of homeopathy as 'Green Electricity', occasionally checked the attack, conjured away the pain, as it were, and almost subdued the spasms, but these successes were deceptive; after working for a short while the mysterious water lost its efficacy.

Jacques was staring pensively at his wife, who had buried her face in her pillow, her ice-cold body writhing under the covers; and having gone back to the source of her illness, his thoughts were now following the progress of its attacks, catching up with it in the present, identifying it here at the Château de Lourps, anticipating it even, estimating its passage into the unknown regions of the future.

From when did it date and from what disasters was this disconcerting derangement of the nerves born? No one knew;

after their marriage, no doubt, in the wake of one of those internal problems that a misplaced sense of shame had concealed for as long as possible from the tentative diagnoses of the doctors and the untimely approaches of her husband; all this had dragged on for years, though initially only affecting her physical health, but then, bit by bit, it infiltrated her mind, sapping it at its base, ending up by establishing a pitiful equilibrium between the metritis induced lethargy on the one hand and her mental lassitude on the other, between fainting fits brought on by a ravaged stomach and the listlessness of a broken will.

And so little by little, a crack formed in the keel of the household, a crack through which their money drained. Louise, so attentive on her watch, had since the wedding fallen asleep, leaving the maid to pilot the ship. They immediately sprung a leak of brackish water. From the day the maid began doing the shopping, it was as if Jacques's wallet was blockaded by a flotilla of old battleaxes, supplying vegetables rescued from the gutter, worm-eaten pears as full of black spots as a snuff box, and maggoty apples with flesh as mushy as wool chewed by a cat; the fish became dodgy and the meat pallid, its blood despicably drained off to be sold separately.

Their meals were both expensive and unsavoury at the same time; as if afflicted by an unrelenting chorea, the maid led Louise a merry dance whenever it came to the shopping, and this jig didn't go unnoticed by the tradesmen; the coal merchant tampered with his weights and reduced the size of his sacks, the polisher half-heartedly shined the parquet floor and skimped on the wax, the laundrywoman employed the usual tricks of her trade and massacred the linen, or she switched it, forgot to bring it back or lost it, she muddled up the handkerchiefs as well as the invoices and resorted to crafty foldings in order to hide bleach stains and iron burns.

Louise felt powerless to respond, letting herself be pushed around, frightened by the idea of making a fuss, of venturing an opinion, or starting a quarrel; but this disarray nevertheless gnawed at her like a regret, disturbing her sleep and aggravating her nervous condition with its constant needling.

She wore herself out in this inner struggle, gave herself orders she wasn't able to obey, ended up depressed, burying her head in the sand like a child, wanting to believe that these swindles would cease to exist if she closed her eyes and didn't see them.

Jacques had not been without his own complaints during this fiasco, but the distressed face of his wife, the mute supplication in her eyes, disarmed him; noticing that whenever he scowled, Louise's state deteriorated, he too consented to do nothing, frightened by her failing energy, by the heartrending silence of a woman who'd once been lively and alert in her work.

He thought gloomily about the progressive disarray of his domestic life; Ah, it was beyond repair now. And a silent rebellion surged up inside him. After all, he hadn't married in order to relive the chaos of his bachelor life. What he'd hoped for was some distance from the odious details of domestic life, a peaceful household, a silent kitchen, a cosy atmosphere, a quiet, comfortable home life, a cushioned existence with no sharp edges that might attract his attention to his worries; he'd wanted a blissful haven, a well-furnished ark, sheltered from the winds, and what's more, he'd also wanted a woman's company, her skirts whisking away the irritation of trivial cares, protecting him, like a mosquito net, from the stings of life's minor concerns, keeping the room at an even, regulated temperature; he wanted everything to hand, without having to wait or go to the shops: love and food, laundry and books.

Solitary that he was, standoffish and not very open to new

faces, having a horror of society, having succeeded, finally, in reaping the exceptional benefits of the bearish reputation he'd acquired because, tired of his refusals, people were now sparing him the vexation of making excuses by not inviting him anymore, he had realised his dream of quietude by marrying a girl without a sou, with neither father nor mother, with no family to visit, who was quiet and devoted, practical and honest, who would let him flick through his books in peace, who revolved around his idiosyncrasies, protecting them rather than disturbing them.

How far away all that seemed now! The contentment of living side by side with a wife not given to verbosity, and therefore tolerable, and who felt no need to go out to parties or the theatre – how short-lived that had been!

From the first premonitory symptoms of her inexplicable illness, the atmosphere at home had changed rapidly. That slightly overcast morning feel that he liked so much was transformed into a long and dreary winter's evening. Louise, uncommunicative, reserved, would still smile, proving to Jacques that her affection remained intact, but it was with a hesitant, beseeching look, like that of a cat lying on one's clothes, imploring to be left alone, not chased away, not forced to search for another place.

And he grew irritated at this irruption of his memories, each one of which, in passing, touched the tender spot of his wound. Was it his fault if he was formed in such a way that he couldn't bear to live adrift, and that, with all his interests and passions, he needed peace of mind at all costs? He was a man who, reading in a newspaper or book one day some bizarre phrase about religion, science, history, art or whatever it might be, immediately gets carried away and rushes headlong into the study of it, hurling himself into antiquity, straining to probe its depths, to remember his Latin, swotting up like a maniac, then drops it all, suddenly disgusted for no reason with his work and his researches; a man who one morning throws himself into contemporary literature, swallowing the contents of numerous books, thinking about nothing but this particular art, not even sleeping, until he abandons it, too, the next morning, in a sudden volte-face, and now bored, daydreams while waiting for another subject on which to pounce. Ancient myths, theology, the Kabbala, each in its turn had demanded and held his attention. He had scoured libraries, worked through boxes of old papers, cluttered up his intellect skimming the surface of this jumble, and all this from idleness, from a momentary attraction, with no aim or useful purpose in mind.

In the course of this game he had acquired an enormous amount of muddled knowledge that was slightly more than conjecture, but less than certitude. A lack of energy, a curiosity that was too sharp and easily blunted, a failure to see ideas through, a weakness in the supports of his mind which buckled too easily, an excessive eagerness to dash down diverging roads or to abandon new paths as soon as he'd started out on them, an intellectual dyspepsia that demanded a variety of dishes, then quickly tired of the foods desired, almost digesting it all, but badly – that's how it was with him.

Pirouetting around like this amid the dust of time he'd spent some delightful hours, but ever since Louise's provident ways had dissipated, worn down by the rasp of her nerves, he'd been left dismayed, defenceless against the money worries that froze his intellectual infatuations and brutally threw him back into the inextricable spider's web of real life.

And now that he had no money left at all, what was going to happen? He shook his head in desperation; 'Moral and physical collapse, utter poverty,' he said to himself, and he took a perverse delight in exaggerating the horrors of the future, going straight to beggary, to starvation, the poorhouse for his wife, the lowest depths of destitution for himself.

As always happens with unfortunate and anxious people who jump to extremes and even feel a kind of consolation in realising they can fall no further, Jacques stepped back and calmed down, assuring himself of the extravagance of his fears. 'Everything works out in the end.' This axiom, dear to those poor devils who, despite everything, end up managing to eat and live even though they cannot, realistically, expect to get anything more, he now repeated to himself, banking on the unknown, counting on the future, putting his trust in providence or in chance.

'Anyway,' he said, 'my affairs could work themselves out without my having to resort to illusions. When I get back to Paris, I'll perhaps recover a few debts and then move to a quieter neighbourhood.'

He pursued this line of thought: 'I could sell most of my furniture and my books.' He went through them in his mind, first sacrificing the things he was least attached to, then hesitating for a few seconds over some of the others. 'That's enough!' he concluded, 'it's imperative to get rid of things and keep only what's needed to furnish two rooms.'

And it wasn't without a certain pleasure that he gave himself up to the selection of his books and his belongings; his predilections, spread over entire bookshelves and rooms, began to focus themselves, turning to the rare objects he was preparing to keep; he desired them even more now, and this new burst of affection for certain volumes, for certain pieces of furniture, almost made him wish that, today and without delay, he could get rid of the others which he suddenly no longer cared for.

It would be delightful, he thought, to furnish, with the pick of my possessions, a little kitchen and two small rooms, and he imagined them, wide rather than long, brightly lit against the backdrop of a garden that sheltered them from the noise of the streets. He would concede the expense of some wallpaper, not a blossom or floral pattern, but dark and with a matte finish. Over here, his bed, which he would keep, and his bedside table of kingwood and *bois d'anis*; over there, his writing desk, two armchairs, three chairs, a rug, and a firescreen; then, in the hearth, his wrought iron firedogs with splayed feet and pear-shaped heads; finally, on the mantelpiece, a carved and painted wooden bust from the late Middle Ages of a peasant praying, his hands clasped over a book, his pleading, anguished eyes raised towards the heavens; on either side of this bust, two burnished copper candlestick holders, and two pharmacy jars decorated with the coat of arms of a monastery, jars that had no doubt contained electuaries, such as diascordium or theriac, from some ancient convent.

In the other room he would arrange his books on simple wooden shelves, painted black, forming a kind of dining-room-cum-library.

He smiled, eager – almost impatient – to realise this intimate living space; it seemed to him that he would be snugger, more at home, more at ease in these suburban rooms than in his Parisian apartment with its vast rooms.

But no, it wasn't possible! He tumbled from the heights of fancy back down to earth. 'I can't even retire to some cheap room, can't hide myself away in some hole and live a working man's life because to realise that modest dream I'd need to have the one resource other people who've come down in the world have, a frugal, healthy wife! and since her illness Louise has been good for nothing. What could I do with a disabled wife, seated in a corner and tapping the floor with her foot? And what was next…what was next…who knows if her health won't get worse, and with no money to care for her I'll have to become her sick-nurse?'

Oh, if only he were alone, how much simpler his life would be! If he had to do it all over again, he certainly wouldn't get married. And supposing, in fact, that Louise did die, once the tears had dried, he could wait for something to turn up without too much hardship; he could get by until he found a job; he might perhaps find a woman, strong, dependable, expert at running a household, a woman who'd once been a priest's housekeeper, and what's more, one who'd be his mistress, one who didn't impose such lengthy fasts on her lover! Yes, he had to admit he was suffering from this sexual abstinence his wife's illness was making him endure.

He wouldn't mind her being a bit stout, this mistress, though not too rosy-cheeked, he'd like her to be…

Ah, now I'm becoming simply vile, he thought, as if woken abruptly from a dream and seeing Louise, eyes closed, in a state of suffering. He sat motionless, dazed by this burst of lust that had suddenly detonated inside him, because he sincerely loved his wife and would have given everything he possessed to cure her.

At the thought that he could lose her, a sob rose to his lips; he leaned over and kissed her, as if to compensate her for this involuntary explosion of selfishness, as if to deny to himself the baseness of his reflections.

She smiled at him – and at that moment she too was going back over her life, mourning over her miserable body, over her wasted existence, disoriented by the onset of poverty.

She acknowledged that her husband would never amount to anything. To be sure, she couldn't complain; he was good, affectionate, almost doting some days, even when absorbed in his books, as he usually was, and distracted from amorous attentions by his studies; but how careless he was when it came to money! She had frequently been worried about his investments, being shrewder and less trusting than he was in these matters. But he would just shrug his shoulders. Oh, what an idiot to let himself be swindled by a banker who he respected for the single fact that this dodgy dealer never talked about money and was interested in art! How many times she'd been exasperated by her husband, who was perhaps a superior man when it came to things she'd never heard of, but who was certainly a fool in practical affairs!

What could she do? she'd tried for years to save the household from these pitfalls and hazards, but whenever it was a question of money she continually came up against a husband who wouldn't answer her, who'd bury his nose in his books and grumble impatiently; but she'd had to refrain from any further reproaches, telling herself that, after all, his little fortune wasn't hers, feeling herself in the awkward position of someone taking a share of profits that don't, so to speak, actually belong to them.

Now ruin had come upon them, total ruin, and she felt the fury of a housewife towards a husband who didn't know how to berth his ship; she was amazed at herself for having imagined she hadn't the right to assert her convictions, to speak out. To be blunt, ever since the wedding his savings belonged to her. If she hadn't brought Jacques any dowry, she had at least surrendered to him the bounty of her sex, and what largesse was great enough to pay for that! Although she was neither enamoured of herself nor besotted with pride, she inevitably thought, as all women do, that the possession of her body was an inestimable gift; and again like all women, whether wives, daughters or mistresses, she thought that husbands, fathers and lovers had been put on this earth to supply a woman's needs, to support her, to be, in a word, her breadwinner.

And besides hadn't she been pretty and desirable when he'd married her, hadn't she been the bestower of some delirious nights, and hadn't she always been gentle, alert and attentive to Jacques's wishes? When all was said and done she'd made a fool's bargain in marrying him, because he'd cheated her; through his carelessness, he'd robbed her of a happy life and criminally aggravated the anxieties of her illness with the menacing prospect of poverty.

Ah, if she had her time over again, she certainly wouldn't get married! Then a gleam of common sense came to her: what would have become of her then, a woman with no family and no dowry? But her fate had been more than she could have hoped for; she'd married a man whom she liked and who, in a world obsessed with filthy lucre, had chosen her, poor as she was. All in all, apart from his lack of interest in real life, what could she reproach him with? Nothing, not even, during the carnal lenten fast he was having to put up with, a brief fling!

She regretted her unfairness. Raising herself a little in the bed, she called to Jacques and kissed him, as if to compensate him for this involuntary explosion of selfishness, as if to deny to herself the baseness of her reflections.

And yet, despite these sudden fits of self-interest that had so brutally shaken them, Jacques and Louise were nonetheless good people, happy to live together, unsuited to deception and false pretences, incapable of infidelity, each ready to sacrifice themselves for the other without a second thought.

Caught off-guard, taken unawares by a force independent of their will, they embodied a pitiful illustration of the baseness of the unconscious in otherwise decent people. They were, in short, victims of those terrible thoughts that worm into the minds of even the noblest, that make a son who adores his parents, not so much yearn to be rid of them, but muse involuntarily about their deaths with a certain sense of satisfaction.

Obviously this painful thought upsets him; he is stirred to the pit of his stomach by a sudden vision of the laying out of the coffins; he sees himself weeping hot tears, but he also immediately feels a pleasant sensation flowing slowly through him when he imagines himself at the cemetery, surrounded by people who stare at him, who arouse by their very presence his desire to be the centre of attention and his satisfaction at being pitied, who appease that need for a touch of drama that everyone harbours within themselves, without even suspecting it.

Then, inevitably, once the terrible spectacle of the funeral has faded, he envisages his future, awards himself, so to speak, a down payment of his inheritance and the comfortable existence he'll be able to lead when he comes of age.

It's this same ferment of surreptitious ideas that makes a widower living with his children unable to stop ruminating about how different his lot would be if he lived alone; he plunges into conjectures, into dreams of the future, he constructs an unfettered existence for himself, delights in the evocation of a new way of life, obviously not going so far as to wish that his children would disappear, but giving in to the appeal of the idea that they're no longer there, and leaving it at that.

However resolute and strong-willed one might be, no one escapes these mysterious impulses that circumscribe the outer limits of desire, that are nurtured, cultivated and sheltered in the most secret sewers of the soul.

And these irrational, morbid, bottled-up urges, these simulacra of temptation – these diabolical suggestions as a believer would say – surface especially in those unfortunates whose life is dismasted, because it is in the nature of anguish to fix on those lofty souls it humbles by insinuating the seeds of unworthy thoughts in them.

Ashamed and full of pity, Louise and Jacques looked at each another without speaking.

'My poor dear,' Louise said finally, 'you must be hungry

and I can't get up to light the fire. See if there's any meat left over from yesterday; anyway, the little girl from Savin will be here soon. Oh, if only I could move!'

'Don't worry yourself about me; look, here's some veal, some bread, and some wine, I don't need anything else.'

He moved the table closer to the bed and, without much appetite, made hard work of the tasteless veal and the stale bread.

There was a sound of footsteps coming up the stairs.

'It's the child,' said Louise, sitting up; 'give her the list of provisions to buy, it's there, on the side of the mantelpiece.'

A little girl entered, fair-haired, with a hooked nose covered in freckles and bulging blue and white eyes; she squirmed about, sniffing and scratching her pinafore with her fingernails.

'There, darling,' said Louise, 'here's a list for your mamma; you're to bring back the purchases this afternoon.'

The child hung her head and didn't move.

'Your pappa's a grocer, isn't he? Do you know if he has any gruyère?'

She looked up wide-eyed and, like a carp, opened her mouth from which no sound emerged.

'Do you know what gruyère is?'

'My mamma does washing she told me to say to the lady,' the little girl blurted out in one go.

'Oh, good,' replied Louise, who had been concerned about the question of the laundry for the last couple of days. 'You can tell your mamma that she's to come and see me tomorrow.'

The child nodded her head. 'Wha'sat?' she exclaimed suddenly, pointing at a pot of face powder.

'Ah, she's made up her mind to talk,' exclaimed Jacques. He held the unstoppered pot under her nose, but the child recoiled with a grimace and made a gagging noise, like a cat in front of a plate of liver that's gone off.

She declared that the smell of the powder was making her sick.

'Go and get some air, that'll sort you out, and don't forget our shopping. Hello, here's the postman. Have you got a letter?'

'I don't reckon so, I've a paper,' and the man sat down, put his straw hat on the floor, stuck his stick between his legs, took the satchel off his back and held out a newspaper to Jacques, all the while staring attentively at the veal left on the plate.

He seemed even more drunk than usual.

Jacques offered him a glass of wine.

He raised it to wish everyone good health, and knocked it back in a single swig.

'That's good, but it don't half give you an appetite,' he said, still staring fixedly at the plate.

Louise invited him to sit at the table; so he drew up a chair, pulled out his penknife, sliced off a hunk of bread, opened it up, shoved a piece of meat into it, and, with a frightful chewing noise, wolfed down both the bread and the veal.

He licked the blade of his knife before closing it, and, his eye like a small skylight through which the flames smouldering beneath his tanned skin escaped, he winked and said to Louise: 'Are you sick then, my little lady?'

'Yes, she's suffering with her legs,' replied Jacques.

'Ah, don't talk to me about that, there's no worse illness. I've been there m'self, weeks flat on my back unable to move, couldn't even lift a finger as they say, all from a fall I had – I thought I was done for – it's nearly two years since it 'appened and I'm still limping from it; I tell you, they picked me up on the Donnemarie road out of a ditch; I was as good as dead, they said, not a breath, nothing. They were calling out: old Mignot! old Mignot! I didn't hear a thing, Constant's son and big François can tell you…'

'Were you well looked after, at least?' asked Louise.

'Oh I was indeed, it was election time; Pathelin was for the reds and Berthulot was for the royalists, they each sent their doctors to see me twice a day. And it was good Bordeaux, first rate stuff, they brought me; once the voting was over, as true as I'm sitting here, I never saw those doctors or the wine again, and I had to look after myself at my own expense! Now then, what time is it, if you don't mind me asking?'

'Half past twelve.'

The postman rose and picked up his stick again. 'Til next time,' he said, waving with his back to them, and he went downstairs.

Louise had fallen back, exhausted, onto her bed. 'If I could only sleep…' she sighed.

'I'll leave you in peace,' said Jacques, 'you should have time for a nap until the girl gets back from Savin.'

He was just getting ready to go out when hurried steps shook the staircase and the postman reappeared, bareheaded, carrying his hat, brim folded, its two sides pressed together in his hand, as if it were a straw basket.

He opened it out on the floor and something startled leapt out, a strange creature with enormous claws, grey and hooked, grafted onto a very small body wrapped in white down and topped by a ghastly, grimacing head with round, motionless eyes and the beak of an eagle, which was making its scared old monkey face scowl.

'It's a little screech owl what's tumbled out of its nest into the nettles at the foot of the church.'

And the postman touched it with the tip of his boot. The creature walked with difficulty, sideways like a crab, ending up in a corner of the room where it stopped, its beak pressed against the wall.

'But what do you expect me to do with this animal?' asked Jacques.

'Well, if you don't want it, I'll take it to the priest in Chalmaison; he'll give me twenty sous for it. I'm telling you, that man he's got butterflies, he's got birds, he got moles...the things he stuffs! He's got some – oh, they're real funny – that look like they're dancing...and frogs standing up fighting each other!'

'I don't want anyone to kill it,' said Louise, 'it must be taken back to the church, its mother will come for it.'

'I don't reckon so; kids'll find it and throw stones at it.'

And picking up the creature, still motionless in the corner, he carried it over to the bed, trembling with fear, its eyes vacant, blinded by the daylight, its wings still covered in a cocoon of incredibly fine fluff of an unimaginable whiteness.

'So he's not for you then? Come on, Pierrot, let's go and see the priest,' he said, enclosing it in his straw hat again; 'I'll need to get a move on, because it's a long walk. Are you sure you don't want him?'

'No thanks,' said Jacques.

'You should have given him twenty sous for him to take that owl back to the church,' Louise said, after the postman had gone downstairs.

Jacques shrugged and unexpectedly showed a bit of nous: 'He would have just taken the twenty sous and still have gone to Chalmaison.'

In order to let his wife get some rest, he went out and wandered aimlessly around the lanes; then he made his way over to Aunt Norine's and found the door closed. Both husband and wife were in the fields.

Ah, there's no use expecting any help from them when

you're ill, he thought, they must be at the Graffignes vineyard; I suppose I could go and meet them.

But he didn't even make a start because he remembered the extraordinary difference there was between Aunt Norine and Uncle Antoine sitting at home, and Aunt Norine and Uncle Antoine when they were working their land; relaxing, they were amiable people, attentive to their niece and helpful; at work, they were haughty, would barely reply to you, ill concealing their complete disdain. They gave the impression they were fulfilling some kind of calling when paddling around in liquid manure and that they alone, in the whole world, knew what work was; they were sarcastic, too, and although ordinarily very humble would cast insolent glances at the Parisian who didn't even know 'how wheat grows'.

'Aye, they don't teach you that in Paris, I shouldn't think,' Norine would sneer, while Antoine would explain things Jacques hadn't asked him about in that pompous tone of his:

'You see, nephew, soil isn't like the pavement in your cities; it works, but it's also like us in that it needs its rest; if, one year, it's given us wheat, well, the coming year we sow it with oats, and the next year following we plant it with potatoes or beet, then we go back to wheat again, and sometimes it even needs to lie fallow for a whole year after harvest without being touched at all; it's all very well being some know-it-all from Paris, but you can't learn about soil in a day.'

And what's more, thought Jacques, they'll shower me with their litany of complaints again, and I'll have to hear them repeat that they're aching all over, that it's really hard breaking their backs at their age while I earn as much money as I want doing practically nothing.

Oh yes, I earn money, he thought bitterly, it's astonishing how much I earn, and how much I'm capable of earning! And he wondered, as he did every day, how he was going to live once he returned to Paris; but this question remained unanswered, because he had to admit quite simply that he was good for nothing. And at the château? Here, his money was dwindling and the next delivery of wine ordered in from Bray would empty out his purse. All things considered, it would have been better not to have run off to the countryside but to have stood up to his besieging creditors, to struggle along in Paris, to start afresh some way or other, and not to idly waste what little money he had at the Château de Lourps. But he'd been so tired and Louise was so ill! Besides, he'd counted on collecting the debts owed to him at Ormes.

Oh, and what about that friend he'd once done a favour for, who now refused to reimburse him? And I know he's rich, he said to himself angrily; yet in the past he'd been so generous. How the provinces reveal a man!

God, I'm so bored, he sighed; and like all people at their wit's end, he dreamed of being somewhere else, wished he could flee far from Lourps, abroad, no matter where, to leave his worries and cares in dry dock, to forget about his life, to reinvent himself body and soul. But it would be exactly the same everywhere else, he said to himself; one would need to be transported to another planet, but even then, as soon as it became habitable poverty would arrive there, too. And he smiled, because this idea of another planet reminded him of his dream the night before, his journey across the moon; this time, he thought, it's clear what the source of my dream was, the link is easier to follow than that of Esther because the evening before my departure for the old planet I looked up at the stars and the moon and I remember that at that moment I could recall quite clearly the details of the selenographic maps I have.

And then in the course of these rambling reflections, he

suddenly recollected that he needed to draw some water for the household cleaning.

After making his way to the well he came to the conclusion that the winch would have figured highly among the instruments of torture in the Middle Ages: you had to hang onto it, to brace yourself while turning the handle, in order to prevent the terrifying plummet of the pail into the void from fear of detaching the rope, which was fixed to the winch's wooden spindle by a single nail; then you had to turn the other way around and, ears deafened by the screeching of the dry pulley, wind the pail which weighed at least a hundred pounds all the way back up. He turned and turned, exhausted, watching the rope, hoping it would finally come up wet from the hole, thus announcing the imminent arrival of the pail.

It's never going to end. It's very strange all the same, he said to himself, because it seems lighter than usual; ah, here's the rope…but it isn't even wet! He reached for the pail, which appeared at the level of the curbing stones; it was empty.

'That's all I need,' he said, 'the well has probably dried up; we're in a right mess now!'

He sat down, despondent. 'Let's see, I'll have to warn Uncle Antoine; he knows the vagaries of wells better than I do.'

But neither old Antoine nor his wife had returned from the fields.

He didn't see them again until the evening, when, tempted by the idea of a drink, they decided to visit their niece.

'Well, what's up with you then? Oh my, oh my, would you believe it!' they exclaimed when Louise suddenly kicked out her leg. 'It must scare you to death being jerked around like that!' And they began to worry about their wooden bed; then, with a deliberate, almost defiant air, they gulped down their glasses of cassis and left, saying that 'all in all them Parisian illnesses were right peculiar'.

'Whatever's she got, I ask you, to make her jerk around like that?' pondered Norine, once they'd left.

'It's the rich what has them sorts of things; then there's... you know...the château, it brings bad luck to those what live in it; the marquis died there, that's proof of that...'

'And as for his wife, when the moon was full she'd just talk and talk...she went completely mad.'

'Now then,' continued Uncle Antoine, 'Jacques's complaining that the barrel hasn't arrived. While they're waiting for it, you've notched up on the wood by the fireplace how many litres of wine we've lent them?'

The old woman nodded her head.

'Aye, to be sure,' she said, 'they'll have to give us more than half the barrel for what we've let them have.' Then, after a pause: 'One last thing, husband ...'

'What's that then?'

'You told Bénoni that when he arrives from Bray he's to bring the barrel straight to us, not to the château?'

'Aye,' and they both smiled, thinking about the profitable arrangement they were preparing: draw wine from the barrel and store as many litres as they could in the cellar, then make up the Parisians' share by diluting it with some large bowls of water.

VII

One morning, Jacques noticed Uncle Antoine making his way through the garden wearing a long, dark blue smock, shining as if varnished and brocaded with arabesques of white thread forming epaulettes on either side of the collar. A peremptory soaping had lightened the natural skin colour of his cheeks, on which toothbrush-like whiskers were bristling, a last wipe with a dishcloth having flattened their tips down in the direction of his mouth.

'Where am I going, my boy? Why, I'm going to get myself a shave, because today's Sunday.'

'Oh,' said Jacques, who had lost all track of time since coming to Lourps. 'Tell me, do they celebrate mass there?' and he pointed beyond the orchard wall to the old church.

'No doubt they say mass for the women of Longueville.'

'But you, you don't go?'

'Me? what good would that do me? Mass, that's the priest's job, isn't it? He prays for everybody he does, it's all he's got to do!'

'And where's Norine?'

'She's gone to the meadow up on Renardière hill.' And after a pause, he added: 'There's another one! look my boy, see how many wasps there are. It's a good sign because it means we'll have a lot of wine this year.'

Talking as they went, they left the garden and found themselves on higher ground, near the church, opposite the Path of Fire.

'See you later,' cried old Antoine, and he went down the slope.

Jacques followed him with his eyes, then sat down on the

embankment and contemplated the same countryside he had glimpsed at dusk the day of his arrival at Lourps.

Let's see, he thought, recalling the names of the hills that had been dinned into his ears on a daily basis thanks to Norine, there in the distance, the far distance, are the forests of Tachy, then Grateloup and Froidsculs knoll; over here, where I am, are the slopes of Renardière and Graffignes, and further down, at the bottom of this corrie edged with woods, the small red and white village of Jutigny, with its whitewashed walls and terracotta roofs, then, almost right behind me, the black and green countryside of Longueville, with its peat bogs and its trees; finally, crossing the ploughed earth of the corrie like a stripe of chalk is the dull flat road that leads to Bray.

He looked up and probed the horizon.

Way up high, over Tachy, the sky was drizzling an imperceptible mist of iron filings, very pale blue, almost lilac in tone, like the dusty haze sifted through sultry morning skies which darkens as the afternoon progresses. The trees enclosing this view stretched out in nebulous, mouse-grey clumps, attenuated by the mauve ash that was quivering in the air; little by little, this ash dispersed and tree trunks appeared, like a dark hedge, though their tops still remained blurred with not even a hint of green; further below, rising up in tiers one above the other, were fields like carpets, a speckled motley of autumn-leaf-browns and rust-reds, and roads climbing interminably, running right up to the borders of the forest, separating these squares of dyed wool like strips of linen bandage.

Then, above the horizon, behind the shapeless tufts of the woods, a great white cloud loomed up, expanding as it rose, bits breaking off and floating away like puffs of steam from a train into the sky, which passed through infinite gradations from russet red to soft violet and, as it escaped the valley, turned completely blue.

And in the distance, villages exchanged glances from the hillsides; at the ends of those ribbons of linen, at the edges of those carpets, were little clusters of houses the roofs of which remained invisible, lost in the shimmering air, but whose walls blazed with the dazzling unpretentiousness of crude whitewash; the mist was clearing still more, hilltops were being tinged with yellow, gilded by rays of sunlight that struck complete hamlets but spared the dull carpet of fields and spurned the muted colour of the dry, ploughed earth.

In its turn, the wind rose, breaking the silence of the plain, sweeping away the bluish mists that were veiling the hillsides.

Then the horizon dug deep notches into the treetops, the green of which could now be seen; tiny hamlets and pathways, indistinct until a moment ago, became solid and no longer seemed to drift along the ground but to plant themselves firmly into the earth. The silent, motionless poplars, constricted for the most part, with their bushy tops, their bald patches and their tight clumps of leaves, began to swell, to stretch and roll in the wind with a noise like a sluicegate opening. And once again the sky changed; the sun disappeared, abandoning the villages shivering on their slopes; clouds scurried past, sketching out continents amid the sea of the heavens, the blue of which looked like ragged gulfs in these promontories of vapour. And there were holes thrust into this alluvium of space, funnel-shaped holes, russet-red, through which filtered a light like that from a bull's-eye lantern, a crepuscular light that blanched the landscape, making the melancholy, lukewarm colours seem more threadbare, more diluted, so to speak, and by contrast accentuating the garish tones which, left untouched, advanced haltingly over the valley.

The air was stifling; oppressive furnace blasts were coming in on the wind, inflating the shiny smock of Uncle Antoine, who could be seen far off in the distance, very small, swollen into a hunchback by the rising smock, which let billows of dust through his legs that periodically shrouded him from behind.

Jacques, who was laid low by the merciless blue of August skies but who delighted in the bleakness of a grey November, remained indifferent to this haggling of the weather, which was fretful and cheerful by turns but unleashed neither real melancholy nor genuine pleasure. He returned and walked around the château's garden. He sat down on the ancient lawn, but this posture irritated him; he stretched out on his belly and, thinking of nothing at all, amused himself picking flowers. There wasn't one among those he could reach that a horticulturist would have tolerated in their garden, because they belonged to that gang of plants that spring up on roadsides, an unhealthy flora, uncouth flowers, some of which, such as wild chicory, were nevertheless attractive with their star-shaped petals of pale blue azure.

Some had broken through the crust of moss and survived on their own; others had formed little groups and inhabited minuscule districts in which their tribe were comfortably encamped.

In amongst them, Jacques recognised strains of opium poppy, their nodding seedpods topped, like those of the common poppy, by a flat, pointed crown of grey seagreen, flecked with pink; then, separated by ant-hills, were stems of wild mint and he amused himself by crushing their leaves between his fingers then smelling them and savouring the changes in the scent it gave off, first its initial perfume, then a distinct odour of paraffin, and, to finish off when the essence grew fainter, a light musky whiff of armpit.

He turned over, absolutely unable to stay in one position. He got up, smoked a cigarette, walked down pathways. In the midst of this tangle of verdure he was finding new shrubs and plants every day. This time, against the old ditches at the bottom of the garden near the iron gate, he noticed magnificent hedges of thistle and bushes of holly, their metallic green leaves speckled with yellow tears like blobs of liver of sulphur. The sight of these bushes stopped him in his tracks, because, scrolled and spiralled like the arabesques in old ironwork, wreathed with finials and flourishes like the Gothic letters in ancient charters, they reminded him of certain German engravings from the end of the fifteenth century, whose heraldic air set him daydreaming.

The screech of the winch over the well being set in motion dragged him from his reflections. He could see, through a screen of leaves, Aunt Norine in her clogs, furiously turning the handle.

'So what were you saying, nephew, about the well being dry?' she cried, when she caught sight of him in the distance; 'don't be afraid, come on out, there's still enough water in there to drown a bigger man than you; here, look' – and with an arm of iron, she drew up an enormous bucket full of cold blue water, in which the reflection of the well's pulley shimmered.

And she explained to him how it should be done. You had to lower the bucket carefully, but once you'd come to the end of the rope you had to give it a little jerk, so that it submerged and didn't just float.

'Damn!' exclaimed Jacques, annoyed by this lecture and a little vexed at his incompetence, which the old woman had capitalised on to make fun of him. He went back up to his room; the table was laid.

'Oh no, not veal again!'

'What do you want me to do? I can't just throw it all away!' And Louise told him the way the butcher operated: you ordered one pound of meat from her and she sent three, declaring that you had to take it or leave it, seeing as it was too small an amount to be worth her slaughtering and selling her animal for; and to think that, for want of another butcher, one had to agree to such conditions out of fear of starvation.

'With the result that we're forced to eat the same meat for several days, or throw it away, which is what we do in fact. I'm telling you, these ruses will end up costing us dear!'

And he flew into a rage when he learned that the house-keeping money was almost spent.

They started to exchange bitter words when the sound of voices echoed in the stairwell. Then they fell silent; she, clearing the table; he, thinking about the fresh attempts his friend must have made in Paris to get his invoices finally settled.

Old Antoine appeared, freshly shaved, wearing a baggy cap, then Norine, her face practically scrubbed clean, her hair wrapped in a headscarf patterned with large black squares.

'I'm taking you to Jutigny, nephew,' said Uncle Antoine, 'today's the day I go to Parisot's for a hand of cards and a drink.'

'But I don't play.'

'What difference does that make? You can watch us…Well, I won't say no to that,' he said to Louise, who was offering him a brandy.

'And enjoy yourselves!' cried Aunt Norine after they'd clinked glasses; then the two men got up and left.

'Parisot, now there's a chap who's doing alright,' Uncle Antoine explained on the way, 'added to which his inn ain't 'alf worth some money,' and he pointed to a large two-storey building, standing on the road from Longueville to Bray, at the head of the village.

They went through a door, above which dangled a pine branch, into an indescribable uproar. You'd have sworn that all these peasants, who were laughing and jostling one against another, were arguing and about to come to blows. They cheered old Antoine, and some of them stepped back to make room for him and Jacques.

'What'll you have?' asked Parisot, a tall, cheery man whose bald head had something of the beadle and the simpleton about it.

'Give us some cassis and wine, my good man, and some cold water,' replied old Antoine.

While the old man, elbows on the table, was studying the game going on around him, Jacques took in the room with a glance, a large room, with walls painted sea green, and the skirting boards and mouldings chocolate-brown. Here and there were insurance certificates and handbills advertising manure; a copy of the law against drunkenness was stuck up with a blob of wax in each corner, and a framed set of the rules of billiards and of *boules* was hanging on the rail used to keep the scores.

On the ceiling, a few schist oil lamps; all around the room, school benches and tables covered in frayed, threadbare oilcloth.

In the middle, a sturdy billiard table with First Empire brass fittings and, in a corner, a row of white cues with chestnut patterns.

A cloud of smoke filled the room; nearly all the peasants were puffing away – on cigarettes if they were young, or on the seasoned stems of pipes, if they were old.

Jacques studied them; essentially they all looked the same: the old had mops of wiry hair, large hairy ears with pierced but ringless lobes, sideburns, rheumy eyes, big bulbous noses with bristles sprouting from the nostrils over a shaved upper lip, wine-stained lips, and firm chins over which they would continually rub their fingers.

In short, they all resembled the second-rate actors who

impersonated them, with their toothless smiles, their walnut complexions, and their rambling unfunny stories; only their swollen hands, the blackened knuckles, the crushed, split and eternally dirty nails, the callused, scabby palms, and the wrinkled leather on the backs of fists the colour of onion-skins, indicated that they genuinely worked on the land.

All the young men were a cross between pimps and soldiers. They didn't have big bushy sideburns but clipped moustaches and closely cropped hair. From their heads alone, they looked as if they belonged in the army; but taken as a whole, from head to foot, in their peaked caps, in their great blue smocks hanging down to their ankles, open at the front revealing shiny waistcoats decorated with stippled buttons that looked as if they were carved from some kind of hard Italian cheese, in their grey trousers and their fancy slip-ons, they could have been mistaken for pimps from the suburbs of Paris, with their rolling hips and their swinging arms.

They swarmed round the billiard table, crossing their cues like swords, jumping on a mate's shoulders to try and make his legs buckle, slapping their thighs, striking matches on the seat of their pants, and they were arguing like men about to cut each other's throats, shouting, mouths in each other's faces, making gestures as if they were going to fight or punch someone, but which ended up in friendly shoves and huge roars of laughter.

For their part, the old men were yelling just as loudly, banging their fists on the table every time they threw down a card; or else stopping, half pulling a card out of the fan in their hands, then pushing it back, the skin of their dewlaps contracting with a grimace: 'We 'aven't got all day!' the others would shout.

And then, once the trick was taken, the recriminations would begin:

'You should've played a heart!'

'No way!'

'Yes you should.'

'Bloody fool! Is that what you'd have done in my position? But I told you before, spades were trumps!'

'Water!'

'An absinthe for me!'

'Parisot, a shot of *Picon* over here!'

And the innkeeper, shambling over, would bring the drink in a glass, while his son, a tall, gangly lad who was half-asleep, wandered around the room with a carafe of water.

'Hey, over here, you dope!'

'Of course, of course, everyone's happier that way.'

'Well, they didn't believe a word he said…'

'I'm telling you he's a liar.'

'To tell you the truth, she was a bit too young…'

'No, I go there on Sundays, but not during the week.'

'Ay, ay, that's that then!'

Jacques was bewildered by all these interjections, these snatches of gossip that reached his ears, interspersed by the sizzle of a chip-pan squalling in a neighbouring room and by the successive turns of the billiard players, whose cues threatened to blind him with every back stroke.

He stared at Uncle Antoine; he was placidly sipping his mixture of cassis and wine and marking the points of the game on the table with a stub of chalk.

Jacques was starting to get inordinately annoyed amid all this noise. An odour of old flannel waistcoats, of filthy sawdust and wood shavings, a smell of cowsheds and wine dregs enveloped him, while thousands of flies buzzed around him, swooping down *en masse* onto the sugar, sucking up the stains on the table, landing on his cheeks or brushing their wings against the tip of his nose.

He waved them away, but they returned immediately, buzzing more loudly and more persistently.

I'd really like to go, he thought, but Uncle Antoine was beginning a game of piquet. He'd switched places, so Jacques now had next to him an ancient peasant with a 'chinstrap' beard like some great ape; he had to lean away from him because the nose of this man, who had the face of an oriental professor, was dripping like a coffee filter over the table, and over his neighbours whenever he turned his head.

'There you go,' cried Uncle Antoine as he dealt the cards, licking his thumb before each one, as all the others did when they were dealing.

Jacques was just beginning to doze off when he heard some fragments of conversation the meaning of which he tried hard to make sense of, but one of the two peasants talking was speaking so fast and using so much slang it was almost impossible to follow. It was something about a Parisian woman, and at first Jacques wondered if they weren't referring to Louise; but no, they were recounting a scene that had happened the Sunday before at this very inn, at Parisot's. The two peasants were crying with laughter, and Uncle Antoine, distracted for a moment from his game by these guffaws and catching the drift of the story by a phrase he heard, burst out laughing too.

I'm so bored! Jacques said to himself, I'd have been better off staying at Lourps. He stood up, and then knelt on the bench so as to look out the window.

Practically all the women of the surrounding area were gathered on the road, and not one, not a single one, had any breasts! And how awful most of them looked, roughhewn as if sculpted with a billhook, washed-out, their looks gone by the age of twenty, scruffy as slatterns in their drawstring blouses, their grey skirts and their workhouse stockings, worn with a pair of slippers!

God, what frights! thought Jacques. Even the girls seemed prematurely old, with their sharp features and their air of maturity. Holding hands in groups of six, they'd formed a circle and were singing in their shrill voices:

I'm off to see my aunt
Who's got some chickens to sell,
Black ones and white ones,
Four sous,
Four sous,
Won't you turn back, Ma'moiselle!

At this they turned around and, back to back, thrust out their backsides and shrieked.

Jacques began to take an interest in these little female monkeys, who at least had a vague hint of rosiness around the lips and a twinkle in their eyes; then more girls ran up, the youngest of which were almost pretty in their striped pinafores. And the circle expanded and re-formed, while in the middle, spinning round alone, an older girl began a lament about the Massacre of the Innocents and the Virgin:

Mary, Mary, you'd best be away,
Great King Herod's a-coming to slay
All the small children in bed where they lie
Including those who are here today!

And the revolving circle sped up, flying round, the smallest girls being lifted up by the arms, their feet no longer touching the ground, and their hats, falling off backwards, danced around, held on by elastic around their necks.

Amid the cloud of dust they were kicking up, Jacques could no longer make out the girl, whose plaintive, trailing refrain was being repeated by the circle in a variety of voices:

Mary went up to her dressing room
And clothed herself in white and blue
All her finest things she wore,
Then carried off her son in her –

Everything stopped, the rotating circle and the song; slaps echoed out, accompanied by the sound of shrill sobbing; a peasant woman was furiously smacking one of the little girls who had lost her shoe and had continued to jump around in her stockings.

'Now then, nephew,' said Uncle Antoine, tugging Jacques's sleeve, 'it's time we made our way back to Lourps.'

'I'm ready,' the young man replied, delighted to be leaving the inn, and they departed.

On the way, he asked the old man to tell him the story about the Parisian woman which had made the peasants recounting it laugh so much.

'Oh, it's nothing!' said old Antoine, 'it was a lady who has her little'un with a wet nurse round here – oh, she ain't no rich lady, mind. So she comes here with her other child, but as there's no place to stay at old Catherine's where the little'un is, she rented a room at Parisot's.

'But Sunday, now that was the village fair weren't it, and at Parisot's that evening at nine o'clock when she came back to go to bed, he told her he couldn't let her in, 'cause her room's the love room, that is, the one the lads and lassies use. But this lady wanted to stay, 'cause it was pitch-black and raining and she didn't know where else she could sleep, so he said to her: "Well, there ain't no other rooms, but there's two beds in yours, so you can sleep there with your little'un and the lads won't bother you, they'll go on the other bed with the girls." And she made such a face that those who were there still crease themselves over it – anyways, in the end she went over to old Catherine, who to top it all was ill, so the lady spent the night in a chair!'

'But I don't find it funny,' said Jacques, 'to throw a woman and child out on the street when it's raining and night's fallen.'

'All the same, he has to make money out of the room does Parisot, since the others were taken by paying customers who'd come for the fair. He couldn't miss out on his wine sales just for one Parisian lady; it was bad luck for her that she happened to be there that day. Anyway, she could easily have slept in that bed, the lads they mess around with their fillies, but they wouldn't 'ave done her no harm, 'cause they were too busy elsewhere. Foolin' around, having a good time, if you know what I mean! They have a few drinks – and then if they get the urge, no word of a lie, they just go out and head off into the fields.'

'But if that's the case,' replied Jacques, 'the village must be full of pregnant girls.'

'It is indeed, it is indeed – and they has to get married…the craftier lads,' he added after a pause and with a wink of his eye, 'they try to get the well-to-do girls in the family way…'

'And is it the same everywhere round here?'

'Of course, what did you expect?'

'Fair enough,' said Jacques, a little taken aback by this story, which summed up the hatred those in the countryside felt towards Parisians, as well as their money-grubbing instincts and their lack of morals.

On returning that evening, he recounted it all to Louise. He expected to see her protest against the cynical greed and the impudent sarcasm of the innkeeper. She felt sorry for the woman and pitied the child, but she just shrugged her shoulders. 'Anyone else would have done the same as Parisot,' she said, 'here, money is everything, and anyway, it has to be said that the evening of the village fair is the time of the year when the inn makes most of its profits, so…'

'Ah…' exclaimed Jacques, and stared in surprise at his wife.

VIII

The long-awaited barrel arrived one evening. Jacques learned this news the following day from Aunt Norine who, with a tight-lipped, almost shifty air, informed him that Uncle Antoine was just finishing putting the wine in bottles.

'The sly dog,' Jacques exclaimed, 'he didn't waste much time.'

'What else should he have done, my dear boy? It's only so that you, who haven't any bottles at all, can have your share sooner: we'll leave yours in the barrel and Antoine will bring it over to you as soon as he can.'

Jacques and Louise wanted to taste the wine. They went over to see Uncle Antoine, who they found pretending to be busy and jabbering away to himself, boasting about how he'd driven a hard bargain, telling them that this quality wine had come from Sens and declaring it was a right good drop.

Faced with this effusive gush of words and the old couple's obvious embarrassment, Jacques realised straightaway that he was being conned.

'Let's have a look,' he said, turning the spigot, and he and his wife tasted the wine. It was a brash, cheap wine that initially strove to invoke the flavour of grapes, but then, after you'd swallowed it, left you with the bouquet of a cask that had been rinsed out with pump water.

He glanced at the bottles that had already been drawn, thinking that those ones seemed to be less diluted.

'There, that's our lot,' said Aunt Norine, 'that's sixty-two litres, which is the half that we'll pay you for, plus twenty extra to make up for what we lent you while you were waiting for Bénoni to bring the cask. It's all there by my reckoning. So you see, all the rest is yours.'

'I don't care,' said Louise, 'it's like dishwater this wine, your friend Bénoni is a crook.'

'Oh no, that's not true!' protested the old couple, and they tried to persuade their niece that the lightness of the wine was a sign of Bénoni's honesty, since if he'd been crooked he'd have adulterated it so as to make it darker.

'Come on, it'll do,' said Jacques. 'But where are we going to put the barrel?'

'You'll see, my boy,' said the old man, who laid it in a wheelbarrow, rolled it as far as the château, and unloaded it onto one of the steps, propping up the part that was overhanging with a pile of stones placed on the paving beneath.

'If you want my opinion,' Jacques said to his wife when they were alone, 'that uncle of yours is a wily old fox.'

Then all of a sudden she lost her temper, reproaching her relatives for this hospitality that consisted in loaning them a room that didn't even belong to them: and, for the first time, she poured out all her grievances, revealing that Norine gave them potatoes and plums, but not a single peach, because that was a fruit that sold well at Provins market every Saturday. 'No, you don't invite people to stay and then leave them to feed themselves at their own expense; and I know for a fact they're rich, very rich,' she concluded, listing all the land they owned for five leagues around.

Jacques was surprised by the sudden bitterness of her reproaches.

'Let's not get carried away,' he said, 'it's not worth the effort; the only thing that annoys me is the incompetence of these misers; if they'd just stolen a few litres, it wouldn't have done much harm, but they've ruined what they left us by watering it down so as to cover up their fraud.'

'At least, Norine won't be able to take it with her when she goes,' his wife concluded.

'True…but, in the meantime…' Jacques said hesitantly, 'they've no doubt paid their friend Bénoni. Can we reimburse them right away?'

'Right now? No.'

'Ah…'

'Obviously, since you don't have any money.'

'I'm waiting for a letter from Moran, who's handling our financial affairs.'

'Oh, Moran!'

'What? he's a friend, the only one who's remained faithful to us in this whole debacle and you're sneering at him!'

'Me? What gives you the impression that I'm sneering at him?'

'The scornful tone in your voice of course!'

Louise shrugged her shoulders.

'Right, I'm going for a walk.' And, once outside, he mused over the change that was taking place in his wife, sought to unravel what was going on inside her.

That's three phases, he said to himself, after a moment's reflection. After the wedding: a decent girl, loving and devoted, thrifty but not penny-pinching…and in good health it should be said; then, after the nervous disorders began, improvident, wasteful, almost submissive; and now, selfish and bitter. He thought again about the way she'd received the story of the Parisian woman driven out of the inn, and that rage she'd suddenly exhibited when she realised about Norine and Antoine's scheming. In the past she would have laughed.

It's true that we're poor now and she's right to defend our interests; but this reflection didn't really convince him. He felt that some new, indefinable element was insinuating itself between them, a hint of defiance and resentment. But she's ill, he protested, and this second thought reassured him even less. No, there was something in particular, a new state of mind: on the one hand an impatience he'd never seen in her before, and on the other an attempt to assert herself, clothed in a series of vague reproaches, a sort of reaction against her role in the relationship which up until now had been so passive, a reaction that inevitably implied a disdain for men and a certain vain confidence in herself.

Not only are you dropped by casual acquaintances and colleagues when you fall into poverty, he thought to himself bitterly, you're even abandoned by those closest to you; then he smiled, realising the banality of his observation.

'What's to be done?' he said to himself. 'Play for time with my wife and handle the relatives with kid gloves, otherwise life will be unbearable.' And, as it turned out, from time to time he did need to act as a buffer in order to ameliorate their conflicts.

A coldness developed between his wife and Norine, between Uncle Antoine and himself; and the cause of this awkwardness, this reserve, this continual reticence, was the old couple themselves and Jacques was obliged to conciliate them so as not to break with them completely.

So it was that, without wanting it, without even suspecting it, the peasants drifted away from their niece. In the first place, they had behaved badly towards her and were therefore on the defensive, knowing full well that the Parisians hadn't been completely taken in by the theft of the wine; then an uneasiness, almost a repulsion, ever since they'd seen her ill and kicking her feet, had distanced them further from Louise. They weren't far off thinking her possessed or mad, even fearing that perhaps her illness was contagious and that they could catch it. They also thought the money they were owed for the barrel should have been paid straightaway and that, in short, they'd been deprived of the feasting and the generosity they'd counted on when inviting them down; finally, the harvest season had arrived and, for them, there was no time for family, friends or acquaintances anymore; they were entirely preoccupied by financial issues, obsessed by anxieties over the weather and bringing in the corn.

They didn't pay any attention to the Parisians, who they looked down on as good-for-nothings, and didn't even come to visit them anymore; these circumstances helped to avert an out and out quarrel. But bored of living alone, Jacques and Louise made advances to Norine and Antoine, went to see them; and the need the old couple felt to complain about their lot – and to boast about their hard work – resulted in a welcome whose kindness increased, because the mean tricks one inflicts on people give rise, in those who commit them, to a slight distancing at first, then to a movement in the opposite direction, a desire to smooth things over, to draw in one's claws, no doubt in order to set more traps in the future.

Jacques was pleased that things hadn't turned out worse, because now that his period of sluggishness, a torpor caused by the fresh air, had come to an end, he was overwhelmed by boredom; inevitably he daydreamed wistfully about his work, his books, his life in Paris, about those stimulating surroundings the charm of which he exaggerated now that he was no longer being subjected to them.

Then a heatwave struck; the weather, uncertain for several days, finally settled. Stripped of its clouds, the naked sky burned a ferocious, harsh blue, inundating the countryside with flames, ravaging the landscape. The earth dried up, turned as yellow as a fire brick, and parched knolls cracked; under dusty clumps of grass, the baked roads crumbled.

Like most highly-strung people, Jacques suffered

unspeakable tortures in weather like this, which liquifies your brain, soaks your palms with sweat and turns your underwear into a hip bath. Horrible sensations, of shirts riding up his back, of soaking collars and damp vests, of trousers sticking to his knees and feet swelling in his boots, the tiresomeness of sweat running down his skin as if from a water jug, forming into drops beneath his hair and gumming up his temples, overwhelmed him.

And all of a sudden his appetite deserted him; this diet of never-ending meat dishes poorly masked by tasteless sauces made him feel sick. He ransacked the vegetable garden, looking for herbs. There weren't any, neither chervil, nor thyme, nor burnet, nor bay leaves, not even cloves of garlic, the foul smell of which he found disgusting anyway, nothing but a few shallots – and their fiery, mineral taste revolted him. He stopped eating, and then the stomach upsets began.

He trailed through the rooms looking for somewhere a little cooler, but in the dark in which he shut himself away his melancholy became unbearable. He would walk around, going into less enclosed spaces, but there the heat would get in, the air vents blasting him with hot gusts, gusts that stank of mouldy parquet floors and musty rooms.

He waited until the abominable sun had set before going out, but the air was still thick with a heavy haze.

As for Louise, she kept to her room, dozing placidly on a chair, losing what little energy she had in the depressing atmosphere of the heatwave. She rarely came downstairs in the evening, despite Jacques's entreaties, and in order to distract her he would inveigle her into walking a little, just as far as Norine's.

The distraction was, it has to be said, pretty poor. Norine and old Antoine moaned endlessly about the workers they'd hired, explaining that for the harvest they'd taken on some of the Belgian labourers who roam the north and east of France at this time of year, and complaining that having to pay and feed these men would be the ruin of them.

'They're a scourge,' Norine was saying, 'they're good-for-nothings, you have to do everything for them. Oh, it's very hard for us all right. But them folks what don't grow their own crops, they wouldn't know about that!

'But,' said Jacques, 'couldn't you cut the wheat yourselves?'

'Oh dear me, no! besides, my dear boy, after the grain harvest be finished there's the grape harvest, too. This'll be going on for the next three months.'

And the old man ended up admitting that the Belgians, with their short-handled sickles and their billhooks, were quicker at the job and worked harder than all the men in the region put together.

'Us, we ain't skilled at it; we're just "mowers". We work with the big scythe that's over there in the corner, but it's slow work and as for the wheat that's been beaten down, you can't cut it and it gets wasted.'

One afternoon, tired of the solitude, Jacques left the château and walked along the slopes of Renardière hill, looking for Uncle Antoine.

Everywhere, from the tops of the hills to the bottom of the valleys, people were reaping, and, the sound carrying despite the distance, he could distinctly hear the rustle of stalks, followed by the metallic ring of the sickle cutting the wheat. The life of the landscape changed from hill to hill. Near Tachy the harvest was over, the stooks were piled up in heaps like beehives on the pale ground, which bristled with the short stalks of spared wheat, carts were circling round being loaded with sheafs, and hayricks rose up like enormous pies covered in straw. On Renardière hill they were only just beginning to reap and you could make out a few large hats, not a single head, occasionally a glimpse of back, but everywhere clusters of buttocks swaying slowly to-and-fro, above splayed legs.

Jacques eventually recognised Aunt Norine and Uncle Antoine fussing about near the men they'd hired. They stopped when they saw him. Jacques, still dazzled by the sun and sweating by the bucketful, was amazed to see that the Belgians were perfectly dry, flattening the wheat with their billhooks in one hand, and cutting it with their sickles in the other.

They were strapping fellows with blond beards, tanned complexions, and blond eyelashes, ersatz albinos coated with a brown patina by the fiery weather. They were wearing coarse, striped smocks, as thick and rough as hair shirts, and attached to the leather belts of their trousers, and hanging over their lower abdomens, were tin horns full of water and straw to moisten the whetstone that sharpened the sickle and prevent it from jolting about.

They didn't breathe a word, and as they were reaping wheat that had been flattened by the rains, they were toiling away, spitting into their hands, their scythes screeching against the wheat, which fell with a sound like a length of cloth being torn.

'Aye, lads, it's a tough job when the wheat's flat like that,' sighed Uncle Antoine, and he added this comment which didn't please Jacques very much: 'You've certainly worked up a sweat doing nothing, nephew!'

It's like an oven! thought the young man, who sat down cross-legged and huddled himself up, trying to shelter his body under the circle of shade cast by the brim of his large straw hat. And as for 'golden wheat', what a joke that is, he said to himself, looking into the distance at the dirty orange bales piled up in a heap. No matter how hard he tried, he couldn't come round to seeing this picture of the harvest, so endlessly celebrated by painters and poets, as truly noble. Beneath a predictable blue sky, hairy, barechested men stinking of sweat were sawing in unison through rusty brushwood. How paltry this picture seemed next to a scene of a foundry or the belly of a steamer, lit by the fires of a forge!

After all, next to the abominable magnificence of machines, the sole beauty the modern world has managed to create, what was this innocuous labour in the fields? What was an ordinary harvest, the natural fecundity of a benevolent earth, the painless birth of a soil fertilised by seed strewn from the hand of a brute, in comparison to the accouchement of cast iron inseminated by man, to those embryos of steel, born from the wombs of furnaces and taking shape, growing, expanding, crying out in raucous groans, and then flying along rails, raising mountains and crushing rocks!

The life bread of these machines – hard anthracite, dark oil, the whole black harvest reaped from the very bowels of the earth in pitch darkness – was so much more grievous, so much more grand.

And he reciprocated some of the contempt they had shown him, these whining peasants whose easy-going life would have seemed like an incomparable Eden to a miner, to a mechanic, or to any of the labourers in a city, not to mention the fact that, in the winter, these peasants just sit around gossiping and warming themselves, while workers in the city slave away and freeze. Yes, go on, moan, he said to himself, mentally addressing Uncle Antoine, who was complaining, arms folded across his belly, sighing: 'It's really very hard when the wheat's flat like that.'

'Eh now, what's the matter with you?' he said after a pause, looking at Jacques. 'What's got into you?'

'I'm being eaten alive, and all over at the same time,' cried the young man. It was a sudden outbreak of scabies, an atrocious itch that the scratching of his nails couldn't arrest. He felt as if his body was being enveloped by a low flame and, little by little, the fleeting pleasure of skin being scratched until it bleeds was giving way to a more acute burning sensation, an irritation that made you scream, a tickling pain that drove you mad!

'It's harvest mites,' said Aunt Norine, with a laugh, 'they just turned up yesterday. Here, look,' and she tilted her head and pulled apart two folds of flesh on her neck, between which Jacques could make out, deep under the skin, a red spot the size of a millet seed.

'But it's nothing, it's sort of like having fleas,' added Uncle Antoine, 'they'll go soon enough once it rains.'

Jacques envied the grained leather skin of these people who were hardly suffering at all, while he was having to grit his teeth as he raked his flesh.

To hell with the countryside! he said to himself as he left the harvesters. He needed to undress so he could lacerate himself more freely. He turned back towards the château, but he didn't have the strength of will to wait, to go any further; he stripped off behind a clump of trees, almost crying it hurt so much; he started ripping off flakes of skin and couldn't get enough of the painful pleasure of pinching himself, of scraping, tearing and grating his body, but as soon as he'd gouged one place, an intolerable burning sensation began again in another, flaring up everywhere at the same time, interrupting him, forcing him to scratch all over with both hands, returning to old bites that were already bleeding.

He tidied himself up as best he could, then went upstairs to the bedroom like a man in the grip of delirium and found Louise, practically naked, in tears; with her the irritation had progressed so rapidly that her hands were trembling, and at the same time hiccups and gurgles were welling from between the rows of her chattering teeth.

He suddenly remembered the cure for prurigo: vegetable oil soap; he rushed downstairs, ran over to Norine's, pushed open the badly fitting window, went in, and finally found some soap in a pot, and returning, he rubbed it vigorously over his wife's body in spite of her cries of pain, then he furiously coated himself with this congealed fat. He felt a sensation as if someone were sticking thousands of pins all over his body, but these sharp darts, this unequivocal pain, seemed delicious to him in comparison to that ambiguous itching, to those roving shooting pains, to the exasperating seething of scabies.

And Louise was calmer too, though the vegetable oil soap wasn't strong enough to get rid of the harvest mites entirely; they thought of dislodging them using the point of a needle, to root them out from the burrows they were digging, but there were so many of them that this subcutaneous hunt became impossible. 'We need sulphur, Emmerich ointment, and hot spring baths,' Jacques kept saying to himself in despair.

And Aunt Norine and Uncle Antoine just stared at them that evening, containing their laughter, amazed that Parisians had such delicate skin.

'What's the matter with you?' exclaimed the old woman to her niece, 'I ask you…harvest mites are just like a heat rash, they're only wee pimples!'

'Besides, they're good for the blood, they purge you,' added Uncle Antoine. 'Look, nephew, you kill 'em like you do tapeworms, by drinking rum,' and he emptied the carafe and toasted their health.

That night was terrible. Once in bed, the itching, which had eased a little during the evening, began again. Worn out, in a state of over-stimulation that made him clench his fists, Jacques got up, stifling with the heat, while Louise scratched at the sheets and bit the pillow to stop herself screaming.

Then she finally succumbed and fell asleep. And, in his turn, Jacques, away from the warmth of the bed, calmed down too. Sitting naked at his writing desk, he mulled over his troubles and exhorted himself, as soon as he received a little money, to go back to Paris as quickly as possible. I've had enough of this countryside, he thought, especially its mites! And he counted the days; his friend had finally discovered a bank that had agreed to cash his promissory notes. But there was a pile of papers to sign, a proxy to prepare, an agreement to leave a small deposit as a guarantee, a whole mass of formalities that seemed as if they'd never end. Another week here, and then Paris can do with me what it likes, as long as I'm away from here…Besides, it's obvious that the countryside isn't doing Louise any good. She's constantly shut up inside and doesn't want to go out; and the sinister aspect of the château is clearly having an effect on her…

And he, too, since the tedium of the countryside had gained the upper hand, was again feeling in the grip of that vague unease, of that obscure sense of dread that had oppressed him so forcefully when he first arrived at Lourps.

The situation was this. After he'd recovered from the fatigue of the journey and accustomed himself to his new way of life, the instinctive repulsion he'd felt for the château had died away. As for the nocturnal noises that filled this ruin – the bird fights in the dark rooms on the upper floors that could be heard distinctly, the howling of the wind sweeping through the corridors, playing harmonica through the cracks in the tiles and blowing whistle-blasts under the doors – he no longer noticed them. He would sleep, waking only from time to time to hear poachers beating about in the woods or the call of owls hooting from the rooms opposite.

This was only a minor irritation, disquieting but not actually scary, with no real hint of terror; in short, he would go back to sleep indifferent to those perils whose threat he no longer noticed.

But another situation was taking shape. The drowsiness which the open air was pouring over him had numbed the dream life that had so peculiarly flourished since his arrival at Lourps. Now, he was sleeping undisturbed; every now and again he would feel himself roaming again on the borders of a dream, but, as was previously the case in Paris, when he awoke he couldn't remember anything of these wanderings in the land of delirium, or rather he could only recall scraps of these forays, devoid of sense.

Boredom was beginning to disrupt this animal-like serenity. Already the night before, he'd drifted in his sleep amid incoherent and meaningless events. He remembered only having dreamed, but couldn't rearrange the outlines of the dream which had dispersed with the dawn; but now, this very night, irritated by the burning of his skin and worn out with pain, he was gripped again by fear, a mysterious, impulsive fear, a kind of waking dream, the images of which were coming so quickly they were overlapping one another, scrambling themselves up, a fear whose relation to the dread aroused by a bad dream seemed unmistakable. As for the forgotten noises of the château, he could hear them now with an absolute and intense clarity.

His sluggishness of spirit and dullness of mind – which are the most significant factors in bravery, because a man's courage in the face of danger almost always stems from a crudeness in his nervous make-up, the lumbering mechanism of which doesn't falter for an instant – had come to an end. Wound-up and greased by boredom, the machinery of his brain had gone into action, and that lifeblood of nightmares and fears, the imagination, had immediately carried him away, prompting him to exaggerations, multiplying the appearance of danger, coursing in every direction through a delicate nervous system that shuddered at every jolt and discharged its energy. He sat there at his desk, stirred by this inner tempest in which the beginnings of unfinished thoughts floated to the surface, along with the debris of ideas whose ramshackle structure resembled that of certain dreams.

As if woken by her husband's silence, Louise, eyes wide open, sat up in bed and burst into tears.

He tried to take her hands but she kept putting them up to her face, and, when he did catch a glimpse of her eyes between the fingers he'd prized apart, he discerned an ambiguous expression beneath the veil of tears, an expression of both dreadful anguish and of contempt.

He let go of her fingers, which covered her face again like the grilled visor of a helmet, and sat down at the foot of the bed.

A perfect lucidity suddenly illuminated him, sweeping away the surge of his anxieties and fears and taking possession of his whole mind through the force of the idea's clarity. He understood now that, for the three years they had been married, neither of them had really known the other. Him, because, in spite of all his efforts, he'd never had the chance to examine his wife in one of those moments when the depths of the soul rise to the surface; her, because she'd never had the need, in the calm surroundings of the city, of a protector.

Jacques saw clearly enough inside them both at that moment to notice their reciprocal lack of esteem. He was discovering in Louise the hereditary greed of the peasant, forgotten in Paris but nurtured by this return to her original surroundings and hastened by apprehensions of an imminent poverty. She was suddenly discovering a failure of nerve in her husband, one of those weaknesses of a refined soul, the agitated workings of which women find unbearable.

And far removed now from his puerile fears and his hollow dreams, all pushed aside in a stroke, Jacques gloomily thought of this mutual solitude which, like iodoform, had stained the pustules of their most secret, spiritual maladies and made them visible, forever unforgettable to one another.

IX

To the great despair of the peasants, who had been cursing and swearing since dawn, the weather broke. Almost without transition the white hot sky turned cold again beneath a mass of ash-coloured clouds, and, slowly and imperturbably, the rain fell.

This rain, deadly to harvest mites, which immediately disappeared, and a palliative to energies sapped by the heatwave, seemed delightful to Jacques, putting his mind back on an even keel; however, after two days of indefatigable showers some unforeseen difficulties arose.

One morning a thin peasant woman with a gammy hip and a sumptuously protruding pregnant belly entered, declared that she was the mother of the child from Savin who ran their errands, went on at great length about her daughter's delicate health, and finished by announcing that if 'the lady' didn't give her forty sous a day, she'd no longer send her child out to carry provisions to the château during this rainy weather.

'But,' Louise pointed out, 'what we pay you for drink, jam, cheese, everything in fact, is twice as much as it costs in Paris; it seems to me that with a profit like that, and the twenty sous we give your daughter every morning, you could show a bit more gratitude.'

The woman complained about the cost of the shoes the child was wearing out, pushed out her pregnant-woman's belly still more, accused her husband of being a drunkard, and whined so much that the exhausted Parisians gave in.

Then the question of bread came up. Just as Jacques had foreseen, water seeped into the basket at the end of the avenue in which the baker from Ormes left their loaves, and they had to chew on soggy bread, bite into a soft putty in which their knives were turning rusty and losing their sharpness.

Disgust for this pap overcame Jacques's self-respect and he forced himself to keep a watch on the time, to go down through the mud in the heaviest of showers, in order to collect the bread from the baker's own hands and bring it back, more or less dry, under his coat.

The well joined in, too; spoiled by the downpours, its blue water turned yellow, came up muddy, sprinkled with leaves and tadpoles, and they had to filter it through a dishcloth to make it just about drinkable.

And lastly, the château revealed its worst aspect. Rain came in everywhere, rooms oozed; food kept in the cupboards went mouldy and a smell of the mire blew up the weeping stairwell.

Jacques and Louise constantly felt as if a damp cloak was weighing on their backs, and in the evenings, shivering, they got into a bed the sheets of which seemed to be drenched.

They lit brushwood and pine cones, but the chimney, which had no doubt been decapitated at roof level, hardly drew at all.

Life was unbearable in this ice house; Louise, out of sorts, got up only to prepare the food and then went back to bed again. Jacques wandered aimlessly through the rooms.

He had received a few books from his friend Moran, his favourite books, intoxicating and intense; but an odd thing happened as soon as he tried to reread them; the phrases that had captivated him in Paris loosened and unravelled here in the countryside; taken out of its proper setting, this heady literature lost its flavour; its venison paled, its juices lost their gaminess and vigour; wild boar-like sentences became tame and stank of lard; ideas obtained through rigorous selection now grated like wrong notes. The atmosphere of Lourps was actively changing his perspective, blunting the cutting edge of his mind, and rendering any sense of refinement impossible. He could no longer read Baudelaire and had to content himself with flicking through the out-of-date newspapers he was receiving; and even though he took no interest in them, he waited impatiently for them, always hoping for the arrival of the postman at midday with some letters.

This legendary drunkard played a role in Jacques's state of listlessness; he made Jacques talk while he was licking the plates clean and gulping down great draughts of wine, but the postman's conversation hardly varied; he was always complaining about the length of his round and decrying his poverty; then he'd start spreading gossip he'd gathered in Donnemarie or Savin, announcing the marriages of people Jacques didn't know, confiding that the girl's bulging belly, noticed by the priest, had been redeemed just in time by the mayor.

Jacques would end up yawning, and the postman, a little drunker than when he arrived, left without even a stagger, squelching through the ruts and puddles.

Then Jacques would stay for hours on end at the window to watch the falling rain; it streamed down continuously, streaking the air with its threads, unravelling its transparent skein in diagonal lines, splashing the steps, smacking against the windows, pattering on the zinc pipes, liquifying the distant plain, dissolving the higher ground, and churning up the roads.

The empty hull of the château sang during these downpours; sometimes, a continuous glug-glugging could even be heard from the stairwell, the steps of which formed a waterfall, or sometimes a sound as of a cavalry regiment on the march shook the paving stones in the hallways, as surges of water poured from the broken gutters.

The countryside looked ominous; under a low grey sky, clouds like billows of smoke from a fire were rapidly scudding away and wringing themselves out over the distant hills, whose scree-covered slopes were oozing streams of mud. Sometimes screaming gusts of wind would shake the woods opposite, surrounding the noises inside the château with the roaring sound of waves; and bent trees would spring upright again, creaking under chains of ivy as taut as rigging, losing their ruffled leaves which would fly off like birds on the wing, high above the treetops.

It became increasingly impossible to put a foot outside without getting bogged down. Jacques fell into a terrible despondency, hitting the depths of depression in a single stroke. In this state of complete distress, his wife was no help to him whatever; she even made things worse, because relations between them now lacked openness, were full of reticence; added to which Louise's silence exasperated him; that way she had, whenever he received a letter from Paris, of staring at the paper without paying attention to the news it had brought, offended him; he sensed, in this aspect of her behaviour, her absolute disdain for his clumsy attempts at practicality; moreover it seemed to him that the mental change that had come over Louise was being reflected in her face. Under the force of this idea, he succeeded in distorting his perceptions, convincing himself that his wife's features were becoming peasant-like; she had once been rather pleasant, with her dark eyes and brown hair, her slightly large mouth, and her fresh if somewhat anxious looking face, as long as a billhook blade. Now her lips seemed to him to have become thinner, her nose was sharper, her complexion had become ruddy and an icy water was seeping into her eyes. By dint of staring at Aunt Norine and his wife, looking for similarities in their traits and gestures, he eventually persuaded himself that they resembled one another; he saw in Norine what his wife would look like when old, and he was horrified.

An adept at self-torment, he went back over his memories; he recalled Louise's family, he'd briefly met her father, who died shortly after their wedding, an upright man, a retired customs official, to whom one of his cousins, now also dead, had introduced him; there persisted, deep down in this business-like and quietly stubborn old man, the vestiges of peasant blood, a whiff of his lowly origins – and a thousand little details recurred to Jacques, such as his wife's reproaches when he used to bring back some curio or expensive book.

Obsessed by his *idée fixe,* he compared this concern for household economy, which he once thought admirable, to her present full-blown instinct of greed. By reasoning this way, endlessly chewing over the same reflections in solitude, he ended up misrepresenting their real meaning and attributing to facts of no importance an enormous value.

I'm changing too, he thought one morning as he was looking at himself in a small mirror; his skin was turning yellow, becoming wrinkled around the eyes, white hairs salted his beard; though not very tall he'd always hunched a little, now he stooped.

Even though he wasn't exactly enamoured of his looks, he was saddened to see himself so old at thirty. He felt as if he'd come to the end, he and his wife were drained to the marrow, incapable of any effort of will, totally unable to spring back.

For her part, Louise was worn out, sick and frail, terrified by this incurable disease that consumed her. Tired of their state of abandon, she could think of nothing else, growing increasingly annoyed at not seeing any money arrive. She couldn't understand the interminable red tape of the banks, had no idea about how difficult it was to discount bills, attributed the desperate situation that had overwhelmed her to Moran's bad faith; and she no longer ventured to say anything either, not wanting to make their stay in the château hateful by provoking quarrels.

Fortunately, an animal insinuated itself into their lives and reunited them; it was Aunt Norine's cat, a mangy tom cat, malnourished and ugly, but affectionate; this animal, wild at first, was quickly tamed; the arrival of the Parisians had been a godsend for it, it would eat the remains of their meat and their soup, though only for a short while as Aunt Norine began to hold on to the leftovers her niece put aside for the cat and devour them herself.

After realising what she was up to, the Parisians gave their scraps directly to the animal which followed them around and, tired of being starved and kicked, settled down with them in the château.

It was a case of who could pamper it the most; the cat became a soothing subject of conversation, a bond between them with no risk of bitterness, and its antics brightened up the glacial solitude of the rooms.

In the end it lay on the bed next to Louise, occasionally taking her neck between its two paws and affectionately butting its head against her cheek.

The rain persisted. Jacques began to walk through the building again. He returned to the marquise's bedroom, hoping to escape the boredom of the present by stepping back a century, but no sooner had the desire come to him than the impossibility of satisfying it became obvious; moreover, the sensations he'd experienced the first time he'd entered the room didn't recur. The smell of ether that had so deceptively intoxicated him when he'd opened the door the first time had long ago disappeared. No amatory thoughts would ever again insinuate themselves in this hovel, the decomposition of which was hastening amid the premature decay of a season gone bad. He closed the door behind him determined never to visit it again, and bored by the other rooms, he resolved to explore the cellars.

He borrowed a lantern from Uncle Antoine, who protested loudly, declaring it would bring bad luck to go beneath the château. He emphatically refused to follow Jacques, who struggled on his own against a door the lock of which scraped at every push. Finally he broke it down by shoving against it with his shoulders and kicking it with his feet, and found himself opposite a staircase that seemed to have no end, under a massive vault hanging with spiderwebs, like torn veils of dark muslin; he descended the warm, dank spiral staircase and emerged into a kind of portico, its ribbed vault supported by columns whose blocks, yellowish grey and speckled with black spots, were like those stones, worn smooth by time, that serve to relieve the austere bulk of ancient portals. The antiquity of this château, whose foundations went back to the Gothic period, was obvious from the moment he entered the cellar.

He strolled through long dungeons with enormous walls and arched ceilings that bristled with metal spikes and hooks like grappling irons. He wondered what these instruments that slashed the air had been used for, and he stared in amazement at the surprising thickness of the walls in which, every now and again at the back of niches at least six feet deep, he could make out ventilation holes in the shape of a capital I.

All the cellars were identical, connected one to another by doorways minus their doors. But, he thought, that can't be all there is; and indeed given the size of the château this row of rooms barely accounted for the area beneath one of the wings. Moreover, when he struck the ground it sounded hollow; everything had been blocked up. He looked for places for communicating corridors, but the walls were uniformly black and the bare earth floor seemed as if it was composed of soot; besides, the lantern wasn't bright enough for him to be able to examine closely any gaps in the wall or to check the patina of the stones.

In short, he thought he'd find immense corridors, underground passages as far as the eye could see; but everything was sealed up.

'But nephew, of course there are underground passages, everybody knows about them round 'ere. I reckon they go as far as Séveille – the village that's in shooting distance of Savin. They say, too, that they go all the way under the church; oh, they've been blocked up for years, since I don't know when…'

'What if we unblocked them?' proposed Jacques.

'Eh? But you must be mad, my boy, why would anyone want to do that I ask you?'

'You might find buried treasure under the paving,' Jacques replied seriously.

'Well, I'll be…' and old Antoine scratched his head; 'I suppose there could be all the same. I've had the same idea from time to time, but in the first place the owner wouldn't like it; and secondly neither me nor anyone else round 'ere would be stupid enough to go down there… No,' he added after a pause, as if he'd made up his mind, 'there's bilious gases down there that'll choke you.'

Jacques returned to the subject on several occasions, hoping to convince the old man to start digging, because in the absence of treasure, which he didn't really believe in, he'd have liked to unearth some interesting relics. And besides, it would be something to do, a diversion from the emptiness of his life here. But although Uncle Antoine was tempted by the prospect of treasure, he didn't give way. His greed was conquered by his fear; he limited himself to shaking his head and replying 'No doubt…no doubt,' but refused even to examine the entrance to the cellars.

In any case, he was laid up in bed for a few days, complaining of a dizziness in his head. His niece advised him to see a doctor, but he and Norine threw up their arms in horror: 'I ain't got money to fritter away on their drugs!' he cried, and he made do with drinking the local panacea: green mint tea.

This illness was a real stroke of luck for Jacques, who could spend the day outside the château in order to visit the 'in-laws'. For hours on end he calmly smoked cigarettes by their hearth.

Besides, the atmosphere in this little cottage was less hostile than that of the château. He felt more at home, warmer, more sheltered, better protected by these snug walls than in that huge bedroom at Lourps, whose high walls appeared to be moving further apart all the better to freeze everything around him.

The single room of this shack diverted him, moreover, with its old copper cauldrons, its antique firedogs on which writhed red snakes of dried firewood, its two alcoves each fitted with a bed and separated by a gigantic dresser of polished walnut, its edelweiss cuckoo clock, its plates daubed with pink and green, and its large frying pans of black cast-iron, with handles that were an ell in length and looped at the end.

All these paltry utensils had harmonised with one another over time, which had softened their crude colours, blending the warm brown of solid walnut with the sooty velvet black of the kettles and the cold bright yellow of the bowls; Jacques took pleasure in examining these furnishings, and in studying the amazing engravings, hanging above the canopy of the fireplace, in wooden frames painted brick-red.

Two in particular, one small, one large, cheered him up. The small one depicted an episode from 'The Storming of the Tuileries, 29 July 1830,' and it included this touching story, printed underneath it:

A student from the École Polytechnique presented himself

*to the officer who was guarding the entrance to the Tuileries and
summoned him to let him through; the latter riposted with a pistol
shot that missed the student, who, pressing the point of his sword
against the officer's chest, said: 'Your life is in my hands but I
do not wish to spill your blood, you are free.' Then, transported
by gratitude, the officer took off his cross and, pinning it on the
hero's chest, said: 'Brave young man, you deserve this for your
courage and your restraint.' But the brave young man refused it
because he did not believe he was yet worthy of it.*

The artist of this Épinal print had obviously got carried
away over this chivalrous theme. The officer was huge, topped
by a shako like a child's chamberpot upsidedown on his head,
and dressed in a jacket with red tails and white trousers. Behind
him smaller, similarly outfitted soldiers, open-mouthed, their
eyes filled with tears, were watching the worthy conduct of this
short-arsed student squinting idiotically in front of the massive
wooden figure of the officer. And behind the hero, decked out
in a cocked hat and dressed in blue, was the crowd, represented
by two people: a bourgeois wearing a fur-trimmed Bolivar hat,
and a proletarian dwarfed by a pie-shaped cap, both huddling
together and brandishing a tricolour, above trees splodged in
mushy pea green and stuck onto a police blue sky, embellished
with clouds the colour of wine vomit.

The other print, equally colourful, was less martial but
more practical. Of fairly recent date it was entitled 'The Home
Doctor.' This engraving, the printed border of which contained
recipes for liniments and herbal teas, was divided into a series of
small pictures describing the accidents and afflictions of people
sporting the pale blue jackets, full-fall trousers, high cravats and
whiskers and quiffs of the Louis-Philippe period. In a woeful
litany of grimacing faces one below the other, it presented the
painful spectacle of people with fishbones stuck in their throats,

splinters in their hands, lice in their ears, foreign bodies in their eyes, and verrucas on their feet.

'They're a couple of paintings old Parisot gave us for our wedding,' the old man said to Jacques, who was standing on a chair in order to get a closer look at these works of art.

And so the days drained away in warming his feet and chatting with Uncle Antoine. Jacques would question him about the château, but the old man muddled up his explanations and didn't really know anything anyway.

The château had formerly belonged to the aristocracy; people in the region recalled a family from Saint-Phal, who had also owned a château in the neighborhood at Saint-Loup; they were buried behind the church, but the tombs had been neglected and their descendants, even supposing they still existed, had never reappeared in the area; in the course of the last eighty years the estate had been broken up, its woods and land being bought by farmers and the château itself sold as it stood to some people from Paris, who couldn't decide whether to restore it or not and were constantly trying to resell it. Because of its dilapidated state and its lack of water, no one would agree to buy it now. The reserve price of 20,000 francs hadn't even been reached at the last 'candle auction'.

Sometimes Antoine would talk about the 1870 war, recalling the fraternal relations between the farmers and the Prussians. 'Oh yes, nephew, they were nice lads, the ones I lodged here; never a harsh word with one another, and they were men with real spirit! When they had to march on Paris, they cried saying: 'Papa Antoine, we kaput! kaput!' And what's more, they had no equal when it came to looking after the cattle.'

'So you didn't suffer during the invasion?' asked Jacques.

'Why no, of course not. The Prussians paid for everything they took; as proved by Parisot making a fortune at the time.

What's more there was a colonel that everyone liked, too. Every morning he'd assemble the regiment out on the road and say: "Is there anyone here who has a complaint against my soldiers?" And we'd all reply: "Certainly not," and shout at the tops of our voices: "Long live the Prussians!"'

Jacques let him run on, sometimes listening to him, sometimes staring out of the window at the bedraggled antics of animals in the rain. Just recently, Uncle Antoine had procured a flock of geese that constantly roamed around the courtyard in a solemn and idiotic fashion. They would stop in front of the house, the gander at their head, honking with their imbecilic, self-satisfied little laughs, drinking from a barrel stuck in the ground, lifting up their heads in unison as if trying to make the water go down easier, and then suddenly, for no reason, they'd rise up on their feet, flap their wings, and rush off straight for the stable making a frightful noise.

On other occasions, Aunt Norine would come back during the day, and whenever her niece, who she felt a bit constrained by, wasn't there, she'd indulge in saucy conversations that made her clear, watery eyes sparkle; Jacques learned with amazement that Uncle Antoine was a bit of a ladies' man, acting the lover every night, and he was completely floored when the old lady said, with an expression that was half suggestive, half apologetic: 'And why not, eh, if it does you good?'

Jacques felt the lacklustre carnal instincts that stirred within him from time to time evaporate completely; he was even gripped by an immense disgust for those ridiculous contortions, which he could no longer think about without the abominable image immediately surging up of these two old people fumbling about in their nightcaps, and going to sleep afterwards sated by their own filthiness.

In any case he was beginning to tire of the cottage, of

the old couple, of their exploits and their geese, when Uncle Antoine, back on his feet, returned to work in the fields. So he began his walks through the château again, reached such a degree of lethargy that in order to occupy his mind he examined the bunches of keys that hung in a cupboard and tried them in the locks of all the armoires and doors. Then, when his fascination with this futile task had worn off, he had to content himself with the cat, playing hide-and-seek with it in the corridors, but the animal, which was at first amused by these chases and ambushes, quickly got tired of it. Moreover, it seemed to be ill, its right ear was lying flat, leaning to one side like the flap of a soldier's fatigue cap, and it stared imploringly and mewed. It ended up by not running or jumping any more; unsteady on its paws, it seemed to be suffering from rheumatism in its hindquarters.

Louise carried it around, stroked it and smothered it in caresses, because she'd become attached to this cat which followed her and her husband around like a little dog.

She talked of taking it to Paris in order to safeguard it from the dampness of the countryside, and she was genuinely indignant with Jacques for bemoaning that the animal was so exceedingly ugly.

The fact is that this cat, all skin and bone, had a misshapen, elongated head, and to make it worse, black lips; its coat was an ash grey colour streaked with rust, a street cat's coat with drab, dry fur. Its bald tail looked like a piece of twine with a little tassel on the end, and a flap of fur on its belly, no doubt detached in a fall, hung like a dewlap, its matted hairs brushing the ground.

If it weren't for its large imploring eyes, in the green waters of which flecks of gold continually swirled, it would have been, with its paltry, saggy skin, the runt of the gutter cat species, an unspeakably ugly cat.

'I'm dying of boredom,' Jacques said to himself when the

animal refused to play anymore. 'There's nothing to do here, not even an armchair to sit on! it's impossible, like at the seaside, to smoke a cigarette that isn't damp – and to not even feel like reading!'

Even if he went to bed at nine o'clock, the evenings still seemed endless. He bought some cards in Jutigny and forced himself to take an interest in bezique, but he and his wife got fed up with it after two hands.

One evening, however, he felt in a better mood, more at ease. It was blowing fit to raise the roof, and the corridors of the château were booming like bass tubas and whistling sporadically like flutes. It was dark; Jacques loaded the fire with pine cones and twigs, and by the sparkling light of flames that blossomed into bunches of pink and blue tulips against the sparse black lilies on the old fireback in the hearth, he drank a glass of rum and rolled cigarettes, which he left to dry out.

Louise was in bed and was stroking the cat stretched out on her chest. Jacques, seated with his elbows on the table, was dozing, staring vacantly, thinking about nothing. He roused himself, pushed the two tall candles that, along with the fire, illuminated the room a bit closer, and began to flip through a few journals his friend Moran had sent him from Paris that very morning.

One article interested him and propelled him into a long daydream. What a fine thing is science! he thought, here's this Professor Selmi from Bologna who's discovered an alkaloid – ptomaine – in rotting corpses, which appears in the form of a colourless oil and gives off faint but lingering scents of hawthorn, musk, seringa, orange blossom or rose.

These are the only fragrances they've been able to discover up to now in a rotting organism, but others will no doubt turn up; in the meantime, in order to satisfy the demands of this eminently practical century – which perfunctorily buries destitute Parisians out at Ivry and finds a use for everything: bodily liquids, waste matter, the guts of decaying carcasses and old bones – they could convert cemeteries into factories that would prepare to order, for the families of the rich, concentrated extracts of their ancestors, essential oils of their dead children, bouquets of their late fathers.

This would be what you'd call in the trade a deluxe item; but for the needs of the working class – which it would be out of the question to neglect – they could supplement these luxury dispensaries with industrial laboratories that would manufacture perfumes wholesale; it would be possible, in fact, to distil them from the remains of communal graves that no one had claimed; this would be the art of perfumery, but founded on new lines, within the reach of everyone, this would be a cut-price item, a perfume to be sold in cheap stores, since the raw materials would be abundant and the only cost, so to speak, would be the expense of a gravedigger and a chemist.

Ah, I know a lot of working women who'd be happy to buy for a few sous whole pots of pomade or cakes of soap, perfumed with the essence of prole!

And what a constant aid to one's remembrances, how eternally fresh one's memories would be with these concentrated emanations of the dead! At the present time when two people love each other and one happens to die, the other can only preserve a photograph of them and tend their grave on All Saints' Day. But thanks to the invention of ptomaines, it'll be possible from now on to keep the wife you adored in your own home, in your very pocket, in a volatile, spirituous form, to transmute your loved one into a bottle of smelling-salts, to condense her into a quintessence, to put her, in powdered form, into a sachet embroidered with a mournful epitaph, to take a deep breath of her on sad days, or take a light sniff of her on your handkerchief on happier days.

Not to mention that as far as sexual mind-games are concerned we might perhaps finally be spared hearing the ineviable 'appeal to mother' when the crucial moment comes and she swoons calling for her help, because she knows full well she cannot come since that redoubtable lady would be already there, reposing unseen in the form of a beauty spot, or mixed in white skin cream on her daughter's breast.

And in the near future, with the aid of progress, ptomaines, which at the moment are tremendously poisonous, will no doubt be consumed without any danger at all; so why couldn't they flavour certain foods with their essences? Why not use this scented oil the same way one uses essences of almond and cinnamon, vanilla and cloves, in order to make cake fillings so delicious? The same as with perfumery, a new avenue would be opened up in the art of the pastry chef and the confectioner, one that would be both economical and emotionally beneficial.

In short, those august family ties which are being loosened and undone in this present wretched age of disrespect would assuredly be reinforced and retied through ptomaines. Thanks to them, there'd be an affectionate coming together of distant generations, shoulder to shoulder with an ever-renewing sense of tenderness. Ptomaines would constantly inspire a fitting atmosphere in which to recall the lives of the dead and to cite them as an example to their children, whose gluttony would help preserve their memory with perfect clarity.

So it is that on All Souls' Day, in the evening, in a little dining room furnished with a sideboard of pale wood veneer and black beading, by the light of a table lamp dimmed by a shade, a family is seated. The mother is a decent woman, the father is a cashier in a commercial firm or a bank, the child, still quite young, just recovered from a bout of whooping cough and impetigo, subdued by the threat of being deprived of dessert, has finally consented not to tap his soup bowl with his spoon and to eat his meat with a bit of bread.

Motionless, he watches his calm and collected parents. The maid enters, bringing in a ptomaine cream cake. That morning, the mother had respectfully taken from the Empire-style mahogany writing desk, adorned with a trefoil-shaped lock, a glass-stoppered vial containing the precious liquid extracted from grandfather's decomposed viscera. With an eyedropper she had herself infused a few drops of this perfume which was now flavouring the cream.

The child's eyes shine, but as he waits for them to serve him he must listen to eulogies of the old man who has bequeathed him, so it seems, besides certain facial features, this posthumous rose flavour, on which he is about to stuff himself.

'Oh, he was a man of sober tastes, a prudent, hard-working man, was grandpapa Jules. He arrived in Paris in clogs but he always put a bit aside, even when he was only earning a hundred francs a month. He wasn't the kind of man to lend money at no interest or without guarantees, he wasn't such a fool! business before everything, cash up front; and how respectful he was to the rich! And so he died revered by all his children, to whom he left gilt-edged investments, real assets!'

'You remember grandfather don't you my dear?'

'Yum, yum, grandfather!' cries the brat, ancestral cream smeared all over his cheeks and nose.

'And your grandmother, you remember her too, don't you my sweetheart?'

The child thinks for a moment. On the anniversary of this fine old lady's death, they prepare a rice pudding which they flavour with the bodily essence of the dead woman, who smelt of snuff while she was alive but, by a curious phenomenon, exudes orange blossom since her death.

'Yum, yum, grandma too!' cries the child.

'And which one do you like best, tell me, your grandma or your grandpa?'

Like all kids, who prefer what they haven't got to what's in front of them, the child dreams of the far-off rice pudding and admits that he likes his grandmother best; nevertheless he holds his plate out again for more grandfather.

Fearing he'll get indigestion from so much filial love, the provident mother has the cream dessert taken away.

What a delightful and touching family scene, thought Jacques, rubbing his eyes. But he wondered if, in his present state of mind, dozing face down on his journal, he hadn't dreamt what the scientific article had said about the discovery of ptomaines.

X

He was groping his way up in the gloom, the next day, following the curve of a spiral staircase. Suddenly, in a beam of bluish light, he saw a man standing, drawn up to his full height, wrapped in an ancient houppelande, of that green peculiar to parmesan, dotted with pink peppercorns instead of buttons, very tight at the waist and flaring out at the back, forming a filigreed bustle of metallic braid, painted with red lead.

From the V-shaped funnel of the lapels – parted to reveal two small, bare breasts, nipples covered by thimbles – sprang a concertina neck, pleated like the bellows of an accordion, and a head encased in a blue enamel slop bucket, held in place by its handle, like a strap under the chin, and adorned with a plume from a catafalque.

Little by little, as his eyes were emptied of the darkness that filled them, Jacques made out this man's face: beneath a forehead ringed with pink by the pressure of the bucket, two paintbrush bristle brows rose up over eyes dilated by belladonna, separated by a nose teeming with ripe boils, connected by a hairy philtrum to an ace of hearts mouth, propped up by the corbel of a chin punctuated with a comma of red hair, like that of a furniture mover's.

And a nervous tic was agitating this monstrous, cadaverous face, a tic that would tweak the inflamed tip of the nose, flicking up the eyes and snatching at the lips in the same spasm, dragging the lower jaw with it, revealing an Adam's apple stippled with dots, like the plucked flesh of a chicken.

Jacques followed this man into an enormous room with clay walls, illuminated almost at the level of the ceiling by semicircular windows. High up, near the cornices, ran pipes covered in a green fabric, like extravagant speaking tubes or the siphon from an enormous enema. But there was neither a rosewood mouthpiece to blow into, nor a spigot to connect it up, nothing. The apparatus just traversed the room for no apparent reason. Beneath the tubes, hanging from figure of eight hooks, were boiled calves' heads, very white, all sticking their tongues out to the right; and under them, attached by long nails, were pistachio-coloured schapskas with gooseberry mortarboards and visorless shakos like butter pots.

In a corner, on a cast-iron stove, an earthenware pot was whistling, its lid lifting up and spitting little bubbles.

The man plunged his arm into the pocket of his houppelande and brought out a handful of crystals that made a crunching noise as he ground them in his fist, and staring straight at Jacques with his dilated pupils, he said in a voice that managed to be both grating and ice-cold at the same time:

'I scatter the menstrua of the earth into this pot which, along with the giblets of a hare, simmers with that venison of vegetables, that wild fowl of peas, the broad bean.'

'Quite so,' said Jacques, without batting an eye. 'I've read the ancient books of the Kabbala, and I'm well aware that the expression "menstrua of the earth" simply refers to common salt...'

At this, the man bellowed and the receptacle on top of his head fell off. Covering the pear-shaped cranium that had completely filled the bucket was a thick mass of hair, bright red like the horsehair plumes that embellish trumpeters' helmets in certain cavalry regiments. He raised an index finger in the air like some Buddha; powerful rumblings coursed through the green woollen snakes that stretched around beneath the ceiling; excited tongues flicked in and out of the calves' withered mouths, simulating the screech of a wood plane; the butter-pot shakos beat out a drum roll, then everything fell silent.

Jacques blanched. Ah, it was all clear now; an anonymous decree, but one whose terms were categorical, had ordered him to deliver his watch, against a written receipt, into the hands of this man, and this on pain of the most lingering torture! He knew it now, but he'd left his watch at Lourps, hanging on the wall by the head of the bed! He opened his mouth to apologise, to ask for more time, to beg for mercy; but he stood frozen to the spot, speechless, because the man's terrifying eyes were lighting up the room like the headlamps of a tram, burning like pharmacy bulbs, blazing like the lights of a transatlantic liner.

He had only one aim, to run away; he dashed down the stairs, found himself suddenly at the bottom of a well that was blocked up at the top but illuminated the length of its shaft by folding wooden shutters, set like the slats of enormous venetian blinds.

Not a sound, a diffuse half-light, the light of an eclipse or the glow of dawn on a rainy day in October.

He looked up. High above was a gigantic scaffolding, beams interlaced and intersected with each another, enclosing within an inextricable cage a huge bell. Ladders zigzagged amid this network of planks, running up into the roof timbers, descending suddenly, breaking apart, losing their rungs, resting on wooden platforms, then climbing back up, suspended without any visible means of support in the void.

Without knowing how, Jacques found himself on a kind of poop deck, next to some gigantic blinds which he took to be louvres.

I'm in a bell tower, he thought; it plunged away beneath him, a formidable black vat in which swam shapes like Italian pasta – phosphorescent stars, crescents, diamonds and hearts – a whole subterranean night sky constellated with edible stars that terrified him; he looked through the slats of the louvres; an incalculable distance away, he could make out the Place Saint-Sulpice, deserted, with a shoeshiner's stand next to the fountain. No one around except a policeman, hatless, practically bald, sporting a tuft of white hair on the top of his head, like a leek. Jacques wondered if he should ask for his help, demand his protection. He rushed down a long ladder in order to catch up with him, and entered a well-tended arcade, planted with pumpkins.

All were palpitating, ardently straining upwards, tugging at the stems that attached them to the ground. Jacques's first impression was that he was looking at a field of Mongolian buttocks, a garden of backsides belonging to that yellow race.

He examined the deep, well-rounded clefts that sank into these plump-skinned, bright-orange spheres. Then a dirty-minded curiosity came over him. He stretched out his hand; but, as if cut beforehand by a provident greengrocer, the pumpkins fell open, divided into slices, revealing their entrails of white seeds, arrayed in clusters within the yellow rotunda of their empty bowels.

Must I be so beastly? And suddenly, for no reason, he felt appalled, thinking of the trapped pieces of sky that were scudding along under the stone vault of the room; he was gripped by an immense pity for those scraps of firmament which had no doubt been stolen and interned, perhaps for centuries, in this very arcade. He went up to a window to open it, but the sound of footsteps and voices could be heard; they're looking for me, he thought; the noise was getting closer; he could distinctly hear the rattle of rifles being cocked and the heavy thud of butts against wood. He wanted to run away, but the door, battered by a furious hail, was cracking. Oh! they were there, behind that door, just as he'd imagined them without ever having seen them, those demons conjured up in the night by deviant young girls, monsters in search of nubile orifices, pallid, uncanny incubi with icy sperm! In a sudden flash he realised what kind of abominable harem he'd strayed into, for a phrase he'd read long ago in the *Disquisitionum Magicarum* by the exorcist Del Rio came back to him, insistent and clear: 'Demons practise sodomy with magicians.' With magicians! Yes, that field of pumpkins was undoubtedly a sabbath of sorcerers, squatting, buried in the ground and wriggling about in order to try and disinter their heads and bodies! He recoiled; no, he didn't want to witness the disgusting ejaculations of these living fruits and those evil spirits at any price! He took another step backwards, felt the ground give way beneath him, and found himself, in a daze, standing in the tower, underneath the bell.

The bell was swinging but its clapper wasn't striking the metal at all, and yet strange sounds could be heard, reverberated by the echoes in the tower.

He looked up in the air and gawped.

An old woman wearing a calash bonnet, a nankeen camisole splattered with dirt, and a blue pinafore on which jiggled the heart-shaped brass badge of a costermonger, was sitting on a beam, legs dangling, and under her raised petticoats he caught a glimpse of her enormous thighs, carefully squeezed into tight surgical stockings.

On a dancing master's pocket violin, she was playing the tune *Oh, How You Hurt Me, Handsome Grenadier*, big tears streaming down her face, the Queen Amélie curls that corkscrewed around her temples jumping in time to the music, as did her large feet in their cloth slippers of choirboy-red.

Opposite her, sitting upright in a wooden bowl resting on a beam, was a legless cripple, a chamberpot on his head like a white porcelain beret; he was dressed in a child's striped cotton pinafore, fastened at the back, leaving room for arms that were covered from wrist to elbow in calico oversleeves, held in place, like those of a butcher, by wide bands of light blue elastic.

And this man was blowing into a set of bagpipes so hard that his green eyes were disappearing, like tiny capers, behind the pink balloons formed by his two cheeks, which bore the name of a shop across them.

Jacques reflected for a moment. He was in a bell tower and it was only natural, since he didn't have any money, that he'd accepted this job as bell ringer in a church. These are no doubt my assistants, he thought, contemplating the two bizarre creatures who were making such a row up in the rafters. But why is she crying like that? he added, watching the salty cataracts of tears that were streaming down the old woman's desolate face. She'll have quarrelled with her husband, that legless cripple, perhaps. This explanation seemed to satisfy him. Then he jumped to another idea. There can't be any water in this tower, so how can I move in? The fact is, the old lady would probably agree, for a small fee, to bring up a few buckets, let's ask her; he wanted to get closer, ventured out onto a beam, but, scared by the void, he buckled, throat constricted, forehead covered in sweat. He neither dared to go forward, nor back; bending double, he fell onto all fours and then sat astride the beam, which he gripped furiously between his legs, and he shut his eyes because his head was spinning; but anxiety made him open them again; slowly, as if covered in soap, the beam was sliding between his thighs. He saw it receding, he felt the end slip from under his belly, he cried out, beat the air with his arms, and fell into the abyss.

Then, on the Rue Honoré-Chevalier, along which he was striding, he was struck by a thought. Where's my cane? he said to himself. At this particular moment, this insignificant event took on enormous importance. He knew, categorically, that his life, his whole life, depended on that cane. He hesitated, panic-stricken, retraced his steps, ran from one side of the road to the other, unable to collect his thoughts: But I had it only a moment ago! My God! My God! Where have I lost it? Ah! – suddenly, an absolute certainty imposed itself. His cane was there, behind that half-open door, there, in a courtyard he'd never been in!

He entered what looked like a ship's bilge. The place was deserted, but the air was teeming with inhabited shadows, filled with invisible bodies. He realised he was surrounded, being spied on. What could he do? And now the courtyard was growing brighter and the huge wall at the end that supported a neighbouring house was changing into an immense sheet of glass, behind which lapped a turbulent mass of water.

A sharp click, similar to that made by those little machines that stamp tickets at a train or bus station, rang out. The noise came from the translucent wall, low down. Jacques was examining the ground when, at the level of the paving slabs, behind the glass partition, a head surged up in the water, a woman's head tipped back, rising up in slow, jerky movements.

The neck emerged in its turn, then tiny breasts with erect nipples, then a whole firm torso, a little crimped at the flank, lastly a raised leg, half hiding a quivering belly, small and bulging, a smooth-skinned belly as yet spared from the ravages of childbirth.

At the same time, the iron jaws of an enormous crane rose up with her, clamped onto her hips. These jaws were biting into her skin, which was bleeding and the turbulent water was dotted with red spots. Jacques looked for the woman's face and saw in it a solemn and tragic beauty, proud and tender; but almost immediately an unspeakable suffering, a silent, implacable torture clouded her pale face, which her mouth defied with a cruel, languid smile of unbearable sensuality.

He was moved, stirred to his very soul; he leapt forward to rescue this unfortunate, when he suddenly heard two sharp clicks from behind the glass wall, like the sound of two marbles bouncing on a hard surface. And the woman's eyes, her blue, staring eyes had disappeared. Nothing remained in their place but two red hollows, which were blazing like firebrands in the green water. And then the eyes reappeared, unblinking, only to detach themselves and bounce again, like little balls, without the water deadening their sound. Alternately, in this suffering and tender face, crimson holes and blue eyeballs, falling into this vertical Seine, in the depths of a courtyard.

Oh, this succession of azure stares and eye sockets drowned in blood was dreadful! This creature, magnificent while she remained intact, repulsive as soon as her unstuck eyes flew out, left him gasping. The horror of this constantly interrupted beauty that came so close to the most frightful ugliness, with its purple gouges and its lips that, without moving a muscle, became hideous as soon as the equilibrium of the face was lost, was unspeakable. At those moments, Jacques wanted to escape, but as soon as the eyes were shining in their place again, he wanted to throw himself on this woman, carry her off, save her from the invisible hands that were torturing her, and so he stood there, distraught, while the woman was rising and rising, borne up by the claw which was digging into her hip and which bit into her more deeply the higher she rose.

Finally, she reached the height of the wall and appeared, streaming with water, in the air, above the rooftops, in the darkness, displaying her torn flank, like a drowned woman rent by boat hooks.

Jacques closed his eyes; wails of distress, sobs of compassion, cries of pity were choking him; an intense dread froze him to the marrow, buckling his legs.

He looked up in spite of himself and, almost fainting, staggered backwards.

The woman was now sitting on the ledge of one of the towers of Saint Sulpice; but what a woman! a filthy slut, laughing in a lewd and jeering fashion, the hair on top of her head tied up with a rag into buns, like a bunch of shallots, a fiery red fringe of hair, watery eyes with bags underneath, a bridgeless nose squashed at the tip and a ruined mouth, toothless at the front and rotten at the back, outlined like a clown's with two streaks of blood.

She looked like a cross between an army whore and an itinerant chair mender, and she was amusing herself, tapping the tower with her heels, ogling the sky, and, high above the square, flaunting her old saddlebag breasts, a paunch that bulged like badly-closed shutters, and her vast thighs like wrinkled wineskins, between which sprouted the dry tuft of an unspeakable mat of kelp.

What is all this? Jacques wondered, dismayed. Then he pulled himself together, tried to be reasonable, succeeded in persuading himself that this tower was really a well, a well that rose into the air instead of plunging into the ground, but a well none the less; an iron-ringed wooden bucket that stood on the coping stone testified to the fact; then everything fell into place; this loathsome slut was Truth.

How worn out she was! though it was true men had been passing her down one to another through the centuries; in fact it wasn't so surprising, wasn't Truth the great Whore of the mind, the Streetwalker of the soul? Indeed, God only knows but ever since Genesis she's probably been noisily prostituting herself with the first man who comes along: artists and popes, yokels and kings, all had had her and each one had acquired the assurance that he alone possessed her, and at the slightest doubt, furnished unanswerable arguments and irrefutable, conclusive proofs.

Otherworldy to some, all too worldly to others, she sowed conviction indiscriminately, whether in the civilised minds of Mesopotamia or in the wily fools of Sologne; she caressed each according to his temperament, each according to his delusions and his manias, each according to his age, offering herself to his lust for certitude, in whatever position or in whatever form he preferred.

'There's nothing more to be said, she's as false as a counterfeit coin,' Jacques concluded.

'How stupid you are!' said a slightly drunken voice. He turned around and saw a coachman wrapped in a grey box coat with a triple collar, his whip hanging round his neck.

'You don't recognise her then? Why, it's one of Ma Eustache's girls!'

Jacques, surprised, didn't reply. In spite of the fact he had a patriarchal look about him, the coachman started yelling terrible blasphemies, then as if in the grip of delirium, he hopped on one foot and spat tomato sauce into a High Court President's cap, which happened to be on the ground close by, and resolutely, his sleeves rolled up, he rushed with fists outstretched at Jacques, who woke up with a start in his bed, exhausted, faint, and soaked in sweat.

Several nights followed during which his soul, set free from its miserable prison, flitted through the smoky catacombs of dream. Jacques's nightmares were desolate and foreboding, leaving him with a gloomy sensation on awaking that induced melancholy thoughts, already weary from their constant repetition amid the surroundings of this empty château during his waking state. He had no precise memory of his excursions into these domains of terror, only a vague recollection of painful events shot through with alarming conjectures.

In the mornings, Jacques would feel feverish, the dizziness of a drunken man stumbling through his recollections, a general sense of unease, a lassitude throughout his whole body. Once again he became anxious about the causes that were dividing his life into two like this, rendering it sometimes incoherent, sometimes lucid. At a loss for an explanation and thinking about one of Louise's periodic indispositions, he wondered if that extraordinary phrase from Paracelsus, 'the menstrual blood of women engenders phantoms,' weren't true; then he smiled and shrugged, but from then on he abstained from drinking alcohol, waited until he'd digested his food before going to bed, and covered himself with lighter blankets – and as a result obtained, if not a completely undisturbed sleep, one with more obscure, more agreeable visions.

The fine weather having returned again, he forced himself to go for walks, visited the neighbouring villages, went to Savin where he discovered a small hamlet comprised of two lanes lined with shacks surrounded by dead hedges. All he was able to ascertain was that these walks outside the château were entirely devoid of interest. Everywhere there were great dusty roads, planted here and there with milestones and walnut trees, often criss-crossed in the air by telegraph wires, roads pock-marked every hundred yards with heaps of stones, and all leading, after a more or less lengthy march, to identical towns inhabited by identical peasants.

You needed to go several miles further to reach the woods; it was easier to wander in the garden at Lourps and to doze in the shade of its pines.

Then, for a few hours one day, he had a new and unforeseen experience. The priest, who'd come to Lourps on Sunday, had left the key to the church at Uncle Antoine's so he could give it to the locksmith, who had to repair some hinges. Jacques borrowed it.

This key didn't fit the main door of the church, which opened onto the road by the château. He had to skirt around the gate, to go in through the graveyard, enclosed by railings, full of tangled weeds and crosses of black wood and rust-eaten iron. He looked for the graves of the marquises that old Antoine had talked about, but he couldn't find them; creeping ulcers of lichen and moss were gnawing away at the gravestones whose engraved inscriptions had been clogged up long ago; perhaps it was under one of these stones that the abandoned remains of the Saint-Phals lay?

The graveyard looked very plush with the sunlight falling on it. It was a riot of grass, a tumult of branches in the middle of which, on stems armed with claws, bloomed indolent buds of wild rose. On this plot of land sheltered by the church, the air seemed warmer; bumblebees were humming, bent double over flowers that swung from side to side and drooped under their weight; butterflies fluttered around as if intoxicated by the breeze, and a couple of wild pigeons from the château flew past in a rustle of wings.

Jacques regretted not having known earlier about this little corner, so peaceful and cosy; it seemed to him that only here could he come to terms with his fears and lull to sleep the insomnia of his forlorn thoughts. Here, one was so far away from everything, so hidden, so alone. Through the tall grass, he followed a wavering path that led to a door carved into the side of the church; with his key he opened it and emerged into a whitewashed nave.

The church was elongated, without transept simulating the arms of a cross, formed simply by four walls along which slender columns, disposed in groups, shot up into the arched vaulting. It was illuminated by rows of windows facing each other, ogival windows with short lancets, but what a state they were in! The arched points of the lancets were broken, patched up with cement and bits of brick, the stained glass had been replaced by panes divided into fake lozenges by lead foil or just left as they were, empty, and the weather-beaten vault was losing scabs of its plaster skin, sagging and straining under the weight of the roof.

He found himself in an old Gothic chapel, battered by time and mutilated by masons. Above the choir stalls, traversing the building from one side to the other, a square beam supported an immense crucifix, the base of which was fixed to the beam with iron screws. The crudely carved Christ, smeared with a layer of pink paint, had the air of a thief daubed with watery blood; barely attached to his cross, he rocked at the slightest breeze, groaning on his loosening nails; from head to foot, he was streaked with long trickles of bird droppings that accumulated near the wound in his side, making its darker colour stand out even more. Screech owls and crows would enter the church freely through the holes in the windows, perch on this Christ figure and, flapping their wings, swing him about as they inundated him with their digested jets of ammonia and lime. All over the sanctuary floor, over the rotten wooden pews, over the very altar itself, was a mass of white excrement, the filthy evacuations of carnivorous birds.

Jacques approached the altar, the roughly planed planks of which could be seen beneath linen starched by guano and pissed on by bursts of rain; it was surmounted by a tabernacle, spangled like the biscuit wrappers in a hospital with silver stars on a blue background, by candlesticks fitted with fake cardboard candles, and by chipped vases empty of flowers.

A whiff of carrion was wafting from the altar. Guided by this smell, Jacques went behind the tabernacle and saw, on the ground, the remains of shrews and field mice, headless carcasses, bits of tails, lumps of fur, a screech owl's entire pantry was lying there, next to a half-open pine wardrobe in which were hanging stoles and albs. He was curious to rummage through this wardrobe, and below the coat rail, piled up on a shelf, he could make out a biretta, a chalice, a ciborium, and a badly closed tin box containing a few hosts.

Then he crossed the nave, and at the back, on the baptismal font near the main door, he saw a scrap of newspaper in which some salt was wrapped and an old bottle of Boyer's Melissa Cordial, containing a few drops of water.

A priest who could leave the church in which he celebrated mass in such a neglected state must be a very singular priest all the same! He should have at least put away the unleavened bread and the vases, thought Jacques. It's obvious that God spent very little time residing in this place, because the priest was just gobbling down the sacraments, rushing through the mass, hastily invoking his Lord and then dismissing him as soon as he came without a moment's delay. It was a divine service, but in telegraphese, just about sufficient for the three or four people who came from Longueville and who didn't dare to sit down, the pews were so worm-eaten and dirty.

Jacques was about to leave when his eyes were drawn to the floor of the choir stalls; among the irregular sized paving stones, he noticed some regular slabs that looked like the flat slabs of gravestones. He knelt down and scraped at them, revealing inscriptions in Gothic characters, some completely worn down, others still visible, amid the vague escutcheons and outlines of figures lying prone with their feet together and their hands joined.

He returned to the château, brought back a bowl of water and a cloth, and from beneath the muck he scrubbed off, complete letters appeared.

Word by word, he deciphered one of these stones:

'Here lyes Louys Le Gouz, esquyre, yn his lyfe Lord of Loups yn Brye and Chimez yn Thouz. Ye 21st daye of December, one thowsant fyve hondreth fyve and twynti. Pray ye for him.'

On another, he read:

'Here lyeth Charles de Champagne, knight, Baron of Lours, who dyed ye 2nd February one thousand six hundred fifty and five, the sonne of Robert de Champagne, knight, Lord of Séveille and Sainte Colombe, &c. *Requiescat in pace.*'

As for the others, older still no doubt, they were so eroded that despite all his efforts he couldn't make out their letters.

He was slightly surprised. No one in the surrounding countryside knew about these tombs, which on Sundays weren't exactly trampled on by this negligent priest and his indifferent flock. And here he was walking all over the old feudal overlords, lying forgotten in their own ancient chapel at the Château de Lourps. How long ago all that seemed…even the name had altered. 'Loups' and 'Lours' had ended up being merged together and written as 'Lourps'. Oh, if only Uncle Antoine would agree to open up the château's cellars and break into the church's crypt through the underground tunnels, perhaps then they'd discover some interesting remains.

He left, and thinking to prevail on Aunt Norine to convince her husband to let him carry out his excavations, he made his way towards the cottage.

But he had to put off opening his campaign until later, because the old woman was grumbling, irritated, her nose buried in a calendar, an ear cocked, listening to the lowing of her cow.

'Is Uncle Antoine all right?' asked Jacques.

'Aye, he's in the byre; there, d'y hear that?'

Indeed, one could hear a voice swearing and the crack of a whip.

'Oh, bloody hell!' said Norine, 'there…Patch hasn't taken, she's back on heat. That's three weeks gone by I reckon,' and she added up again, the tip of her finger following the dates in the almanac. 'What's more Beauty's started trying to mount her, and that's a sign. Ever since yesterday she's been bellowing so much she's stopped us getting any kip. There's nowt else to do, we'll have to take her back to the stud.'

And in answer to Jacques's questions, she explained that Patch was a difficult cow to impregnate. They almost always had to go back to the bull, and it was tedious because it made them unpopular with the herdsman who didn't like them tiring out his beast.

'It's 'cause you don't press 'ard enough on her rump when the bull mounts her, and with that damned mule's spine of hers it stops her from taking it,' cried Uncle Antoine who appeared, furious, pulling the cow by a rope as it bellowed and butted its horns at everything in sight.

'Oh, it's all very well you talkin' like that, if you're so clever why don't you go over to François and put your hand on the cow's back yourself, then you'll see how easy it is.'

The old man shrugged his shoulders: 'Alright, I'll go,' he said. 'Hey, take that you ol' bitch!' and he administered a solid blow with the handle of his whip to the skull of the snorting animal.

Jacques followed him out; they walked slowly down the Path of Fire.

'We're a bit early,' said Uncle Antoine, 'at this hour the herdsman'll be keeping a watch on his cows in the meadow; anyway it doesn't matter, we'll leave Patch off at his place on the way and then go and fetch him.'

They crossed the main road to Bray and rejoined the lane to Jutigny village; every gateway they passed there were 'Good days' and 'Hellos' from headscarfed old women, darning by windows that framed them like busts. On the doorsteps of the houses sulked brats as dirty as pigs, hair down to their eyes, holding sandwiches scalloped with bite-marks.

They stopped in front of a new cottage with a courtyard, in one corner of which swayed blood-red hollyhocks, or 'stick roses' as Uncle Antoine called them.

They lifted the latch of a lattice gate, tied Patch to a post in the courtyard, then, closing the gate behind them, they went down an elm-lined alley at the next bend in the road.

They came out into an immense meadow. Jacques was taken aback at the expanse of this countryside, lying flat under a sky whose curve seemed to touch the earth at the horizon, far off in a remote distance adorned by clumps of trees.

Through the middle of this meadow ran a path bordered by willows with squat trunks and with bluish leaves that wafted like smoke whenever the wind blew.

As he got closer, he noticed that between this narrow hedge of willows ran a tiny river, the Voulzie, mottled with dark circles formed by the erratic movements of water spiders. The river made famous by Hégésippe Moreau snaked around in cool, silent meanders, coiling itself up in certain places into completely blue loops, in the depths of which quivered the eddying reflections of branches on the riverbanks, before unwinding and stretching out in a straight line, carrying off with it a whole stream of sky between its two verges.

A ray of sunlight gilded the meadow's fleece; the wind quickened the flight of clouds clotting like curdled milk in the distance and drove them over the Voulzie, dappling its azure with white stains. A cool smell of grass, a dull odour lightly spiced with ochre, rose from this green earth stamped with the brown imprint of cattle hooves.

They crossed the Voulzie by a plank bridge and then, behind the curtain of willows, another section of meadow stretched out, trampled all over by a herd of cows. They were of every colour, every shade: tans and bays, whites and browns, and friesians whose irregular black patches resembled splashes from a spilt inkwell. Some, seen head-on, slavered as they lowed, horns like the tines of a fork, dewlaps hanging, bright eyes staring into a sky that was shimmering in the dusty-blue daylight; others, seen from behind, displayed, beneath the two hollows of the rump, nothing but a tail that swung like a pendulum in front of the swollen mass of their pink udders.

Dispersed over the plain, they formed a rough circle around which wandered two Alsatians, their tongues hanging out.

'There's Papillon and Ramoneau,' said old Antoine, pointing at the two dogs; 'the herdsman's over there,' and indeed they could now see him, crouched down, poking at crushed clods of earth with his stick.

'Eh, now then François, how goes it with you?'

He lifted his dour, clean-shaven face, wiped a hand over his aquiline nose, and in a toneless voice that nevertheless contained a hint of mockery, said:

'Oh not bad…not bad…but what of it, old Antoine, I've an idea you ain't here for my sake but for Patch's.'

Uncle Antoine started to laugh.

'Ah, you know what's what, you do; you ain't no idiot, you see right away what's goin' on.'

The herdsman shrugged his shoulders.

'Aye, that I do. All the same, I can't say I'd lose much sleep if that bloody cow of yours dropped dead,' he said. He stood up, looked at the sun, and grabbing the tin horn slung bandolier-fashion over his shoulder blew three long, shrill blasts on it.

Immediately, the dogs rounded up the cows into a single heaving mass; then, divided into two columns, they walked off in single file along two different paths.

'He warns the village about the return of the cattle with his horn,' explained Uncle Antoine, and seeing Jacques's astonishment at the unconcerned François, who wasn't taking any further notice of his animals, he added: 'Oh, they know the way to their cowshed, there's no need for him to lead 'em!'

'Heel!' shouted the herdsman to his dogs, which began snarling, hair bristling and teeth bared, as soon as they came near Jacques.

And they left for the herdsman's place. As soon as they arrived, François went up to Patch, who was lowing, untied her, and by kicking her with his boots and punching her with his fists, managed to push her head through a kind of wooden guillotine, set up near the cowshed.

The stunned cow was no longer struggling; suddenly the door of the cowshed opened, and a fawn coloured mass, with a muzzled snout, a squat neck, an enormous head and short horns, slowly emerged, restrained by a cable unwinding from a winch.

A shudder rippled across the skin of the cow whose eyes bulged. The bull approached her, sniffed her, and with a detached air stared at the sky.

'Come on!' shouted François, coming out of the cowshed armed with a whip.

'Come on, boy, up, up, up!'

The bull remained still.

'Come on, we haven't got all day.'

The bull sniffed, his legs braced, his two pendulous balls, which seemed to be attached to his belly by a huge vein ending in a tuft of hair, dangling under his rump.

'Go on, get on top of 'er!' yelled Uncle Antoine.

Again François hissed in his toneless voice: 'Up, up, up, boy!'

And still the animal didn't move.

'Come on, you idle good-for-nothing!' and the herdsman lashed the bull with a great crack of his whip.

The bull lowered his head, shifted his feet one after the other, and with an unconcerned eye surveyed the farmyard.

Uncle Antoine went over to Patch and lifted up her tail. Slowly, the bull took a step forward, sniffed the cow's behind, gave it a quick lick, but still didn't move.

Then François sprang forward, using the handle of his whip.

'You worthless bugger, you're only good for making stew!' yelled Uncle Antoine, joining in, violently whacking the animal with his cane.

And suddenly the bull heaved itself up and clumsily straddled the cow. Uncle Antoine let go of his cane, rushed up to Patch and flattened her back with his hands, just as something red and misshapen, long and thin shot out from the tuft of hairs underneath the bull, striking the cow. And that was it; without so much as a pant, without a bellow, without a spasm, the bull fell back on his feet and, dragged by its cable, returned to the cowshed, while Patch, who hadn't felt anything, who, overcome with fear, hadn't even dared breathe, looked around her with frightened, seething eyes.

'That's it?' Jacques couldn't help exclaiming. The whole scene hadn't lasted five minutes.

Uncle Antoine and the herdsman burst out laughing.

'Well, as for his bull,' said Jacques on the way back with Uncle Antoine, 'it's impotent.'

'No, it's a good stud; François gives him too much fodder and not enough oats, but he's a fiery lad all the same!'

'And is it like that every time you take a cow to a bull? is it always so organised and so quick?'

'Certainly, my boy; sooner or later the bull wants to do it and once 'e starts, 'e don't hang around any longer than what you saw just now.'

Jacques was beginning to think that, like 'golden wheat', the epic grandeur of the bull was just an old commonplace of the Romantics, one of those hackneyed images endlessly touched up by the would-be poets and second-rate novelists of the present day. No, really, there was nothing here to get carried away by, nothing to put your riding boots on and blow your horn for! It was neither dignified nor elevating. As for lyricism, the coupling consisted of amassing two types of meat which they thrashed, piled on top of one another and then dragged apart as soon as they'd touched, beating them again as they went!

Without saying a word, they were now striding along the main road to Longueville, followed by the cow, which Uncle Antoine was pulling behind him on the end of a rope.

All of a sudden, the old man coughed, then started complaining about the difficulty he was having getting money; after his usual lamentations, he coughed again and added: 'If only those who owe you money didn't take so long to pay you back, one would be happy enough, all the same…'

As Jacques didn't respond, he went on: 'I'd be very happy if I just got thirty francs back…'

'You'll have them tomorrow, uncle,' said Jacques; 'you'll be paid for your half of the barrel you can be sure of that.'

'Oh, no doubt, no doubt…but what about the interest they'd have given me in Provins if I'd taken the money there?'

'With interest, then.'

'Well, well, well…you're a real gentleman!'

Jacques was turning things over in his mind. The money will arrive tomorrow without fail; Moran collected the sums that were owed to me the day before yesterday. By paying off the overdue amounts, as has been agreed, and reimbursing the most vocal of the creditors, he should have been able to stop the repossessions I was threatened with. It's a respite. There must be about 300 francs due to me; I'll have enough, he concluded, to settle up here and in three or four days take the Belfort to Paris express with Louise.

This idea that he was finally going to leave Lourps, return to Paris, rediscover his own rooms, his own bathroom, his *objets d'art* and his books, elated him; but would his leaving here really silence the litany of melancholy thoughts and decant that spiritual anguish, the cause of which he blamed on his wife's estrangement? He felt that he could not easily forgive Louise for being so distant with him at a time when he'd wanted to hold her close. Then there was also the terrible question of living together. Up until then they'd lived unconstrained, in separate rooms, each had their own space; they'd avoided the embarrassment of those ridiculous necessities of life, the shame of intimate ablutions. At the château it had been necessary to live together, to go to bed and get up in the same room, and, as stupid as it was, he thought less of his wife now, felt an embarrassment, almost an aversion on certain days, at the touch of her body.

On his return to Paris he'd go and find them a cheap flat, but he couldn't reasonably hope, as in the past, to have his own bedroom; the prospect of not being able to relax on his own, to get a moment's peace, overwhelmed him. Besides, he well knew that if a man isn't repelled by his wife's intimate complaints it's because carnal passion, like a refractive medium that distorts the reality of things, deludes him and makes of a woman's body an instrument of such excessive pleasure that he overlooks the poverty of her wares.

With Louise, sick and tired, tense and unresponsive, desire was no longer possible; the hereditary stain of woman was all that remained, with no compensatory element of any kind.

This stay at Lourps will have had some really great consequences, he thought bitterly, it'll have initiated us, body and soul, into a mutual abhorrence. Oh, how Louise depresses me.

'Eh, aren't you speaking to me any more, nephew?' said Uncle Antoine.

Jacques stared; he'd reached the door of the château without even being aware of it.

'Goodnight uncle, I'll see you tomorrow.' He climbed the stairs only to find his wife in tears.

'Come now, what is it?' And he learned that Aunt Norine had lost all self-control when her niece had asked if she could borrow some sheets. Norine had refused, saying that she herself didn't change her sheets, and besides theirs were new and that the Parisians might have something wrong with them that would infect the linen. Then in the next breath she'd demanded the money back for the barrel, complaining about people who even though they aren't rich waste food by giving it to the cat.

And she'd wanted to take the creature back.

'He's only good for drowning in the pond,' Norine had shouted and Louise had had to get between her and the cat, which had bared its claws and was trying to scratch her. In short, Norine had become insolent and belligerent, and in front of the pregnant woman from Savin, too, who'd come with her daughter to carry the shopping, and though she'd earlier implored Louise to be the unborn child's godmother, she joined in with Aunt Norine in insulting her as soon as she found out that 'the lady' she was swindling wasn't rich.

'No, I won't put up with being humiliated like that by peasants,' said Louise. 'I want to leave.'

Jacques tried to reason with her; she finally calmed down but declared firmly that as soon as the money arrived she was catching the train.

'So be it,' said Jacques, 'I've had enough of Château de Lourps style hospitality too, and besides leaving a day sooner or later doesn't make any difference to me.'

'It's this poor kitty that worries me,' Louise continued, stroking the cat, which was staring at her imploringly and stretching out its wretched paws. 'I'm scared they'll beat it to death as soon as our backs are turned. Let me bring it back; what do you say?'

'I'd like nothing better, but how? If only it was healthier.'

And Jacques went over to the animal, which got up painfully and whined as soon as he touched it with his fingertips.

'In fact,' he said, 'it's been the only genuinely affectionate creature we've come across here; and yet thanks to Norine, who deprived the animal of the scraps we were keeping for it for so long, we barely even had time to get fond of it.'

XII

'Are you going to blow it out?'

'Yes.' And Louise, who lay on the open side of the bed, leaned over to extinguish the candle.

'Anyway' said Jacques, stretching out as best as he could on the narrow bed, 'soon we're going to be back in Paris on our cosy mattresses. I've definitely had enough of this lumpy sack of beans and this bolster that's so full of needles it feels like it's darning my neck whenever I move.'

He'd finally managed to wedge himself more or less into the space between the bed and the wall, when a whining noise filled the room, a low, drawn-out whine that suddenly burst out into an unmistakeable cry of terrible distress.

'It's the cat,' said Louise. 'My God, what's the matter with it?'

She relit the candle and they could make out the animal lying on the ground, staring fixedly at the floor. Splits were opening up in the matted tufts of its coat as the fur bristled; its flattened ears were pressing down against its skull, and its flanks were heaving like the bellows of a forge.

All of a sudden, it was choked by a furious bout of hiccups; it was as if it was trying to vomit its entrails through a mouth that was opening inordinately wide, leaving its tongue to hang out, its rough wet surface rasping the floor. It retched, eyes bulging out of its head, then, when it managed to catch its breath, let out a desperate howl and a stream of frothy water gushed from its throat.

At the end of its strength, it collapsed, nose in its saliva, and stopped moving.

Trembling all over, Louise leapt out of bed wanting to pick

it up; but shivers coursed over the surface of its coat as soon as she even tried to touch it.

The cat eventually regained consciousness, hesitantly looking to the left, then to the right, tried to raise itself up on its paws, finally managed to stand, limbs trembling, crawled across the room and cowered in a corner; but it couldn't stay in one place, would continually retreat as if to avoid some danger, staring at a point on the wall with a look of pain and confusion, then recoil with a stagger, mewing with fear.

'Kitty, here little kitty,' Louise called softly. It recognised her and then it moaned like a child, casting her looks of such distress that she burst into tears.

It wanted to get up onto her lap, but it could barely climb and clung to her nightdress with its claws, dragging its already lifeless hindquarters behind it.

It whimpered at every effort, but she didn't dare help it because its very body was like a keyboard of pain that sounded wherever she touched it.

Once settled on her lap, it tried to produce a weak purr, but then it stopped and wanted to get down again, slid heavily onto its paws which splayed out, remained motionless, spine arched, tail bristling, ears flattened; then it started to rush around the room again, the bellows of its flanks heaving even harder.

'He's going to have another attack,' said Louise.

And indeed, the hiccups and the vomiting started again. It pounced on itself, threw back its head, made incredible efforts as if to jump out of its skin, then fell on its belly again and froth came out of its mouth and bubbled as it stretched out stiffly, its mouth curled back to reveal its teeth.

'He's really sick,' Louise sighed.

'Well it's not, as we'd thought, rheumatism; it's out-and-out paralysis,' said Jacques, who, leaning out of bed, was examining the animal's upturned muzzle and its rigid hindquarters.

Once again, the cat came to and heaved itself up; its features returned to normal, its mouth closed over its teeth, but a visible pallor bathed its face and there was a pained look in its eyes that revealed an infinite despair, an unbearable suffering.

Louise spread out a petticoat underneath the bed, on which it lay prostrate. It seemed absolutely exhausted, its energy spent, close to death. Nevertheless, it thrust out its claws in front of it, extending and retracting them in clenched paws, and stared around the room with its black, glazed eyes.

Then a rattling noise came from its contorted throat and its eyes closed.

'The attack is over, he'll die peacefully now,' said Jacques. 'Come back to bed, you'll make yourself ill.'

'If I only had some chloroform or something to put him out of his misery, I wouldn't leave him in such agony,' said Louise.

They lay without speaking, lamp extinguished, amazed that a wretched animal could suffer so much.

'Can you still hear him?' said Jacques.

'Yes, listen…'

The cat had abandoned the petticoat and was now trying to climb onto the chair so it could get to the bed. They could hear its laboured breathing and the sound of its claws scratching the wood. Then everything went quiet, but after a short pause it tenaciously continued on its way, hauling itself up with its paws, then falling back and beginning its climb all over again, its whines interspersed with the rattling in its throat.

It reached the bed, tottered, steadied itself, then crawled between Jacques and Louise.

Neither of them dared to move now because the least movement provoked heartrending moans.

It came and sniffed them, still trying to purr so as to show them that it was content to be near them, then, gripped by a convulsion, it got up and passed over Louise, attempted to get down from the bed, fell, and rolled onto the floor with the cry of an animal having its throat cut.

'It's the end this time,' said Jacques; they breathed a sigh of relief. By the light of a match, Louise saw the contorted animal, flaying the air with its claws, vomiting froth and wind.

All of a sudden, terrified, she grabbed her husband by the hand.

'Look, shooting pains…'

And, indeed, the cat's paws were shaking with an irregular juddering motion, and electric shivers ran across its fur in rippling waves, though its body wasn't moving.

The tone of her voice changed and she added: 'It has them, too…so it's paralysis that's coming on.'

Jacques felt himself go cold all over.

'No, not at all, you're just being silly,' and he hastily explained that this quivering of the skin had no connection with the shooting pains she was talking about. 'You have a nervous illness, nothing more; hell, it's a big step from there to locomotor ataxia! Anyway, the best proof is right there: the cat only had those spasms for a minute and now he's dying; whereas you, you've had them for months and yet you're still up and about. And besides, it's silly to try and argue there are similarities between an animal's illness and women's complaints.'

But his voice lacked conviction. In a flash, he saw the tight-lipped doctors, remembered their inscrutable faces, their discreet looks of pity. But no, they knew nothing about it, no more than he did. According to some, it was metritis; according to others, neurosis. They had no idea what it was, one of those nervous complaints which everyone at the present time is baffled by, no matter how clever they are.

He had a feeling that his explanations had been tactless, that this haste in wanting to dissuade her was almost an admission, that his pressing need to argue about it and to convince her clearly revealed that her fears were genuine. He was annoyed with himself, and then with the cat for being the unwitting cause of his anxieties. Oh, I wish it would just die, he thought. Then it occurred to him that it wasn't really helpful for Louise to upset herself by watching the animal's death throes.

'Look, it's late, we can't spend a sleepless night over this animal, especially if we're leaving tomorrow. I think the simplest thing would be to wrap it in your petticoat and carry it into the kitchen.'

But he ran up against his wife's stubborn wilfulness; she became indignant and treated him as if he were being heartless.

He sank back under the covers, cursing. He had only one desire now: that the cat would die. After all, it isn't mine and we don't really know it, he said to himself in order to try and excuse the selfishness of his wishes; and what's more we're catching the express train in a few hours; it's really time this was all over.

The cat no longer moved. Louise was kneeling and looking into its eyes, dull eyes the waters of which had lost their golden flecks and were turning blue, as if frozen by a great cold.

She got back into bed, heartbroken, and extinguished the candle; and in the silence of the room each pretended to be asleep so as not to have to speak.

If only it was five o'clock, I'd get up, thought Jacques. My God, what a night! I'm afraid this will be an irreparable blow to Louise. Moreover, what if it's true? What if the doctors have lied to me? What if those spasms in her legs are a premonitory symptom of ataxia?

And straightaway he glimpsed his wife's distorted features, her open mouth dribbling bubbles, and transposed the agonising symptoms he had seen in the cat to Louise, saw her as she would be in those same moments, in a hallucination of unbearable clarity.

He was on the point of crying out, of calling for help, when he came to; he tried to reason with himself, wanting at all costs to divert the flow of his imaginings, and resolved to count from one to a hundred to make himself sleep. He put his arms outside the covers and pulled down the blankets a bit in order to numb himself with the cold, so that snuggling back under the bedcover would seem warm; but when he reached twenty, the numbers he'd already counted went backwards as if of their own accord, back down the slope he'd set them on, and so, no longer bothering with them, he was driven back into the horror of his thoughts.

That's enough, he said to himself, fighting against them. He coughed lightly.

'Are you asleep?' He was speaking to his wife now, because he was hoping that the sound of his words would dispel the waking nightmares haunting him.

'No,' she said in a muffled voice.

So he babbled on to himself, losing himself in pointless digressions about what packing was to be done, listing the things they'd have to take, worrying about the size of their cases, trying, by any means, to steal a march on the night; but his lips were uttering sounds mechanically, running on by themselves, with no direction from his mind, which despite itself, had retraced its steps and rediscovered the path these subterfuges had tried in vain to make him lose.

Even so, he eventually fell silent and grew drowsy. If he didn't quite go to sleep completely, he at least forgot about his troubles.

Waking suddenly with the dawn, he relived in a flash the

events of the night before and jumped out of bed.

And the cat? He saw it on the petticoat, motionless, prostrate, and called to it in a low voice. The animal didn't move a muscle, but immediately shivers ran over its fur.

My wife is right, we should have the courage to finish it off, he said to himself; faced with the interminable death throes of this animal, he was overcome by pity.

He was eager to escape this cursed room. What nights I've endured here, he thought, the first was horrible, others completely insane, the last unbearable!

He went downstairs and strolled around the garden; and little by little, as he walked, his hatred for Lourps and his desire to leave abated.

It was so pleasant out on this lawn, so warm behind the trellis formed by the leaves. Filtered by the pines, there was a faint smell of turpentine and resin blowing on the breeze; a tannic odour of bark rising up from the churned-up moss on the ground invigorated him like an inhalation of smelling salts. The château, brought back to life by the sunlight, was casting off its surly aspect, looking younger, with a festive, coquettish air, as if for his departure. Even the pigeons, so wild that one never succeeded in getting close to them, were now strutting about in the courtyard and looking at him, without flying off at his approach. It was, in a way, a kind of fond farewell from this abandoned place in which he had drained away so many melancholy hours.

He felt sad at heart, passing for the last time beneath the bower of these deserted pathways, looking at bunches of grapes like sleigh-bells on vines coiled round pagodas of pines, their old cones hanging like cowbells. It was all over; that very evening he would return to Paris and his whole life would change!

All the while he'd postponed his return to some indefinite

date in the future, he'd managed to keep in check his concerns about how he was going to make a living. He would tell himself: 'I'll wait and see,' and then consider various schemes that were more or less certain of success, not so much duping himself with his responses as lulling his anxieties, paring them down, rendering them ineffectual, spacing them out, wearing them away with these simulacra of decisions which, at the time, he almost succeeded in believing.

Now that his return was settled, imminent, he was losing all his courage and was no longer even trying to draw up plans in his mind.

What good would it do? He was entering the unknown; the only things he could reasonably anticipate were these: that he must, as soon as he got back, start to make calls, to make appointments, to renew contact with people he despised in order to procure for himself some advantageous work or position. What a series of snubs, what a succession of humiliations I'll have to endure, he thought; the day of atonement for my contempt of utilitarianism is now at hand.

Solitude certainly had its good side. At least here, apart from the peasants, he didn't have to see anyone; but now, to earn his daily bread, he was going to have to flounder around with the others in the repulsive feeding trough of the masses.

And what then? Even supposing he got used to the turmoil of a life of poverty, what would become of Louise? He imagined her sick and helpless, pictured the terrible consequences of her ataxia, the special cot, rubber undersheets, draw-sheets, dirty linen, all the horrors of an inert body that would have to be attended to; there'd be no way I could even keep her with me since I wouldn't have the money to pay for a nursemaid. So inevitably I'll have to put her in the poorhouse. This thought seemed so hard-hearted to him that tears sprang to his eyes.

However, it was pointless to give in to despair like this before the event; after all, even if Louise is restored to health, aren't the bonds between us already broken? haven't we bruised each other here too much for the memory of our antipathies ever to fade; no, it's really over, whatever happens, the tranquillity of our lives is dead!

But come on, no more of that, he concluded, wiping his eyes; we're leaving in a few hours and we still need to pack the trunks.

He went back upstairs to the bedroom, found his wife up and about, folding her dresses.

'Oh, if it wasn't for the cat, I'd be really happy to be going back to Paris.'

'It only has a couple of hours left to live; look, its eyes have glazed over and it can barely breathe.'

He tidied his papers and sorted out his things, while his wife, in order to prepare lunch, lit the fire.

Unexpectedly, footsteps resounded in the stairwell, and the postman entered.

'I've come earlier than usual,' he said, 'because I've got a nice little letter for you...' And he pulled out the long-awaited envelope, sealed with five official stamps.

A kind of grandeur dignified his sunburnt face and his grey hair seemed almost venerable. The importance of this letter containing money was transfiguring him, ennobling even the old drunkard's toothless laugh.

He sat down, rubbed his head with the palm of his hand, and stared at the barely begun preparations for the meal and the empty table; he was clearly regretting having hurried.

'It's the last letter you'll be bringing us, postman,' Jacques announced, signing the receipt; 'we're leaving for Paris today.'

The old man almost fell off his chair.

215

'Ay, ay, ay, and here was I counting on my Parisians being here until the winter; this news gives my heart a turn, right truly. Oh, it would've meant a longer round, to be sure, but what harm would that do me? I was coming to see generous folk, ain't that true, not stingy at all; why, we're almost friends; and as for you my little lady,' he went on in a doleful voice that almost belied the faint hint of deceit in his eyes, 'you can take ol' Mignot's word for it that you'll be sorely missed, you will. Anyways, that's not going to stop us drinking a last glass of wine to your health now, is it?' and he glanced surreptitiously at the bottle.

Jacques was eager to see him clear off.

'Here, Mignot, here's ten francs for your troubles…and now, to your health,' and he offered him a glass.

With one hand, the postman pocketed the coins, with the other, he tossed the wine down his throat in a single swig; then he asked if he could cut himself a piece of bread, thinking, not without reason, that they wouldn't let him eat like this without giving him more drink.

He knocked back practically the whole bottle in this way, finally he got up, proffered a grubby hand, and in a voice cracked with emotion declared that he'd expect them next year; then, with a look of despondency, he left, jangling the two, hundred-sou coins in his trouser pocket.

'Don't you want no letters to be delivered round 'ere then?' shouted Uncle Antoine, who appeared a few moments after the postman had left.

'Why's that?'

'Why? because he's going to stop at the first inn he sees and drink till he falls over.'

'That's very funny, the whole countryside not getting any letters because Parisians got the postman drunk…but look, we haven't any time to lose because we're catching the express to

Paris at 4.33. We could settle the bill now, if you'd like.'

'The express? You're leaving? Unbelievable! Just like that?'

'Yes, I got some news this morning that obliges me to be in Paris before six o'clock.'

'But Louise, she's staying…isn't that so, my girl?' continued Uncle Antoine, who was looking out of the corner of his eye at the money lying on the table.

'No, I'm leaving too.'

'Well, I'll be…'

'Now let's see,' said Jacques. 'How much do I owe you?'

Then the old man pulled out of his waistcoat pocket a dirty piece of paper, folded in four.

'It's all the figures: Parisot calculated it for me with the interest taken into account. Have a look, my boy, and see if you agree with that.'

'Absolutely…only I don't have any change.'

'That's quickly sorted! I've got some coins here.'

He stood up and pulled out a long purse from the pocket of his overalls.

Knowing I'd been sent some money, the old man's thought of everything, Jacques said to himself.

Uncle Antoine gave him back the change, coin by coin, holding each one between his fingers, grumbling: 'It's hard-earned cash I'm giving you here,' hiding with difficulty an almost mocking satisfaction because he'd just duped the Parisians once more by adding the interest on the money not from the day they'd paid the shopkeeper but from the day he'd ordered the barrel.

'Is that right by your reckoning?'

'Yes, Uncle Antoine.'

'Now my dear boy, if you're leaving, I'll need to get the ol' nag in harness.'

'You mean to say you'd do me a favour…'

'But of course, of course…look, we can't let you leave like this; you should come and have something to eat with us.'

'I've made lunch, it's ready now,' said Louise.

'Well, there you are! I'll carry it for you, then we can all eat it together.'

Louise shot a questioning glance at her husband.

'OK,' he said. 'You're right, Uncle Antoine, the very least we can do before going is have a glass together.'

Uncle Antoine was insistent that he carry the basket in which the provisions were packed. He'd come to the conclusion that he might need his niece in Paris, and drop in on her for a free meal when he went to settle his accounts there at Candlemas.

'They're leaving!' he cried, as he walked through the door of the cottage.

Norine dropped the frying pan in surprise.

'Ah well, that's that then!' And she forced a tear; then, scared of being snubbed by her niece whose contemptuous look unsettled her, she stretched out her long, scrawny arms towards Jacques and mechanically kissed him on both cheeks.

'Ay, ay, what'll we do? What a piece of news…and here was I saying just now that I must make them some *galettes*… you know, nephew, crêpes fried in a pan…there's nowt better! What a pity! Ah, it's too late now, I reckon, now you're going away.'

She muttered away to herself while setting the table: 'It'll seem empty here,' and she sniffed as she rinsed the glasses.

'But you'll come back to see us next year?'

'Of course.'

The meal passed in silence. Norine was snivelling, her nose in her plate; the old man, embarrassed by Jacques and Louise's silence as they sat there looking sad and preoccupied, said only:

'Go on, have another glass, my lad,' filling up the glasses and emptying his own, smacking his lips, which he wiped with the back of his hand.

'We can't delay any longer,' declared Louise; 'I've still got some things to pack at the château, and it'll soon be time for the train.'

'You'll take a rabbit back for later?'

In spite of their protests there was no way of avoiding it. Aunt Norine strangled one of her animals and brought it in, still warm, rolled in straw.

'While Louise has a last look around, we've got time for a glass of brandy, then we'll harness up,' said Uncle Antoine.

They clinked glasses again and, on being begged to write to the old man as soon as he returned to the capital, Jacques – with no intention of keeping his promise – gave his word.

Finally, old Antoine dragged the cart out from the barn, slipped his little donkey into the shafts, and they shambled off to the Château de Lourps.

'I've taken the cat upstairs to another room; I've left my petticoat with it so it won't get cold, and some water to drink if it's thirsty. I'd prefer it to die like that than to think that Aunt Norine had beaten it to death with a stick,' said Louise. 'It isn't suffering anymore, and besides it didn't even recognise me… poor kitty, he's completely stiff.'

'Come on, we're ready to go!' shouted Uncle Antoine, piling the cases and trunks into the cart; 'Now, off we go!' and they jolted off, thrown one against the other, in this rugged cart whose wheels jumped at every stone.

Sitting in the back on a pile of hay, Jacques was studying these peasants who he was hoping never to see again.

That thought will console me for having to leave this miserable haven where I almost found a refuge, he thought, because if I've got to mix with rogues I'd prefer them to be more sharp-witted, and more easy-going.

'Tell me something, nephew...'

'What's that, Aunt Norine?'

'If you've got, you or Louise, any clothes you don't need anymore, we could make use of 'em here, for our Sunday best.'

'There's a proper shortage of old clothes,' said Uncle Antoine.

Jacques, worn out, promised them all they wanted.

'We'll be thinking of you often.'

'And so will we.'

'You're like my own flesh and blood, as they say,' continued Norine in a tearful voice, looking at her niece.

'At last, here's the station,' Jacques murmured to himself. Then, after the luggage had been taken down, the peasants opened their arms and kissed Jacques and Louise extravagantly on both cheeks, with tears in their eyes.

Then, when the Parisians were settled into their carriage, they whipped the donkey and, after a short silence, old Antoine said:

'I heard 'em all right, I heard her telling Jacques she was leaving a petticoat for the dying cat.'

'How stupid!'

'Aye, but it was 'er what said it.'

'Ah well, that's that then!'

And, worried the cat would ruin the fabric with its claws, they drove flat out back to the château.

Figure 1: *'I am holed-up in the moribund Château de Lourps, an aristocratic château with ancient moats, towers and grounds, all of which are in a very sad state.'* (p. 16)
A picture taken sometime in the 1930s, showing one wing of the château and the square tower of the stairwell, with its small six-paned windows.

Figure 2: *'On the hillside, in the distance, a huge building filled the sky, like an enormous barn with its hard, black outline, above which silent streams of red cloud were flowing.'* (p. 47)
The church at Lourps has now been fully renovated after its vault collapsed in 1966.

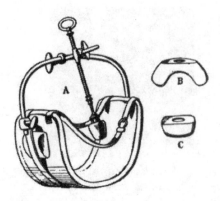

Figure 3: '...*what fantastical ovary compressor...*'(p. 113)
An ovary compressor of the type used by Jean Martin Charcot on his
epileptic and hysterical female patients.

Figure 4: '...*near the cornices, ran pipes covered in a green fabric,
like extravagant speaking tubes or the siphon of an enormous enema.*'
(p. 184)
An enema pump invented by Doctor Maurice Éguisier with its
distinctive siphon covered in a flexible fabric.

Figure 5: '...her navel represented by the Jansen crater, her girl's sex by the great V of a gulf, and the fork of her two spread legs, one clubfooted, by the Sea of Fecundity and the Sea of Nectar.' (p. 112) Huysmans obtained a lunar map to ensure that the physical details of the landscape in Jacques's dream of walking on the moon were accurate.

Figure 6: '...a magisterium concocted by a Bolognese count, Cesare Mattei, and known within the schismatic circles of homeopathy as 'Green Electricity'...' (p. 117) Mattei's 'bizarre medicine' had something of a vogue throughout Europe at the time and Huysmans made further reference to his ideas in his subsequent novel, Là-bas (1891).

Notes

I

45. ...*Night was falling*. The opening scene of *En Rade* has certain affinities with that of Edgar Allan Poe's short story, *The Fall of the House of Usher*, which Huysmans had read in Charles Baudelaire's translation. A number of contemporary reviewers, including Henri de Régnier, referred to the similarity. In a piece of art criticism about the painter Léon Belly, written in 1881, Huysmans specifically mentions the *House of Usher* as having had an enormous impact on him psychologically, and referred to Poe as the "inventor of the mathematical nightmare". He goes on to say that as far back as 1866 he had been reminded by one of Belly's pictures that depicted a stark, melancholic landscape, of this "terror-inducing" story and its memorable conclusion: "...and the deep and dank tarn at my feet closed sullenly over the fragments of the House of Usher."

45. ...*Jacques Marles*. The manuscript version used for the edition published by the *Revue indépendante*, reveals that even at this late stage Huysmans was considering the name 'Gastin de Quélaine' for the main character. The change to the less aristocratic-sounding 'Jacques Marles' signifies a considerable shift in perspective, sociologically and politically, in terms of the issues addressed by the book.

45. ...*Château de Lourps*. In the 1880s, Lourps (the 'p' is not pronounced) was a small hamlet near Jutigny, in the Seine-et-Marne district, about 45 miles south east of Paris. At least part of the château, which Huysmans first visited in 1882, still exists today, one wing having been demolished sometime in the 1930s. For a fuller account of Huysmans' visits to the château, see the introduction. (See Figure 1 on p. 221)

46. ...*periods of wasting*. In the original Huysmans uses the word *étisie*, a medical term for chronic consumption. *Étisie* was also commonly associated with the degenerative disease *tabes dorsalis*, which resulted from an untreated syphilis infection.

Notes

52. ...*Griotte marble.* Griotte marble is named after the griotte cherry because of its distinctive red colour. It is still quarried in the Herault region of France. Griotte marble was famously used by Louis XIV for the fireplaces in the Grand Trianon at Versailles, so Huysmans here is clearly emphasising the former aristocratic splendour of the château.

58. ...*'Ah well, that's that then!'* In the original, Huysmans uses an untranslatable expression, *Ah, ben c'étant!* which he'd no doubt heard used by the local inhabitants of Brie during his visits to Lourps. In the serialised version, the expression appears as *Ah, bien c'étant!*, so it seems as if Huysmans wanted to accentuate Norine and Antoine's rusticity in the novel.

II

61. ...*And this palace.* The section beginning here and ending with the words 'like a poker, thrust into her' was published as a separate 'prose poem', under the heading 'Esther, Fragment' in *La Vogue*, (No.8, 13 to 20 June 1886), some five months before *En Rade* began to be serialised in the *Revue indepéndante*, in November of that year. The piece had clearly been worked on for some time as Huysmans made only a very few changes when it was published in book form nearly a year later. Significantly, in the novel Huysmans changed the description in the opening paragraph from 'its ringed battlements of iron' to 'its towers ringed with battlements of iron', thereby making an explicit allusion to the towers of the Château de Lourps that Jacques noticed on his arrival. This was not the first time Huysmans had inserted such fragments into his novels, having done the same with the 'Pantin' section in *A Rebours*.

61. ...*lamellated with scales.* In the original Huysmans uses the phrase *papelonné d'écailles*. This is actually a tautology as *papelloné* is a heraldic term meaning covered in scales.

62. ...*dangled symbolic pomegranates.* Pomegranates were ancient symbols of female fertility, a point strongly reinforced by the imagery at the end

of the paragraph.

63. *...the king appeared.* This vivid dream sequence is inspired by the Bible story of King Ahasuerus and Esther. The story is a complex one and can be separated into two distinct, but intertwined, narrative strands: the first centres on Ahasuerus' search for a new queen, while the second concerns the deliverance of the Jewish people, after the king has been persuaded to order their massacre. The subject has been treated numerous times in art, with some painters concentrating on the 'beauty contest' element of the story, in which Esther, often depicted naked, appears before the king and he chooses her as his queen, while others concentrate on the 'redemption' aspect of the story, in which Esther again appears before the king, but this time in order to intercede on behalf of the Jews, as she is herself, unbeknown to the king, Jewish. In this latter narrative, the king takes pity on Esther and extends his sceptre to her as a sign of clemency, thereby sparing the Jews. Interestingly, Huysmans conflates these two iconic aspects of the story in his dream sequence and significantly he plays down the political dimension of the story, being drawn to it rather for its aesthetic and sexual potential within the narrative. In many of his novels Huysmans made use of a formal technique known as *ekphrasis*, the literary depiction of an existing work of art, so it seems likely that the imagery of this dream sequence is based on one or more actual paintings. Patrizia Lombardo has remarked that this passage has similarities with Taine's descriptions of Veronesi's *Esther*, in his *Philosophie de l'art* (1866), nevertheless at present no single painting has been found that could serve as a definitive model for the scene. The descriptions and the general tone of the passage are strikingly similar to the descriptions of Gustave Moreau's Salomé paintings in *A Rebours* (*Against Nature*), so it may be that Huysmans is creating an imaginary painting of the scene, in the style of Moreau.

64. *...tissue of the epidermis.* Huysmans had already displayed his knowledge of and fascination with the art of perfumery in *A Rebours*, and the subject of smell recurs numerous times in his work, cf. 'Le Gousset' in *Croquis*

Notes

parisiens ('The Armpit' in *Parisian Sketches*). It is not clear where he found his information about perfumes that altered skin colour, but in the original he refers to its action on the dermis, while in fact it is changes to the upper layer of skin, the epidermis, which actually effect skin colour.

64. ...*red emanations of olibanum.* An example of the specific nature of Huysmans' references to perfume and aromatics is in the use of *oliban* (olibanum) in the original. It is common nowadays to translate *oliban* as frankincense, as both are derived from trees of the genus *Boswellia*, but to use frankincense in this context makes no sense because of the reference to 'red emanations', it being a very pale yellowish resin. By contrast olibanum resin comes from the tree *Boswellia serrata*, and not only has a distinct smell, it is noticeably reddish in colour.

III

72. ...*seething with dandelion heads.* Huysmans recycled the image of the dandelions from an earlier piece he'd published in the *Révue illustrée* in January 1886, called *Autour des fortifications (Around the fortifications).* In his description of a walk around one of the suburbs to the west of Paris, he wrote: "In a field, about the size of a pocket handkerchief, a sign was hanging on the end of a stick: 'It is forbidden to walk on the crops.' What crops! Lord, there was nothing but thistles and briars, and here and there some nice wild dandelions whose delicate heads were moulting in the breeze."

72. ...*moulting.* In the original Huysmans uses his own neologism *s'epoilant*, meaning to lose or shed hair, which he first used in 1879 in *Les Soeurs Vatard (The Vatard Sisters).*

72. ...*crackelured by rain.* In the original Huysmans uses the word *tressaillée*, a term borrowed from painting, referring to the network of cracks that appear on the surface of old paintings. Huysmans frequently made use of the specialised vocabulary of the painter's craft in his descriptions.

73. ...*flamme de punch.* A bluish tint or nuance that had a certain vogue during the nineteenth century. It occurs in the work of Théophile Gautier and Alphonse Daudet, for example, and Claude Monet described his painting *Palmiers à Bordighera* (1884) as being 'all *gorge-de-pigeon* and *flamme de punch*' in a letter to his dealer, Paul Durand-Ruel.

74. ...*he saw an insanely overgrown garden.* As Julia Przybos points out in '*En Rade*, ou Huysmans entre creation et procreation' (CRIN 42, 2003), this scene can be read as a intertextual reference to Zola's *La Faute de l'abbé Mouret*, with Huysmans opposing Zola's optimistic vision of nature thriving in harmony with a pessimistic one of nature degenerating into chaos and sterility.

80. ...*vague Bactrias, hypothetical Cappadocias, speculative Susas.* Bactria was a region of the ancient world that now comprises parts of Afghanistan, Tajikistan, Uzbekistan and Turkmenistan; Cappadocia was an extensive area of Asia Minor, now in modern Turkey; Susa, the ancient capital of the Persian empire, was located in what is now the Khuzestan province of Iran. The events described in the Biblical book of Esther were supposed to have taken place in Susa.

80. ...*by way of Noah.* According to the Bible, Noah was the first tiller of the land and the first to plant a vineyard. He drank the wine, became drunk, and lay naked in his tent where he was seen by his son, Ham, for which 'crime' Ham's son Canaan was cursed by the embarrassed patriarch (Genesis 9: 18-29). The exact meaning of the Biblical passage is not altogether clear, leading to various speculations about the possible sexual nature either of Noah's nakedness or his son's reactions to it. In any event, Marles' interpretation is somewhat tenuous: the real meaning of the dream's symbolism lies in his own psychology rather than his spurious explanation with its superficial gloss of biblical authority.

81. ...*Artemidorus.* Artemidorus Daldianus or Ephesius was a Greek writer of the second century known for a five-volume work on dreams, *Oneirocritica* (The Interpretation of Dreams). Sigmund Freud, in his book *Interpretation of Dreams* (1900), credited Artemidorus for the proto-scientific way in

which he collected dream material through interviews and for taking the circumstances of the dreamer into account in his interpretations.

81. ...*Porphyry.* Porphyry of Tyre (c.233-c.309) was a Neo-Platonic philosopher. An advocate of vegetarianism, he also wrote on a wide variety of subjects including astrology, paganism, Euclidian mathematics and music. Some critics have wondered where Huysmans got his information about Porphyry from, as no book on the subject of dreams at the time made any reference to him. However, it seems almost certain that Huysmans got the details from a rare book published in France in 1747: *Traité de Porphyre, touchant l'abstinence de la chair des animaux, avec la Vie de Plotin par ce philosophe, et une Dissertation sur les génies, par M. de Burigny* (Paris: de Bure, 1747). The book includes an index and the entry for *Songes* (Dreams) gives a page reference and the summary: *"Les bon Génies s'en servent, pour découvrir l'avenir au vrai Philosophe"* (Good Genies help out and reveal the future to the true Philosopher). Huysmans' information is a condensed version of that given in the text itself: *"S'il se trouve réduit dans quelque extrémité fâcheuse, les bon genies accoureront à son secours & lui découvriront l'avenir, soit par des rêves, soit par des préssentimens; ils lui apprendront ce qu'il doit s'éviter."* (If he [the true Philosopher] finds himself in some unfortunate situation, good genies will run to his aid and reveal the future to him, whether by dreams or by premonitions; they teach him this so that he can avoid it.)

82. ...*Wundt.* Wilhelm Wundt (1832-1920) a German medical doctor who was one of the founders of experimental psychology. His *Grundzüge der physiologischen Psychologie (Principles of Physiological Psychology,* 1874) was translated into French in 1886, and the details Huysmans uses are taken from a section dealing with the various physical and mental causes of dreams.

83. ...*Radestock.* Paul Radestock, was a doctoral student of Wundt's. In his *Schlaf und Traum (Sleep and Dream)* published in 1879, he argued that the rays of the sun or moon shining on the sleeper were the cause of dreams of celestial glory in those of a religious temperament.

88. ...*Marquise de Saint-Phal*. According to a pamphlet published by Les Amis de Lourps, the property was bought by the Marquis de Saint-Phalle in 1765 and remained in the family's possession until 1829.

IV

92. ...*the waters 'ave broken*. In the original Huysmans uses a slang term, *la bouteille passe*, the 'bottle' being the sac of amniotic fluid around the foetus. Zola also made use of the term in *La Terre*, which started to appear in installments in *Gil blas* in May 1887, a month after the publication in book form of *En Rade*.

97. ...*But how many cows are there in Jutigny?* Despite Antoine's complaints about the amount of money François is making with his stud bull, the figures do not add up, as Jacques realises and which accounts for his uneasy silence. The most François could have earned from his bull is 450 francs per year and Antoine has already said that the loss of one cow would be nearly 500 francs alone. By comparison, in the early 1880s Huysmans, as a clerk in the Civil Service, was earning 3,000 francs a year, and this was not considered a large amount of money.

102. ...*confessionals of the body*. This euphemism attracted a certain amount of mockery in contemporary reviews, such as that in *La Liberté* (19 August 1887): "Jacques Marles complains that the château of misery lacks one of those 'little rooms' you're familiar with. The author could have called the thing by its name, he does so for many other worse things. But all of a sudden he's in the grip of some scruple of decency." However, the passage is meant to represent the thoughts of Jacques Marles, rather than Huysmans himself, and serves to highlight his alienation from the world of nature and his sense of shame about his own bodily functons. Marles' attitude can perhaps be compared to that of Eugène Lejantel, the narrator of Huysmans' anti-war story *Sac au dos* (1880): "I'm home, in my own bathroom, and I think to myself that you have to have lived in the promiscuity of a hospital or the barracks to appreciate the value of your

231

Notes

own water closet, to savour the solitude of a place where you can drop your trousers in peace."

103. *...sense of distraction.* In the original Huysmans uses the obscure term *évagation*, which according to the *Dictionnaire de l'Académie française* (1832-5) is a devotional term meaning the disposition of the mind to detach itself from the object on which it should be fixed. Interestingly the *Dictionnaire* notes that it is rarely used except in works of ascetic theology.

106. *...like a gaping well.* The imagery and symbolism of the well in *En Rade* has been much discussed, especially in relation to this strange notion of an inverse well. This 'naturalistic' description of the light of the moon looking like a well shaft is mirrored in a later dream sequence, in which Jacques conceives of a tower in terms of a well, one that rises into the air rather than plunging into the ground.

V

107. *...torulous.* A specialised term derived from, and more commonly used in, natural history than in geology, meaning to have a surface covered with swellings or rounded prominences.

108. *...the Moon was a very strange country all the same.* This particular dream sequence in which Marles traverses the landscape of the moon has, understandably, attracted a lot of critical attention, not just for its incredible visual texture, but for its rich seam of psychological imagery. In his contemporary review of *En Rade*, 'Huysmans et son dernier livre' in the Brussels periodical *L'Art moderne* (later published in *Sur la tombe de Huysmans*, Paris, 1913), Léon Bloy described the chapter as an "unimaginable literary tour de force". Huysmans himself was very pleased with it, and in a letter to Arij Prins of August 1886, he describes being "...worn out from working on the Moon – you know that there are some dreams in my new book and among them there's a trip to the moon. I think I'm doing something a bit special, because I'm getting carried

away by my subject – fuck Verne!" Although it was Jules Verne who most famously wrote about a trip to the moon, firstly in *De la terre à la lune* (*From the Earth to the Moon,* 1865) and in a sequel, *Autour de la lune* (*Around the Moon,* 1870), in neither book does anyone actually land on the moon's surface. Huysmans had almost certainly also read Baudelaire's translation of a story by Edgar Allan Poe, 'The Unparalleled Adventure of One Hans Pfaall' (1835), about a balloonist who ventures into space. But here again, the traveller only observes the moon and doesn't land on it, so Huysmans' account of walking on the surface of the moon, even though it is couched in the form of a dream sequence, seems to be fairly radical for the time.

108. ...*merging cordilleras.* The use of the word 'cordilleras' here is an echo of Jacques's impressions of the decaying rooms in the château in which he likens the bulging plaster on the walls to a relief map of 'the peaks of Cordilleras'.

109. ...*countless Chimborazoes.* Chimborazo is an inactive volcano in the Cordillera Occidental range of the Andes. It is the highest summit in Ecuador.

110. ...*Atlas or an Enceladus.* In Greek mythology, Atlas was a Titan who supported the heavens on his back; Enceladus was one of a race of giants, the Gigantes, the children of Gaia (the Earth).

111. ...*Beer and Mädler.* Two German astronomers, Wilhelm Beer (1797-1850), an amateur observer, and Johann Heinrich von Mädler (1794-1874), a professional, worked for four years to produce their *Mappa selenographica* (1834-37), a large-scale and richly detailed map of the moon, which was perhaps the most influential lunar publication of the century. In the letter to Arij Prins quoted in the first note of this chapter, Huysmans complained that he hadn't been able to find a French map of the moon and had to rely on one he'd got from a German bookseller, produced by Justus Perthes. Although most of the names were in Latin, which Huysmans could understand, the key and surrounding text were in German, which he could not. At the end of his letter, therefore, he

listed the German phrases and words from the map's key, and asked Prins to translate them for him. In 1882, in a piece included in the appendix to *L'Art Moderne* (1883), Huysmans compared some of Odilon Redon's images to "the desolate landscapes of a lunar map", a comparison he went on to expand in his imaginative 'review' of an album of work by Redon, which was first published in the *Revue indépendante* in February 1885 and in which he also mentions the Beer and Mädler map by name.

112. *...Acherusia promontory.* Although the Justus Perthes map gives the correct spelling, Huysmans must have copied the name incorrectly as it appears as 'Arechusia' in the novel.

112. *...the contour of which resembled the belly of a pale figure.* (See Figure 5 on p. 224)

112. *...sintered clay.* In the original Huysmans uses the neologism *concréfié*, which has its roots in the word *concréfaction*, referring to the process of sintering or the fusing of materials at temperatures lower than their melting point, rather than the more common *concréter*, to solidify. Huysmans was never afraid of using or adapting words from specialised vocabularies, even if it meant that very few people would have any idea what the word meant.

113. *...what fantastical ovary compressor.* Huysmans' reference to the ovary compressor shows that he was fairly familiar with the work of Jean-Martin Charcot (1825-1893), who sought to establish a physiological cause for 'neurotic' and 'hysterical' symptoms in women. One of Charcot's theories was that there was a connection between diseases or malfunctions of the ovary and incidences of epilepsy and hysteria, and in 1878 he invented an ovary compressor which he claimed could prevent such attacks by applying pressure to the ovaries. (See Figure 3 on p. 223) In *Là-bas* (1891), Huysmans expanded on Charcot's claim that women in the middle ages who were supposedly possessed by the devil were actually misdiagnosed hysterics.

114. *...terrace at Saint-Germain-en-Laye.* The *Grande Terrasse de Saint-Germain-en-Laye* was constructed during the reign of Louis XIV. Nearly

a mile and a half long and situated near the bank of the Seine some seven miles north of Versailles, its elevated position offers a stunning view of Paris and its outlying areas.

VI

116. ...*French kickboxer.* Huysmans uses the phrase *maître de savate*, *savate* being a form of kickboxing introduced into France at the beginning of the nineteenth century. It was popularised by fighters such as Charles Lecour during the mid-1850s, and later by Joseph Charlemont, who not only wrote kickboxing training manuals but established a boxing academy in Paris in 1887. Huysmans also made a reference to *savate* in *A Rebours*. It is possible that he saw an exhibition bout at a suburban fair like the one he describes in *Les Soeurs Vatard (The Vatard Sisters)*.

116. ...*uterine metritis.* An inflammation of the lining of the uterus. In the nineteenth century it was common to associate 'neurotic' or 'hysterical' symptoms with diseases of the womb or uterus.

116. ...*a spell of adynamia.* A medical condition characterised by a loss of strength and vigour.

117. ...*illness whose roots extended everywhere.* This is an obvious play on Pascal's well-known quote about Nature being "an infinite sphere whose centre is everywhere and whose circumference nowhere". However, Pascal had adapted his quote either from Saint Augustine, who in his *Confessions* defined God as being 'wholly everywhere, but nowhere limited in space', or from the twelfth century *Book of Propositions* attributed to the fabled alchemist, Hermes Trismegistus, who defined God as "an infinite sphere whose centre is everywhere and whose circumference is nowhere". As Huysmans was familiar with all three sources it's not clear which author he was specifically pastiching.

117. ...*a magisterium concocted by a Bolognese count.* The German alchemist Martinus Rulandus (1569-1611) defined 'magisterium' in his *Lexicon alchemiae* (*Lexicon of Alchemy*, 1612) as: "a Chemical State which

follows the process of extraction, and in which a matter is developed and exalted by the separation of its external impurities. In this manner are all the parts of natural and homogenous concretion preserved. But they are so exalted that they almost attain the nobility of essences."

117. ...*Count Mattei*. Born in Bologna to a wealthy, aristocratic family, Count Cesare Mattei (1809-1896) studied natural science, anatomy, physiology and pathology, before going on to formulate his theory of electro-homeopathy during the 1870s. Mattei used plant extracts as the active agent of his *materia medica*, which he prepared by a method borrowed from Paracelsus known as cohobation. Mattei made huge claims for his new treatments and they quickly spread throughout Europe during the latter half of the nineteenth century: by 1884, for example, there were 79 distribution centres in 10 European countries. A French translation of Mattei's most famous work, *Électro-homoeopathie, principes d'une science* was published in 1879, (See Figure 6 on p. 224) but it is unlikely that Huysmans had seen a copy before working on *En Rade*, as his descriptions are a little imprecise. In fact Mattei stained his "liquid electric" cures not just green but red, white, straw yellow and blue, in order to distinguish between them. "Green electricity" was intended for use to "calm the pains of cancerous lesions", but could be used "for all sorts of wounds," and above all for "pains in the joints". After *En Rade* was published Huysmans told several of his correspondents, including Zola, Arij Prins and Jules Destrée, that he was reading up on Mattei, and he made further references to him in *Là-bas*.

118. ...*the maid led Louise a merry dance*. In the original, Huysmans uses the phrase *l'anse du panier dansa*, an expression which dates back at least to 1636, but about the origins of which even French etymologists are unclear. In his *Curiosités de l'étymologie française* (1863), Charles Nisard complained he could shed no light on its origins, but the phrase is essentially used to describe a piece of trickery such as when a domestic or employee buys goods on behalf of their employer and then charges him more than they actually paid.

121. ...*Kabbala.* Huysmans had previously made reference to the Kabbala in *A Rebours*, and would do so again in subsequent novels. Here it serves as a symbolic link to Jacques's third dream, showing the way in which events in daily life are transfigured or worked on in the dream state.

121. ...*supports of his mind.* Huysmans uses the specialised word *pal* here, a sharpened stake or picket used as a support for plants or for constructing fences, but which occasionally also doubled as an instrument of torture. The use of the word *pal* is perhaps a playful reference to Léon Bloy's short-lived review, *Le Pal*, which he'd published in 1885, the same year as his visit to Huysmans at Lourps.

122. ...*a little kitchen and two small rooms.* A photograph of Huysmans in his study, taken by Dornac in about 1895, shows a mantlepiece with exactly the same objects, arranged in the same way, as Jacques describes.

123. ...*bois d'anis.* Despite its name this has nothing to do with the anise plant, but is the technical name of the fragrant wood from the avocado tree (*Persea americana*), which has an aniseed smell and was used in furniture making.

123. ...*electuaries, such as diascordium or theriac.* An electuary is a drug mixed into a paste with sugar and water, or honey, suitable for oral administration; diascordium was the name given to a medicinal drug the main components of which were the dried leaves of the plant *Teucrium Scordium* and opium; theriac was a medical concoction that dates back to antiquity, and was believed to be a kind of antidote to all forms of poison.

123. ...*tapping the floor with her foot.* In nineteenth-century medical literature, the involuntary tapping of the foot was described as a symptom of tabes. The idea recurs later in Jacques's dream, in which the prostitute figure sitting on one of the towers of St Sulpice taps her foot against the stonework.

124. ...*who'd once been a priest's housekeeper.* By a strange coincidence Huysmans acquired his own *servante de curé* in 1895, in the form of the eccentric visionary Julie Thibault, her former employer having been

the defrocked abbé, Joseph Boullan. Boullan served as the model for Dr. Johannès in *Là-bas*, and Thibault herself became the prototype of Madame Bavoil in *La Cathédrale* (1898) and *L'Oblat* (1903).

130. ...*The creature walked with difficulty.* The image of the baby screech owl fallen out of its nest clearly has a symbolic component. It recalls that of Baudelaire's poem 'L'Albatros' ('The Albatross'), in which the seabird, the "king of the sky", cannot function once it is taken out of its natural element, and like the poet, becomes a target for the cruelty of ordinary, earthbound men because his "giant wings prevent him from walking".

131. ...*Pierrot.* The figure of the pantomine clown, Pierrot, was a potent one for Huysmans and recurs frequently in his work. In 1881, he and Léon Hennique published their own 'pantomime', *Pierrot Sceptique* (Paris: Rouveyre, 1881), which featured a Pierrot who, unlike the traditional white-costumed Pierrot, was dressed completely in black.

VII

140. ...*liver of sulphur.* A chemical mixture used in alchemy and produced by heating potassium carbonate with sulphur. It is more commonly used to stain or oxidise metals such as silver.

141. ...*dangled a pine branch.* In antiquity the pine was associated with Bacchus, the Roman god of wine. French inns traditionally had a branch of pine, sometimes in the form of a wreath, hanging outside over the door, this functioned both as a sign to potential customers that it was a drinking establishment, and as a good luck charm.

142. ...*law against drunkenness.* To try and combat the problem of public drunkenness in the wake of the Franco-Prussian war and the Commune (1870-71), an act regulating public establishments that served alcohol was passed on 23 February 1873, and a copy had to be displayed by law.

143. ...*suburbs of Paris.* Huysmans uses the phrase *barrières parisiennes*, referring to the old city walls of Paris. As alcohol was cheaper when sold outside the city of Paris, drinking dens tended to thrive just beyond the

barrières, and the surrounding areas became synonymous in the public mind with excessive drinking, violence and prostitution.

144. ...*a shot of Picon*. A strong orange bitter liqueur traditionally added to beer in the north and east of France to create a flavoured and potent drink.

145. ...*a 'chinstrap' beard*. A beard that goes from ear to ear and hangs down like a fringe, with no moustaches or hair covering the chin.

145. ...*face of an oriental professor*. In the original Huysmans qualifies the man's complexion as being *au jus de réglisse*, literally the colour of 'licorice juice'. The term was used fairly frequently during the 1870s and 1880s, especially in descriptions of paintings in popular art criticism, prompted by a reaction to the vogue of 'exotic' orientalism – pictures of Turkish harems, Bedouin tribesmen and so on – many examples of which were exhibited in the annual Salons of the time.

146. ...*I'm off to see my aunt*. This is an adaptation of a traditional children's rhyming game, sometimes known as *J'ai des poules à vendre* (I've got chickens to sell), though there are many variations. The rhyme was included in Eugène Roland's collection of nursery rhymes, *Rimes et jeux de l'enfance* in 1883. Huysmans noted that he heard both this and the rhyme that follows while he was at Lourps, and that he went into the church so he could write them down in his notebook.

146. ...*Mary, Mary, you'd best be away*. Like the previous rhyme, this is also a traditional folk song. It was recorded by the French folklorist Achille Millien (1838-1927), and appeared in one of his many collections of folk songs and poems under the title, *Un ange du ciel a descendu* (An angel descended from heaven). The version Huysmans gives is not the same as in Millien's version, so it may be a local variant. In his notebook, Huysmans included the last words of the rhyme, *son tablier* (her pinafore), that are cut off in the second stanza here. Curiously, the word 'pinafore' recurs several times in *En Rade*, most notably in the dream sequence in Chapter X, where both the old hag and her crippled 'husband' are wearing them. Huysmans' repeated use of the word probably has a sexual significance. One of the first pictures Huysmans published a critical analysis of was

Notes

Jean-Baptiste Greuze's *La Cruche cassée (The Broken Pitcher)*, in which the young maid's broken pot is generally seen as a metaphor for her imminent, if not actual, loss of virginity. Huysmans' description of the picture emphasises the picture's double meaning: "[the girl's hands] rest inert on her pinafore which she gathers up; the pot hangs from her arm revealing its gaping wound".

147. ...*one of the little girls who had lost her shoe*. In the MS, the word *tablier* (pinafore) has been crossed out and *soulier* (shoe) substituted (see note above).

VIII

150. ...*a hard bargain*. In the original Huysmans uses the obscure word *cocheri*. Huysmans' fondness for neologisms and recondite terms sometimes foxes even the most diligent critic: in a note on *cocheri* in a recent French edition of *En Rade* the editor exasperatingly admitted, "We couldn't find this word anywhere".

150. ...*that's sixty-two litres*. It would appear that Aunt Norine, or Huysmans, was mistaken in their calculations. The feuillette was a barrel that held 134 litres or 144 pints, so if Antoine was drawing off the wine in litres he should have syphoned off 77 litres in total: 77 (57+20) + 57 = 134 litres. The figures Huysmans gives are only correct for measurements in French pints (82 (62+20) + 62 = 144 pints).

154. ...*Stripped of its clouds*. Huysmans uses the term *écalé*, meaning peeled or husked.

157. ...*clusters of buttocks*. This image recurs later in Jacques's dream, in the form of a fantasy about a field of pumpkins that turn into palpitating human buttocks.

157. ...*flattening the wheat with their billhooks*. Huysmans' description here is another example of the Naturalist method of using precise and factually accurate detail to give fiction its patina of verisimilitude. Even though

Huysmans himself had never handled a sickle in his life, his account of the reaping method and the tools employed, possibly garnered from observation while at Lourps, matches that of contemporary handbooks on the subject.

160. *...Emmerich ointment.* Presumably a contemporary remedy either manufactured at Emmerich in Germany, or by someone called Emmerich.

160. *...like a heat rash.* In the original Huysmans uses the word *chauboulu*, a dialect form of the term *échauboulure*, meaning an outbreak of pimples or spots.

164. *...iodoform.* In the early nineteenth century iodine was seen as a kind of panacea, and in the form of tincture of iodine, primarily taken internally, was prescribed for a whole range of complaints, including paralysis, dropsy, gout, chilblains, bronchitis, croup, ulcers, asthma and syphilis. Iodoform, developed as an external disinfectant, was first introduced into France in 1878 by Apollinaire Bouchardat, chief pharmacist at the Hôtel-Dieu in Paris. Typically iodoform stains skin a dark yellow or brown colour on contact.

IX

168. *...face, as long as a billhook blade.* In the original Huysmans uses the unusual expression *figure en fer de serpe* to describe Louise's face, a *serpe* being a billhook. In Chapter VII, Huysmans had referred to the peasant women standing in the street as *taillés à coups de serpe* (sculpted with a billhook), a figurative expression he also used in *En Hollande* (1877 and 1886), *L'Art moderne* and *A Rebours*. However, in this instance the reference to the *fer* (blade) makes the allusion a little more opaque, especially as the shape of the *serpe* seems to vary from region to region, some having a large hooked beak like a bird's, some with a little protrusion like a snub nose. As Huysmans had earlier described Norine's face as being "pointed like a blade", it is probable that the allusion serves

to draw a comparison between the two women, especially given Jacques's anxieties about Louise's growing resemblance to her aunt.

169. *...a whiff of his lowly origins.* Huysmans uses the phrase *un relent d'ancienne caque*, a *caque* being a herring barrel. The phrase hints at a popular expression *le caque sent toujours le hareng*, which can be translated as "what's bred in the bone comes out in the flesh", or "you can't escape your roots".

170. *...it was Aunt Norine's cat.* From an interview Huysmans gave in 1893, published in *La Révue indépendante*, it appears that the cat in *En Rade* is a composite of two cats he himself had. The first, *Barre de Rouille* (literally 'dash of rust'), had been subject to fits of epilepsy and Huysmans had to have him put down at the end of November 1886, while he was still in the middle of writing *En Rade*. In a letter to Arij Prins on 2 December, Huysmans remarked that his mistress, Anna, was in tears about it and that "she had adored what she called her ginger child". Huysmans immediately asked his concierge to find him a replacement, and she sent him an affectionate, emaciated and, as he put it, "excessively ugly" cat. This second cat, *Mouche*, which he "described more or less exactly as he was in *En Rade*", also makes an appearance in *Là-bas*.

173. *...A student from the École Polytechnique.* This episode from the Revolution of 1830, in which the Tuileries were stormed and Charles X driven from the palace, is recounted in at least two contemporary accounts of the uprising: Horace Raisson's *Histoire populaire de la Revolution de 1830* (Paris: Jules Lefebure, 1830), and F. Rossignol and J. Pharaon's *Histoire de la révolution de 1830 et des nouvelles barricades* (Paris: Vimont, 1830). Huysmans' description was almost certainly based on an existing Épinal print, as he makes numerous references to these mass-produced, often garishly-coloured, prints in his work. Huysmans' version, whether intentionally or not, leaves out some significant political information that puts the episode in context: the student was actually at the head of a crowd of armed citizens, and demanded entry in the name of the people. The original Épinal print was therefore designed to portray

the student in a heroic light as an exemplar of populist revolt, as he was in the two pro-Revolution history books already mentioned. Huysmans' pejorative comments about the student's size and his idiotic appearance seem designed to subvert the print's original intention.

174. ...*The Home Doctor*. Huysmans' description matches that of a print with the same title produced sometime during the 1850s or 60s. A modern reproduction of it is still on sale today at the Parisian firm Deyrolle.

175. ...*candle auction*. The old-fashioned practice of using a one inch candle stub to time an auction persisted in certain areas of France until the 1890s. It was a form of public auction where the auctioneer only accepted bids for as long as the candle was burning, in other words for about 15 to 20 minutes. The element of uncertainty about when the candle would finally extinguish itself induced higher bids and prevented bidders from simply waiting until the last moment, as in more conventional auctions.

175. ...*the 1870 war*. Huysmans himself had served in the Franco-Prussian war of 1870-71, though he spent much of his time in a military hospital with dysentery. Huysmans' depiction here is the very antithesis of the popular romanticised notion, often associated with the works of writers such as George Sand but in fact diffused through much French culture of the period, that it was the peasantry that represented the 'real', 'honest' values of France. It is hardly surprising, given that Huysmans paints the French peasant as ignorant, medacious and traitorous, that his book caused such an outrage in the area and that he never returned to Lourps after it was published.

176. ...*Jacques felt the lacklustre carnal instincts*. In the light of the various images of impotence and castration that run through the novel it is interesting to note a candid letter Huysmans wrote to Arij Prins in November 1886, while he was mid-way through writing *En Rade*: "As for women – complete peace – nothing. In short, there aren't any really good women in my *quartier*. The best are still the ones we went to. And on the other hand, I can't bring myself to sleep with my own [Anna], having slept with her too much in the old days when she was still young. So I've

become chaste, for lack of favourable opportunities…"

177. *…a soldier's fatigue cap.* In the original Huysmans uses the term *bonnet de police*, the nickname for a soldier's cap, which had a flap that hung loose to the side when the soldier was off-duty. The cap got its name because soldiers who had been put on charge or arrested by the police were required to wear army headgear when the punishment was announced and they invariably had their cap with them when off duty, rather than their helmet or shako.

178. *…One article interested him.* This section, from the beginning of the paragraph to the end of the chapter, was used by André Breton in his famous anthology of black humour, first published in 1930.

178. *…ptomaine.* The word ptomaine began appearing in scientific literature during the early 1880s, following earlier work done by Francesco Selmi (1817-1881), professor of chemical pharmacology and toxicology at the University of Bologna. He discovered that the bacterial putrefaction of protein produced certain alkaloids which he named ptomaines, the word deriving from the Greek *ptoma*, meaning corpse.

X

183. *…belladonna.* Atropa belladonna, commonly known as deadly nightshade, is a perennial herbaceous plant belonging to the Solanaceae family. The hallucinogenic drug atropine is produced from its leaves which, along with the berries, are extremely toxic.

184. *…enema.* In the original Huysmans coins the neologism *éguisier*, taken from the name of Doctor Maurice Èguisier, who in 1846 invented a pumping device for use as a vaginal or anal enema. The rubber tubes of such devices were often covered by a tough outer-layer of woollen fabric – hence the later reference to "green woollen snakes". (See Figure 4 on p. 223)

184. *…schapskas with gooseberry mortarboards and visorless shakos.* The word schapska is of Polish origin and denotes the unusual shaped helmet

worn by the cavalry. During the Franco-Prussian war of 1870 a number of regiments on the Prussian side, such as the Bavarian Uhlans, would have worn the schapska, which is almost as distinctive with its flat mortarboard top, as the Prussian spiked helmet. Given that the shako was the traditional military headwear of the French soldier, the linking of the two types of helmet could be seen as a reference to the Franco-Prussian war, however it is also true that a few regiments of French lancers wore the schapska as well.

186. ...*planted with pumpkins*. The form of the pumpkin must have had some unconscious appeal to Huysmans. In his account of the Salon of 1880 he had written an enthusiastic appraisal of a still life featuring a pumpkin, entitled *Courge*, by Antoine Vollon (1833-1900). His description is striking: "Turgid, swollen, apoplectic, smeared with cinnebar and orange, like a ball of fire exploding in the middle of the weedy paintings around it, crushing everything that surrounds it..." (*La Réforme*, 1880). The version published in *L'Art moderne* (1883) is slightly toned down.

187. ...*incubi*. The occult theory of the incubus – a male spirit who can incarnate himself in order to have sex with a woman – clearly fascinated Huysmans, and not just during the period when he was interested in Satanism. References to incubi or succubi can be found in books written both before and after his period of fascination with the occult during the late 1880s, including *Marthe* (1876), *A Rebours* (1884), *En Rade* (1887), *Certains* (1889), *Là-bas* (1891), *En Route* (1895), and *Sainte Lydwine de Schiedam* (1901).

187. ...*Del Rio*. Martin Antoine Del Rio (1551-1608) was a Jesuit theologian of Spanish descent. He wrote, among other works, his *Disquisitionum magicarum libri sex*, a treatise on magic and the occult pubished at Louvain in about 1600. The quotation in the original is given in Latin: *Demones exerceant cum magicis sodomiam*, which Huysmans, or at least Marles, mistakenly thinks means "with magicians", rather than "by magic". Given the scarcity of books by Del Rio it is most likely that Huysmans got his information from a secondary source on the occult,

Notes

although it is also possible that a friend such as Jules Bobin, who had an extensive collection of rare and esoteric books, had a copy.

187. ...*Oh, How You Hurt Me, Handsome Grenadier.* An air from *La Grande-Duchesse de Gérolstein* an opéra bouffe by Jacques Offenbach (1819-1880). It was first performed at Paris's Théâtre des Variétés on April 12, 1867, and the original French libretto was by Henri Meilhac and Ludovic Halévy. In the first act, Wanda, a young peasant girl, laments the fact that Fritz, her "beau grenadier", is about to go off to war. Aside from the sexual resonances of the piece, Huysmans probably also included it for political reasons. The operetta is a satirical critique of the kind of jingoistic militarism about which he himself was so scathing. After the French defeat in the Franco-Prussian War of 1870-71, the piece was banned for a number of years because of its anti-militaristic sentiments.

187. ...*Queen Amélie.* Marie Amélie Thérèse of Bourbon (1782-1866), consort to King Louis-Philippe, was often portrayed wearing her hair in tight curls.

187. ...*a legless cripple.* Huysmans uses the slang expression *cul-de-jatte*, referring to someone who is legless or lame. This is just one of a number of symbolic images of castration within the dream sequence, in which Marles displaces or externalises his sense of impotence on to others or the objects around him.

188. ...*on the Rue Honoré-Chevalier.* The Rue Honoré-Chevalier is a street in the 6th arrondissement of Paris, but more importantly in the context of the dream is that *chevalier* is French for the courtly figure of the knight, and therefore by implication the courtly lover. The name is another symbolic reference to Marles' impotence, as it is while walking down the street of the courtly lover that he loses his phallic cane.

189. ...*looked like a ship's bilge.* In the original Huysmans uses the word *puisard*, which can refer to a sump, a cesspool or drainage trap, as well as a bilge, the lowest part of a ship formed by its two sides, in which water collects and has to be pumped out. 'A ship's bilge' is slightly more explicit than *puisard* but fits with the general thread of nautical and

maritime metaphor that runs through the novel.

190. *...bounce again, like little balls.* This is perhaps one of the most arresting images in the dream. Huysmans had used it before, in a piece called 'Cauchemar' ('Nightmare') written in 1885, about Odilon Redon's new album of lithographs, *Hommage à Goya*. In his description of a plate called 'Un étrange jongleur' ('A strange juggler'), Huysmans writes of "bulbs in which imperceptibly squinting pupils bounced around like billiard-balls". The main figure in the picture also has one large eye, wide open, while the other seems to be an empty socket.

191. *...like a bunch of shallots.* In *Certains* (1889), in a review of a painting by Albert Bartolomé, Huysmans again used this analogy to describe hair that had been done up into buns.

192. *...civilised minds of Mesopotamia or the wily fools of Sologne.* A slightly convoluted analogy, Mesopotamia being commonly thought of as the 'cradle of civilisation' while Sologne, a marshy region to the south of Paris, was associated with the stereotypical figure of the *niais de Sologne*, the wily fool or shrewd peasant. A French proverb ran, "The fool of Sologne is a fool only for his own profit", it being thought that although the Solognot looked and behaved stupidly, he was nevertheless cunning. In the original text the stress is on Mesopotamia and Sologne as metaphors for contrasting states of mind, rather than as actual locations.

192. *...coachman.* In the original, Huysmans specifies *cocher de l'Urbaine*, the *Urbaine* being one of the two main coach companies of the period, the other being *la Générale*.

192. *...one of Ma Eustache's girls.* Another opaque reference that has long frustrated Huysmans' critics. In the most recent French edition of *En Rade* Dominique Millet-Gérard notes, "We've had no success in deciphering the meaning of this allusion – if it has one." Despite the previous reference to Saint-Sulpice it is unlikely to refer to the church of Saint-Eustache as Eustace was a male saint. There is a possibility that the name derived from a popular ballad, as there is an old song collected in *Les Soirées Chantantes*, a collection of vaudevilles, rhymes and poems,

published pseudonymously by Louis Beffory de Reigny in 1805, entitled
'Des aîles de l'amour' (The Wings of Love), whose first lines run: "C'est
la mère Eustache; / Fille, écoutez ses sermons, / Pour afin qu'on l'sache,
/ J'vous avertissons / Tendrons / Q'faut pas que une fill' s'amourache /
Comm' ça des garçons..." (This is old Mother Eustache, / Girl, listen
to her words / Just so you know, / I'll tell you straight / A girl shouldn't
fall in love / With boys just like that...). Huysmans' phrase *fille à la
mère Eustache* certainly seems to have sexual overtones, *mère* (mother)
being often used as a familiar name for the madame of a brothel and *fille*
(daughter or girl) denoting a whore in street parlance. It is possible, too,
as Per Buvik suggests in *La Luxure et la Pureté* (1989) that the phrase *la
mère Eustache* can be interpreted as an expression of Jacques's castration
anxiety, a *eustache* being a type of kitchen knife. A similar kind of anxiety
underlines des Esseintes' nightmare of the nidularum blades in *Against
Nature*.

XI

193. ...*waking state*. Huysmans uses the expression *à l'état de vielle* (waking
state), a psychological term for a state of distracted daydream or reverie in
which one is receptive to suggestions. Hippolyte Bernheim popularised the
term in his treatise *De la suggestion dans l'état hypnotique et dans l'état
de veille* (1884), which contradicted the ideas of Jean-Martin Charcot on
hypnotism and hysteria, showing that the phenomena of hypnotism were
functions of suggestion and could be implanted in certain waking states
as well. Huysmans refers specifically to Bernheim's work on suggestion
in *Là-bas*.

193. ...*Paracelsus*. Theophrastus Phillippus Aureolus Bombastus von
Hohenheim otherwise known as Paracelsus (1493-1541), was a Swiss
alchemist, physician, occultist and philosopher. In his *De Rerum natura
(Concerning the Nature of Things)*, Paracelsus wrote: "For the basilisk
is engendered and produced from the chief impurity of a woman,

namely from the menstrual blood." However, Huysmans did not get his information directly from the writings of Paracelsus, his quote is lifted straight from *Dogme et rituel de la haute magie* (1855) by the French occultist Alphonse Louis Constant (1810-75), or Eliphas Lévi as he was better known.

195. ...*The crudely carved Christ*. In *Là-bas*, Huysmans used some of the same imagery, and even repeated the same words, in his description of the Matthias Grünewald *Crucifixion*. In both, Huysmans uses the word *bandit* (thief) to refer to Christ, and describes his body as being *barbouillé de sang* (daubed with blood). The church at Lourps (See Figure 2 on p. 222), which was renovated in 1966 after part of the vault collapsed, still has the remains of the original figure of Christ which Huysmans described in the novel.

196. ...*Boyer's Melissa Cordial*. Huysmans refers to the bottle as having contained 'eau de mélisse', a popular remedy for migraine and dyspepsia originally produced by the Carmelites.

198. ...*Beauty's started trying to mount her*. Although Huysmans wasn't a country man himself and had no practical knowledge or experience of farming, his details about cow insemination and behaviour are all carefully researched or closely observed from real life, probably while staying at Lourps.

199. ...*stick roses*. This is a literal translation of both the Dutch (*stokroos*) and the German (*stockrose*) for hollyhock.

200. ...*Hégésippe Moreau*. Pierre-Jacques Roulliot (1810-1838), a French lyric poet and journalist who used the pseudonym Hégésippe Moreau on the publication of his first book of poems in 1829. He was seen as a tragic figure: born illegitimate, his father died of tuberculosis when he was four, his mother died of the same disease five years later, and he lived in poverty for the last years of his life, dying at the early age of 28, also of tuberculosis. The publication of his complete works in 1856 compounded the Romantic myth surrounding his name. His poem 'La Voulzie' appeared in the collection *Le Myosotis* (1838), which was published shortly before

he died. A number of critics have found Huysmans' invocation of the Romantic poet slightly anomalous, given his generally unconventional and anti-Romantic views about nature.

202. ...*something red and misshapen*. This notion of a misshapen or crooked penis is something that clearly unsettled Huysmans; the image also occurs in *A Rebours*, where des Esseintes is obsessed by the Amorphophallus, a flower whose name almost literally translates as 'misshapen penis'.

205. ...*the hereditary stain of woman*. In Christian theology, Eve's punishment for her part in bringing 'original sin' into the world was the 'hereditary stain' of childbirth and menstruation. Although Huysmans was not a Christian at this point, it is clear that Christian mythology served as a symbolic framework that provided an explanation of his misogynistic feelings about women, and that this was a factor in his eventual conversion. *En Route*, the novel which most clearly deals with the period of his conversion, is in many ways an account of Durtal's struggle to contain unruly carnal desire.

XII

210. ...*Look, shooting pains*. The term Huysmans uses in the original is *douleurs fulgurantes*, the same expression Jean-Martin Charcot used in his descriptions of the symptoms of ataxia and tabes, commonly associated with the symptoms of syphilis. Huysmans also uses the expression in the opening chapter, where Marles describes Louise as suffering from shooting pains on the journey to Lourps.

214. ...*What a series of snubs, what a succession of humiliations*. Huysmans was himself worried about money at this point in his life. In 'Obsession', a piece which he wrote in 1885 and added to the enlarged, second edition of *Croquis parisiens*, he deals with the same anxieties of rejection and humiliation in relation to money. Interestingly, the piece opens on a statement of intent on behalf of the narrator to return to Paris from the countryside, where he is staying temporarily, and his references to an "old

church silhouetted against the horizon" show that it was either written at Lourps, or shortly after with Lourps in mind. In a letter to Gabriel Thyébaut in August 1887, Huysmans wrote that the failing bindery business he had inherited from his mother was dragging him into a "rat-trap of difficulties" and that he was having to arrange a "whole heap of meetings to try and find work and money".